TALES FROM A DEAD END WORLD

VOL. 3

by R. E. Sohl

CURIOUS CORVID PUBLISHING

Curious Corvid
PUBLISHING

TABLE OF CONTENTS

MISTRESS OF THE AURORAS

Great witch from the north

She walks forth

In this hour

Clothed in magical power

Yet it was not always so

If only they could know

How the path which brought her here

Was so fraught with fear

Loss and pain

All of it she bravely overcame

Then went on to reclaim

The inner strength that was always there

And triumphed over despair

TEMPTATION

Part One: An Unearthly Encounter (1974)

April McKenna was barely four years old when she first found out that the world was far stranger than most people would ever suspect. That moment is forever etched into her being—her first encounter with the unknown, with the things that should not be, but are. In fact, it's one of her first coherent memories.

Her father had just told her to go to her bedroom to put on her pajamas in preparation for bedtime. She approached the long, dark corridor that led to her room with great trepidation. She was very scared of the dark, of the strange things that might live in those dark places, waiting for her. She could feel them sometimes—cold eyes always watching her from shadowy corners. Unfortunately, she couldn't reach the hallway light switch to make use of its magical ability to dispel all such creatures back to the darkest regions of her imagination where they belonged.

She'd have to make a run for it, as she often did, until she reached the safety of her own room and a light switch located mercifully close to the doorway. Her heart was pounding with excitement as she began her run; she may have been small, but she was also fast. Too fast for any monsters to catch her. She found this nightly race against her fears as exhilarating as it was terrifying, although of course back then she lacked the language to articulate such feelings.

She made it! She came skidding to a halt on the polished wooden floor with her sock-covered feet right in front of the open doorway to her bedroom. That's when she saw it, and her blood went cold.

The lurker in the threshold. The thing that should not be. The thing that had no business being here, that had no place in a sane, rational universe. It stood there in defiance of all logic. It was a shadow in the shape of a man.

It loomed over her childish frame, standing between her room and the hallway. The doorway was aligned with a window right above her bed. Light poured in through that window from a nearby streetlamp. That light also penetrated the shape blocking her way, passing straight through it. With a jolt of horror, she realized that she could see all the murky details of her bedroom behind this thing— the window, the bed. She could see right *through* it!

She stood there, only a few inches from it, completely paralyzed by her fear. Despite her unusual proximity, she could barely make out any distinctive details of its features or clothing. Her father enjoyed photography, often turning their tiny bathroom into a makeshift darkroom, and sometimes she assisted him, fascinated by the look of everything under the red lights. Due to this, even at her young age, she knew what a photographic negative image looked like. That was the closest approximation she could come to likening this thing to, and yet even that wasn't quite adequate to describe its complete otherworldliness. The undeniable feeling that it didn't *belong* there.

The thing made no move towards her. In fact, much like the negative image it resembled, it seemed to be frozen in time. Yet she could feel an unmistakable set of emotions radiating from it. A cruel sort of bemusement at her expense, at the terror it provoked in her. Below that, there was a cool, calculated assessment of her. Years later, when she did finally have the words to try to explain this uncanny encounter, she would tell a friend that she thought it was sizing her up, like a sports team taking stock of their opponents.

They stood like that, mere centimeters away, for what felt like an agonizing eternity, unable to move or even scream. Then, suddenly the spell was broken, and she could control her body once more. Without hesitation she turned and ran from that spot, crying out, "Daddy! Daddy! Help! Help! There's a man!"

She came barreling back into the living room at top speed, nearly crashing into the tackily patterned sofa upon which her father lay, struggling to rise up in response to her screams.

"What's going on?" he demanded grumpily. "I thought I told you to put your pajamas on? Why haven't you done that already?"

"Daddy! Daddy! Come quick! There's a man in my room!" She sputtered the words out between winded breaths.

"*What?*" This, more so than the distress of his young daughter, seemed to capture the immediate attention of her father—the prospect of an invader in his domain. A challenge to the sanctity of his supremacy in his own home. There should be nobody else in the house; his wife was working a night shift as she always did, and his sons were still out running around the neighborhood with their friends, getting themselves into God knows what kind of mischief. Although the boys were due back soon, they would've seen or heard them come back in. He ran into the nearby kitchen and snatched up a broom that was leaning against the wall, brandishing it like a spear as he dashed into the hallway and flipped on the lights.

He cautiously edged down the hallway, April trailing behind him. She had no more fear. Whatever it was that was standing in her doorway, her daddy would sort it out. Nobody was as strong as her daddy was, not even Superman. Her father reached the doorway and peered into the half-light of the room, the broom gripped in his hands so tightly that his mahogany knuckles were turning white. His slightly hunched over battle stance softened, and he stood up straight, a frown painted his face. April thought a part of him had almost been looking forward to giving someone a good ass-whooping. He reached into the room and turned on the light. Its harsh, yellow glow stung April's eyes for a second. She looked inside with squinted eyes.

There was nothing there. Well, nothing aside from the things that were normally there. Nothing and nobody who didn't *belong* there.

Her father had stepped one foot inside and was looking around too. He pulled open the closet door, then slammed it shut. He turned to her. "Girl, what have I told you before about telling stories? You had me half worried to death about a whole lot of nothing!"

"I'm not making it up! I did see a man in here, I really did! I could see through him, too!" She insisted, somewhat incensed at not being taken seriously. April felt her cheeks getting hot with anger. Her daddy, her champion, the person who was always supposed to have her back, thought that she was a liar? It was almost too much to bear.

"Through him? Are you trying to tell me you saw a ghost?" Her father laughed at the idea.

April's brows knitted in confusion. A ghost? Like Casper the Friendly Ghost, who was in the cartoons she sometimes watched? She didn't know of any other ghosts. She didn't really understand why everyone was so scared of Casper; he wasn't scary at all. She felt sorry for him. No, the thing she had just seen didn't remind her of Casper, it was nothing like him at all. What she had seen wasn't friendly or lonely, it was something cold, something completely heartless—something impossibly terrible! If only she'd had the words to convey the sheer depths of the terror it had instilled in her, the fundamental *wrongness* of its very existence, but she didn't, not back then.

"It was real! It was here! I saw it!" She stamped her foot down stubbornly. She knew her father found her spirited display of certainty more amusing than anything else. What would've come off as being true grit and determination in an older person just looked cute on her toddler face. Like a kid pretending to be a grown up, imitating something they'd seen an adult do. Her father laughed again. It was infuriating!

"Sure you did, honey, sure you did." He patted her head, a gesture of casual affection that she would've cherished under other circumstances, but right now it made her want to punch him. How could he just dismiss something so important like this? Like it was nothing? Couldn't he see that this was the strangest, most important thing that had ever happened to her? She pouted. She was four years old, after all.

"Put your pajamas on. I'll be back to tuck you in," he told her and left the room before she could protest. Leaving her standing there alone with her fears.

Part Two: The In-Between Years (1975-85)

The years flew by in the sleeping Calgary suburb where the McKennas made their home. The avocado and harvest gold earth tones of the seventies slowly succumbing to the harsh, neon gaudiness of the eighties. Yet the shadows remained, always watching, sometimes whispering to April. She never saw the Dark Man again, but she could feel him when he was near, draining all the joy from the world like a breeze that chilled her soul. She could often sense him next to her bed at night, looking down at her, his unfettered malevolence washing over her in waves like some dread radiation. She could never bear to try to look at him, she didn't want to look at him, there was no need to—she *knew* he was there. She could see him as clearly in her mind's eye as she could with her physical ones. She huddled there, countless nights, completely covered in her sheets, struggling to breathe through her thick cocoon of safety.

She heard him sometimes, too. In the theater of her mind, she saw him bending down to whisper in her ear. His voice so soft and sweet like honey, but his every word burned with venomous poison. She couldn't make out everything he said. Sometimes it felt like he was speaking to her from the other side of some invisible wall, but what she could understand horrified her. He tried to fill her mind with wicked ideas, pointing out the flaws of her various family members, teachers, and friends. Tried to amplify the outrage of any slight they may have made against her. He constantly urged her to violence, describing in graphic detail all the terrible ways in which she might avenge herself against them for even the smallest of insults. She in turn tried to shut him out of her thoughts, often humming to herself to drown out his polite, gently put diatribes of atrocity.

As she got older, she sometimes wondered if she was going insane. Was it all in her head? Is this what madness looked like? Yet she felt deep in her bones that the thing she had seen on that long-ago night had been as real as anything else she could see around her. The almost nightly visits that were filled with such foreign, hateful ideas felt so real, they *had* to be real. She didn't understand how it could be true, until one Sunday in church when her pastor mentioned demons in his sermon.

A demon? Could that be what haunted her? It seemed possible. Whatever it was, it was certainly a demon to her. Yet she dared not ask for help from anyone. She remembered how her father reacted that night when it had first appeared to her, and his many speeches that made it abundantly clear that he didn't truly believe in anything that he couldn't see, feel, touch or measure. Her mother was a believer, but perhaps too much of one. If she told her of the demon, her mother might wonder what had attracted it to April to begin with—indeed, she often wondered about this herself—and possibly even blame her for it. No, in the end, the only one she felt comfortable asking for help was God himself.

She would pray silently in her head when she felt the demon's acid suggestions penetrating the warm bubble of blankets where she took sanctuary. Pray that God would send her an angel to vanquish this monster and set her free of its torments. But for whatever reason, God did not answer her prayers. He had forsaken her, and the demon laughed at the futility of her efforts. Perhaps what she'd imagined her mother might say was true? Perhaps there was some flaw, some inherent sin within her, a part of her very nature that had attracted this creature to her.

Perhaps she was cursed.

She couldn't bring herself to truly believe this—she could see no good reason for it. She felt like she was generally a pretty good person, or at least she tried to be. She knew she wasn't perfect: sometimes she was too impatient, too quick to anger, and probably too selfish. She did try to be helpful to others, to be a good friend, sister, and daughter. Why should she be punished like this? It wasn't fair, and she was still young and naïve enough to believe that life should be fair.

She was certain, in fact, that if evil was real, then that must also mean that there was something to counterbalance it. How could the Devil be real without God also being real? This one thought got her through many tough days. Yet, if He was real, then where was He? Why didn't He answer her prayers?

This made her suspect that if there was a God, then He was not as humans imagined Him to be in the Bible, or maybe even in any of the other popular holy books. Maybe He wasn't even a He? Maybe He was a She, or some mix of the two? Or something that totally transcended such limiting ideas as gender? She began to take trips to the local library on the sly to look into other religious ideas. If the God of the Bible, Torah, and Koran couldn't or wouldn't help her, then perhaps a different one would? That's when she discovered a book on witchcraft. Thumbing through it, she found instructions on how to protect yourself from negative influences and dark entities. *This* was what she was looking for: clear directions on how to protect herself. She checked the book out and kept it well hidden, knowing that her more traditionally religious mother wouldn't approve, and would probably even see it as a sign of evil within April.

That night, by the illumination of a shaking flashlight, after her parents believed her to be asleep, she crawled out of her bed to perform the ritual that she hoped would protect her. To her great joy and relief, it seemed to work. The Dark Man was still there, still nearby, but he was now separated from her somehow, held back from getting too close. She could barely hear him. His evil words became an unintelligible murmur, easily drowned out by her humming or the rustle of the wind outside her windows. She repeated this routine every night, dismayed that she couldn't completely banish him away, but grateful for the relief she now had from his intrusions. Now he was reduced to nothing but annoying background noise, like someone playing the TV in another room. For the first time in years, she felt free—free of the shadow he'd cast over her life.

Alas, this wonderful feeling was not to last.

Although the Dark Man was now just a manageable annoyance, everything else in her life began to fall apart. Her father began drinking much more heavily. He'd always enjoyed a beer after work here and there, but this was different, this was several every day. Fortunately for the rest of the family, he was a "happy drunk," for the most part. He never laid a finger on any of them, but sometimes something would set him off, and he'd use words that stung as sharply as any slap to the face. April learned to be careful around him, to avoid him when he'd had "one too many" so she wouldn't find herself on the receiving end of his verbal barbs. Once again, she felt dread in her own home. The Dark Man had been relatively easy to defeat, but how did one defeat the kinds of spirits that lived in a bottle? There was no spell for that that she knew of.

One terrible night, her parents went out together and left her in the care of her two brothers, Ron and Ty. April would spend the rest of her life wondering why her mother decided to climb into that car with her father behind the wheel. She must not have been able to tell that he'd already been drinking; he had gotten quite adept at hiding the extent of his problem from her.

They never reached their destination.

They were both killed instantly when the front of the car slammed into a tree. People always say things like that as if it's a comfort, but

April didn't think anyone could ever really know how "instantly" someone else's death happened. How could anyone know how much terror they might have felt as they realized they were off the road and headed straight for a big tree? April already knew from her experience with the Dark Man how time appeared to slow down to a lazy crawl when one was seized by the grip of total fear. Is that what their last moments had been like? Time slowed down while all they could do was watch their own doom looming before them, helpless to do anything to prevent it, and then what? The sound of shattered glass, shattered bones, and twisted Detroit steel? Was there pain? How long did it last before the flame of their lives sputtered out and extinguished?

She didn't want to think about any of that, but she couldn't help it. Who needed a personal demon? Who needed the Dark Man to torture her with such morbid ideas? She was more than capable of tormenting herself with such grim thoughts.

It was more than just her parents that died that day. This was the beginning of the end of her entire family.

Nobody else in her extended family (such as it was) was capable of or interested in taking in two teenage boys and an eleven-year-old girl. They ended up in the foster care system. At first, some effort was made to keep them together. April was able to stay with her big brother Ty. Ron was the oldest, nearly an adult himself. He was placed in a different home until he ran away. Once, after his escape, he tracked her down and visited her. She'd never forget what it was like when she first ran into him again, talking to her furtively from the other side of her school's playground fence. She told Ty, and they helped Ron as much as they could. He was living in a makeshift camp in a patch of woods. They'd sneak cans of food and other supplies to him whenever possible. Then one day, he was just gone. His camp was completely vacant. Years would pass before she ever heard anything about what had become of him.

In the meantime, a few more difficult years lay ahead for April and Ty. The homes they were placed in weren't very welcoming, to say the least. April discovered that the Dark Man still haunted her wherever she lived, but compared to the pain she felt from the loss of both parents, the mystery of what had become of Ron, and the abuses that she and Ty suffered in those foster homes, he almost seemed like a comforting presence. The one reliable thing in her life, the one constant that she could depend on, was that he would be there every night, hovering on the edge of her hearing, whispering his bilious words. He was the one negative thing that she felt she had any kind of power over, that she could keep a safe distance away from. By this time, she didn't need any books. She had memorized the rituals that kept her nemesis at bay and became well practiced at performing them in secret. She could do it in her sleep—literally.

If only it had been so easy to keep away the hands of the people she encountered in those foster homes. Hands that liked to hit her, and sometimes did much worse. Sometimes a foster parent was to blame, and on other occasions it was one of the other kids in the home who preyed upon her. Ty tried to protect her the best that he could, but he wasn't always around to do so, especially when they were inevitably placed in separate homes. For the first time in her life, April was truly on her own. She had no parents, and she might as well have no brothers, either. All she had left was her mysterious enemy constantly trying to corrupt her, the monster that never went away.

Sometimes she felt like just giving up and letting him win. It would be so easy to give in, to do some of the terrible things that she knew he was undoubtedly urging her to do, even if she couldn't quite hear him clearly anymore. A part of her wanted to do it. A part of her was angry enough to believe that she'd find some kind of catharsis in finally releasing all the anger that she'd buried deep inside over the course of the extended nightmare that had become her life. Sometimes she thought she might like it, even if that meant hurting other people—*especially* if it meant that. Yet she didn't let her mind linger in such dark places for very long. In the end, she always rejected such ideas, no matter how tempting they often were. It just wasn't her, it wasn't who she was, or who she wanted to be. There was already far too much suffering in the world; the last thing she wanted to do was add to that suffering by hurting others. Deep down, she didn't want to hurt. She wanted to heal not just herself, but others too, if only she could figure out how.

Was this strength? She didn't think of herself as being particularly strong. She just felt like she was doing whatever it took to survive, to get through this mockery of a childhood and live to make it out to the other side. Once she was a grown-up, once she was able to call the shots, then she could focus on doing more than just getting through each pain-riddled day. Perhaps then she could find a way to thrive, to prosper. Maybe she could buy a house and reunite with her lost brothers? Maybe they could find a way to be a family again?

She knew that it was a long shot, but this was her dream; the one comfort she had was this vision of her future. She clung to this hope like it was a life raft on a turbulent sea. It gave her something to aspire to, to focus on other than her own grief. She became an excellent student, despite being constantly moved from school to school whenever she was placed in a new home. She always adapted to the new school and the new curriculum quickly. Sometimes one school would be ahead of the last one she'd been in, and other times they were behind, which put her ahead of the game. She liked being ahead of the game.

That's how she began to look at it all, too—as a game. She knew the rules and she just had to play along. Too many of her fellow students weren't even interested in playing the game, they were just there because they had to be. They weren't playing to win. The stakes were different for her. If her dream was ever to come true, she would have to excel. She had no choice but to become the teacher's pet, and her peers started taunting her with new names. Unfortunately, she was already used to being called the "n-word," or at least as accustomed to it as one could ever become. Some words never really lose their sting. Now she was labeled with a different kind of n-word: "nerd." There were other names too, like "brain" and "geek." She couldn't see why any of those were bad things, but the other kids sure treated her as if they were. Couldn't they understand that this was her only way out? If she didn't get great grades, she'd never get scholarships to good schools, and without those good schools, she'd never have a job that paid enough to make her dreams come true.

She'd seen how much her parents had struggled to make ends meet. How frequently her mother wasn't around because she was always working night shifts at the hospital as a CNA, how her father worked so hard at the plant that it had turned him into an alcoholic. That wasn't the sort of life she ever wanted for herself. What she wanted most was a stable home, a safe place free from the uncertainty and trauma that ruled her life. In order to get that, she had to be the best student she could be.

Her studies ruled her life. They kept her out of trouble and kept her from focusing too much on all the hurt she'd experienced. She hardly had time to try to make friends, or for boys. She didn't even think that she really liked boys anyway—at least not in *that* way. She only ever felt any sort of attraction towards other girls. These feelings frightened her. She didn't *want* to be different. It was the 1980's, and she was all too aware of how most people looked down on gay people, treating them like pariahs, like they all had AIDS and were somehow going to infect the whole world with it. Yet she couldn't deny the truth of her own feelings either.

She was already different from most of the people around her, anyway. Different because of her race, different because she was an orphan, and different because of her intellect. Oh, and there was also the small matter of the strange demon haunting her that she could only keep away by using witchcraft. She supposed her unconventional spiritual beliefs also separated her from everyone else. That was something she already had to keep a secret. What was one more thing to add to the list? One more secret to keep?

Although she was starting to become more comfortable with the idea that her sexual identity was just one more thing she didn't have in common with other kids, she was still a little saddened by it. Saddened because when she envisioned her future-self living with her brothers in her safe, stable home, she also saw herself as a mother with kids of her own. How could she be a mother and lesbian at the same time? The idea of letting some guy do it with her just so she could get pregnant made her feel ill, so that was definitely not an option. She knew they could make babies in a test tube, she knew about adoption, but would they even let someone do any of those things if they were a gay person? She didn't think that they would. She also had no intentions of living her whole life in the closet. Once she was an adult, once she had a good job and the stability she needed, then there would be no more secrets between herself as the world. She would finally be free to be herself, and damn anyone who couldn't handle the truth of who she really was!

These dreams for the future are what kept her afloat, until one day when her boat struck an iceberg. Someone from social services informed her that her brother Ty, unable to deal with all the loss in his life, unable to escape the abuse that dogged him whenever he went, had given in to temptation and killed himself. He was only seventeen years old. April went through many emotions when she heard the news, but the one she kept on coming back to was anger. White-hot anger. Anger at him for giving up when he was so close to being eighteen, when he would get his shot at freedom from this system that was slowly destroying them. Anger at him for abandoning her. Anger at him for being so *weak*. Was this same weakness within her too? Was it in the McKenna DNA? Was it what had driven her father to drink so much? Was it what had caused her mother to turn a blind eye to her husband's problem?

The anger scared her. The intensity of it. It became harder to focus on her schoolwork as a way of avoiding it. It became harder to avoid the words of the Dark Man, too. Her spells seemed almost ineffective when she was this furious. She could again make out some of the things he said:

You should make them pay! Make them all pay! They're all guilty! The world isn't fair, and the only way to ever get what you want is to take it. Take what's yours! Take your revenge! Kill them all! It would be so easy. It would feel so good. You know you want to!

The madder she got, the clearer the words became, o she focused on releasing her anger instead. She knew that giving the Dark Man what he wanted would be the ultimate show of weakness, and she wasn't weak like Ty had been. The best revenge was to succeed at the game of life. The best revenge was to prove all the people who didn't believe in her wrong. She would be a success, not despite her circumstances, but to *spite* them. She would redirect whatever anger she couldn't release towards more positive goals. The loss of her brother wouldn't sink her boat. It would always hurt her, but she hadn't seen him in nearly three years. In many ways, he was already dead to her—a fading memory from another life, like her image of her parents. They were all becoming nothing but ghosts to her. Ghosts that seemed less real than the actual ghost who'd been haunting her her whole life.

No, she wouldn't let this latest loss destroy her. She would persevere. She would *conquer*. She would go on to someday live free as her authentic self, or die trying.

Part Three: Enter the Wendigo (Late 1986)

At the age of sixteen, it looked like things might finally be starting to turn around for April McKenna. After spending the past five years in more houses (she refused to call them homes, none of them ever felt like home) than she could count on both hands, she had finally hit the jackpot.

Her new foster parents, Rob and Jo Johnson, were some of the sweetest people she'd ever met. At first she didn't believe it. She'd had plenty of foster care experiences that started out pleasant enough before the neglect or outright abuse surfaced. She held her breath, waiting for the inevitable disappointment. She waited, and she waited. Weeks went by, and things were still as great as ever. In the end, she was forced to conclude that the Johnsons were the real deal—genuinely nice people who had a true interest in helping her. Unable to give birth to any children of their own, they treasured her.

They did have one child who was already there when she arrived. Ten-year-old Chris was a First Nations boy they'd adopted years earlier. He'd also started out as a foster, which gave April hope that maybe the Johnsons would, despite her age, adopt her too. She'd already begun to think of Chris, who obviously looked up to her, as her little brother. She hoped that it would become official someday. The idea of being part of a real, loving family again thrilled her.

Then, one day, something occurred which she feared threatened to bring the whole dream crashing down. She was sitting on her bed in her room, reading through a new book of spells that she'd just gotten earlier that day from the local library. The library in this new town had an unusually well stocked Alternative Religion section that delighted her and made her suspect that one of the librarians was also a witch. She'd gotten this book because she was trying to see if there was some way she could communicate with the spirits of her parents. She felt like if she just knew that they were okay, that they were at peace, it would give her a bit more closure. Also, in the back of her mind, she hoped to find a spell that might help her better understand the Dark Man and how to get rid of him for good. She could try asking him who he was and what he wanted with her, but she'd always been afraid to speak to him directly. She felt like if she opened a dialogue with him, she'd also be opening herself up to him in ways that would prove catastrophic for her. It was her number one rule: Don't talk back to the Dark Man. She followed this instinct fanatically, and she felt that doing so had helped keep her alive so far.

As she sat on her bed looking at the book, her foster mother Jo suddenly entered the room. April had carelessly left the door cracked partially opened in her enthusiasm to check out the contents of her new book. She reflexively slammed the cover shut and shoved it behind her back as she saw Jo enter.

"Hey April, I just wanted to tell you that dinner is ready downstairs and—" Jo paused mid-sentence as she spied April's clumsy attempt at performing a sleight-of-hand trick with the book. A bemused smile played around her lips.

"What's that you're trying to hide behind your back?"

"Huh? What? I don't have anything back there. See?" She let go of the book and waved her hands around like she was doing jazz hands while simultaneously shifting herself backwards to sit on the book. She smiled innocently, if unconvincingly.

Jo chuckled. "C'mon, I wasn't born yesterday! What is it? It's okay, you can show me. No secrets in this house, remember?"

No secrets? That would be nice. If only it could be true, April thought sadly.

"I don't know. It's kind of . . . private," April replied hesitantly.

"Oh, I see. You don't think you can trust me yet? I understand, you are still kind of new here. I just want you to know that you can share anything with us that you feel comfortable sharing," Jo said, a bit of hurt creeping into her tone. April didn't think she was trying to guilt-trip her, but it was happening anyway. Jo turned to leave the room.

"It's not that I don't trust you! You and Rob have been so nice to me since I got here, for the first time in forever I feel like I have a real home again. It's just that . . . I'm afraid if you know this thing about me, you won't approve of it . . . or me."

"Oh, honey. I don't know what you could possibly have hidden back there that would make me think any less of you. We'll always accept you just as you are in this house," Jo said earnestly.

Something about the way Jo said those words made April believe her. She *wanted* to believe her. She decided to take a risk, and hoped against hope that the whole thing wouldn't blow up in her face. Slowly, with a deep breath, she pulled the book out from under her butt and showed the cover to Jo.

Jo quickly scanned the cover and grinned. "Oh, is that all? I've read that one, it's a classic!"

April was flabbergasted. "You've read it? But I thought that you and Rob were Christians, like ninety-nine percent of the people in this town?"

"We are—now. But we had a bit of a Wiccan phase back when we first met. I think it's awesome that you're exploring your spirituality."

"So, you don't think that this means I'm the spawn of Satan?"

She laughed. "If you are, then I am too!"

April breathed a sigh of relief. She didn't think of her interest in witchcraft as being an exploration of her spirituality—it was just something she did to survive. It was the only thing that had seemed to yield any actual results against the Dark Man. She hadn't given much thought as to how or why it worked, it was simply enough for her that it did. She did suppose she was beginning to branch out into other applications of it, with her hopes of using it to reach the spirits of her parents and maybe even Ty (although she was still feeling so much anger towards him that she wasn't sure she was ready to try to reach out to him yet).

A wave of gratitude washed over her. She wasn't used to being unconditionally accepted. She was intrigued that Jo and Rob had apparently dabbled with Wicca as well. She felt so incredibly lucky to have ended up in this particular home. Lucky wasn't something she was accustomed to feeling, and it was a feeling she didn't want to lose. The fear of having to leave this wonderful home and go to some other rotten house suddenly gripped her.

Jo must've seen the small change in her expression, and she decided to reassure her further. "The spiritual journey that Rob and I went on together eventually brought us back to Jesus, but it doesn't matter if it does for you or not. Just do whatever resonates with you the most. Everyone is different, and God speaks to us in whatever way He can best reach us. The important thing is that you're asking the big questions."

April fought back the tears that were now welling up. She'd trained herself not to cry in front of others. She didn't want anyone to see something in her that they might think of as a weakness they could tease her about. She stood up and hugged Jo.

"Thanks for being so understanding," she said in a sniffly voice.

Jo squeezed her back, then let her go. "Don't mention it, it's what we're here for. I'll see you downstairs for dinner in a few."

***

When April came down to the dinner table, Rob and her little foster brother Chris were already seated. Jo floated in from the kitchen carrying a pitcher of some sort of drink, probably lemonade.

"So, what's new with everyone?" Rob asked; it was his way to get the nightly dinner conversation going.

"It looks like we've got a witch in the house!" Jo said as she set the pitcher down and took her seat.

Rob almost spat out his food. "Excuse me? Should you really be using that kind of language in front of the kids?"

Jo laughed. "Witch, honey! I said witch with a *w*."

"Oh, I thought you said something else." He chuckled to himself.

"I can guess what you thought I said. No, what I meant is that today I discovered that April here is into Wicca."

Rob's ruddy, plump face brightened. "Really? That's great!" He looked over his forkful of mashed potatoes wistfully, as if viewing some lost horizon. "We used to do a little witchcraft ourselves back when we were younger. Ah, I'll never forget the sight of Jo dancing skyclad in front of a bonfire."

Jo blushed. "You'd better not tell *that* story at this table. It's definitely not appropriate for young ears."

April giggled. She knew what "skyclad" meant. She couldn't imagine her foster parents dancing naked in front of a fire without laughing. She was pleased that Rob was as enthusiastic and supportive of her spiritual choices as Jo was. It made her wonder what else she could trust them with. Would they still be so supportive if they knew that she was gay? Or that an evil spirit had followed her here? She wanted to believe they would be, but she decided to take on one secret at a time. She didn't want to overwhelm them with all the things that made her different. No need to press her luck like that.

"What made you lose interest in Wicca?" she asked her foster parents.

"It wasn't any one thing in particular. We were part of a local coven. Over time, the group just kind of drifted apart, and we didn't find another one that we felt comfortable in. Then we sort of got interested in other things," Jo explained.

Rob nodded in agreement. "Yeah, that about sums it up. But I think it's cool that you're interested in it."

"Thanks. It's really great that you're both so accepting of it. It's something I've felt like I've had to hide about myself for so long."

"We just want you to feel comfortable here, honey. Free to be yourself," Jo reiterated.

"I think it's cool that you're a witch, too. Just like Madame Wendigo!" Chris added.

"Madame who?" April asked in surprise. She had no idea what Chris was talking about.

"He means Mrs. Hairston. She's one of our neighbors, two doors down. Nice old, retired lady. She's a witch too. We should take you over to meet her. Maybe she could mentor you in your spiritual practice," Rob said.

"Uh, yeah sure, that sounds great. When do you think I could meet her?" April couldn't believe how enthusiastic they were about all of this. One of the neighbors was a witch too? Perhaps she wasn't so alone after all. She found the old woman's name interesting. Why on earth was she called Madame Wendigo?

"It's probably too late to bother her tonight. Maybe when you get home from school tomorrow, I can take you over there," Jo mused aloud. Jo would be home when April got back. She had once been a teacher, but now she was a housewife. Rob's job with an advertising firm in the city was enough to cover all their expenses, and Jo was content with devoting herself to creating a nice environment for herself and the kids.

"Sounds awesome, I can't wait!" April couldn't help but think that things were definitely starting to look up, despite her fears of it all slipping away like it always had before.

***

The next day came, although it was hardly soon enough for April. As soon as she got back in the house, she started pestering Jo about taking her over to meet their neighbor with the unusual name. Jo informed her that she'd already called Mrs. Hairston and secured permission to go over there. April wanted to go right away. Jo took her big, puffy orange jacket off its hook by the front door and struggled into it.

"Chris, we're going to see Mrs. Hairston! I expect your homework to be done by the time we get back!" she shouted into the den.

"No fair! I wanna see Madame Wendigo too," his small voice complained.

"Then you should've finished your homework," Jo countered.

"But I *am* done!"

"Really? And is it done correctly? You didn't just rush through it to get it over with?" she asked skeptically.

"I did it right, I swear!"

Jo rolled her eyes. "Okay, you can come, but I'm checking your work when we get back."

"Yaaay!"

"The more the merrier, I guess," Jo said apologetically to April as she took Chris's coat down from the hook.

April shrugged; she really didn't mind him tagging along.

"He just wants to come because he likes the cookies she bakes," Jo whispered.

April smiled at this revelation, which sounded like Chris—always thinking with his stomach.

A moment later, Chris came tearing into the room with the kind of speed and enthusiasm that is a special gift of year-olds. Soon he was all bundled up, and they were on their way. Their boots crunched on the recently fallen snow as they trudged along the sidewalks. Some of them were shoveled and relatively snow free, others ankle-deep in it.

They came to a stop in front of Madame Wendigo's house.

Of course, it would *be this place,* April thought.

Last night, when Rob had said that Madame Wendigo lived two doors down from them, he failed to indicate whether she was two doors to the right or the left. In this case, it was the large Victorian to the right of their house. The old, spooky one that looked like the Munsters or the Addams Family might live there. She had dismissed it as being too much like where someone would expect a witch to live, but it seemed like this particular witch wasn't worried about falling into a stereotype. April couldn't figure out if that was cool or not.

As they walked up to the house, she could see that it was quite well maintained. While much of it was a dull, blue-gray color, there were splashes of lavender highlights here and there which created a nice contrast. April also noticed that she had some cool stone gargoyles perched atop the corners of the house acting as waterspouts, although they were half-covered in snow at the moment.

Madame Wendigo didn't appear to have a doorbell. Instead, there was a heavy brass door knocker in the shape of a snake eating its own tail. From her studies of mythology and witchcraft, April recognized it as being an ouroboros—an ancient symbol of the cycle of death and rebirth. Jo gripped it in her mitten-covered hand and gave it three good, solid, cracking raps.

Shortly after the third rap, the large wooden door swung open with a reluctant creak and a groan to reveal a somewhat wizened-looking black woman with a puffy cloud of white hair held back by a colorful headband. She wore a long dress covered in bright patterns, and over this she'd thrown on a rather plain gray button-up sweater. She wore a variety of necklaces and rings of all kinds that glittered over her knuckles. All of these accouterments clicked and clacked together loudly when she moved. Her face transformed from a serious, severe expression into a wide, welcoming smile at the sight of the three of them on the expansive front porch. April noticed that her teeth looked absolutely perfect—a little too perfect—and wondered if they were dentures. In any case, she was happy to see another black woman in the neighborhood. There were so few people like her in this town, and she often felt like she was the only one.

"Johnsons! Come in, come in! It's too damned cold outside to be hanging out and about." Her voice was high and lilting, almost musical.

"Hello, Helena." Jo beamed at her. She stepped inside, closely followed by the others.

"Hello yourself, Jo. Hello, young Chris. And you must be April." Her eyes twinkled as they appraised her. "I've heard so much about you." Whenever someone said that to her, April never knew if it was a good thing or a bad thing.

Madame Wendigo looked down at their snow-covered feet and grimaced. "Better take those off and leave them on this rug." She gestured to the large oriental rug that they were all standing on, which covered the wooden floorboards of the foyer. "You can hang your coats on that rack over there." She pointed to a wooden coat rack in the corner. A selection of odd hats hung from it. "I've got a fire burning in my parlor that we can warm our bones beside."

As she took off her galoshes, April looked around the interior of the house. It was crammed with unusual knickknacks wherever there was available space. Faded, old oil paintings hung everywhere. Some were portraits of stern-faced people in period costumes, others were landscapes that had an unnatural, surreal quality about them. There were the taxidermic remains of sundry animals bursting from the shadows. April spied a stuffed crow, a fox, and even a black bear lurking in various corners.

Now in socks, they followed Madame Wendigo into her equally eccentrically decorated parlor. It looked for all the world like the den of a fortune teller. The round table that dominated the room had a crystal ball in the center of it, with dark wooden chairs upholstered in opulent red velvet surrounding it. As advertised, a fire roared away in a nearby fireplace. April thought this was peculiar because she hadn't noticed any smoke belching out of the chimney when they'd been outside, yet the fire looked as if it had been burning for some time.

Despite the possibly peculiar nature of the fire, April found it to be effective in warming her up. She hurried over to it and held out her frigid fingers, delighting in the toasty sensation that now suffused them. Soon, Jo and Chris joined her before the blazing hearth. Madame Wendigo hung back, watching them. The dancing flames cast weird shadows over her face.

Chris cocked his head back to address her. "Do you have any of those amazing cookies?"

"Chris!" Jo was aghast.

Madame Wendigo chuckled in amusement. "It's fine. I admire a man who's not afraid to take the direct approach to get what he truly desires. It reminds me of my late husband. Don't worry yourself, young Chris! I made a fresh batch especially for you. If you'll all excuse me for a moment, I'll fetch them from the kitchen. Would the rest of you care for some refreshments? I have some nice hot cocoa."

The three guests all agreed that hot chocolate would really hit the spot. Madame Wendigo seemed to glide out of the room as if she was wearing roller skates under her dress.

"This sure is an interesting old place," April commented as soon as she was out of the room.

Jo nodded enthusiastically as her eyes roved over the photos arranged above the mantle. "She tells me that it's been in her husband's family for generations."

April wondered whatever happened to "Mr. Wendigo," as she preferred to think of him. She had just looked up Wendigos in an encyclopedia at her school's library earlier that day. They were a Native legend; creatures who were consumed by an overwhelming hunger to devour human flesh.

Maybe she ate him? April thought, then giggled at the grimly amusing mental picture that flashed in her head of the kindly, stately old woman gnawing on a severed arm like it was a turkey drumstick at Christmas dinner.

"What's so funny?" Chris asked, never wanting to miss out on a good joke.

April waved a hand at him. "Never mind, you wouldn't understand."

At that instant, Madame Wendigo hovered back into the room carrying a polished silver tray. Piled upon it were three steaming mugs, a large plate full of sugar cookies, and a stack of three smaller plates. She set it down near the crystal ball in the center of the table, then sat down in the chair at the head of the table. The others all crossed the room to sit with her.

"Please, help yourselves," she said invitingly. They all grabbed a mug, a plate, and a few cookies each. Chris took more than the others, studiously ignoring Jo's look of disapproval as he heaped them up.

"You'll forgive me for not partaking in anything myself. I've already eaten this evening, and I'm afraid I'll burst if I have anything else!"

Yup, eating a whole person is very filling, I'll bet, April thought and nearly burst into laughter again. She suddenly became aware of Madame Wendigo's dark eyes upon her, as if she was looking right through her. A chill ran down her spine.

The old woman spoke in her odd accent. "I sense a dark presence around you, child. Always hovering nearby, just on the edge of vision. Its energy is quite unusual . . . unlike anything I've ever experienced before."

April almost choked on her cookie. She gulped down a mouthful of the hot chocolate to wash it down, but it was too hot, and she scorched the inside of her mouth.

"A dark presenth?" she said hastily, her words distorted by her burnt tongue. "I don't know what you mean."

Madame Wendigo stared at her coolly. "That's quite alright. I also sense that you're not ready to discuss such things yet. But perhaps someday you will be ready, eh? Perhaps on that day, you will remember to come to me?"

April's mind was racing. On the one hand, it was good to have someone else finally acknowledging the reality of the Dark Man. On the other, independent confirmation of his existence meant that he was undeniably real and not the figment of her imagination she sometimes liked to pretend he was. Sometimes she thought insanity would be preferable to the existential can of worms that his reality opened up. In either case, Madame Wendigo was correct—she wasn't ready to speak of him to *anyone*.

April noticed a strange look come over Jo's face, as if she wasn't quite sure what to make of any of this. April imagined that Jo must be wondering what all this scary talk about a "dark presence" was. April hoped that she wasn't beginning to fear that bringing her to Madame Wendigo's place had been a terrible mistake.

Madame Wendigo broke the temporary silence that had settled over the table. "So, if I understand the purpose of your visit, young April here fancies herself to be something of a witch, no? And you are hoping that, as a fellow witch, I may be able to offer her some sort of guidance?"

"Yes. That's it exactly, if it wouldn't be too much trouble. Rob and I have lost contact with all of our old friends from our own days as Wiccans, and it's been so long that neither of us feels quite up to doing it ourselves. Besides, we don't want to unduly influence her with our own spiritual ideas. We want her to be free to choose her own path," Jo explained.

"Ah, yes. A noble sentiment," Madame Wendigo replied.

Madame Wendigo then fell silent for a moment, as if weighing what she should say. "Wicca is an earnest attempt to reconstruct lost magical traditions from ancient religions that were suppressed by the Catholic Church. What I practice is . . . different. It's part of a tradition that has existed in an unbroken line since before the dawn of history."

She looked at April appraisingly. "It's not for everyone. I sense in you great potential, but if you decide to walk this path, it will change your life in ways that you can't possibly guess at. I wasn't looking to take on a new apprentice, not at my age, but I've been very lonely since my own children grew up and moved far away. They hardly seem to have any time for old Madame Wendigo these days. It would be nice to have some company and youthful energy in this house again."

April was confused. Madame Wendigo considered herself to be a witch, but not a Wiccan? She'd always assumed the two things to be mutually exclusive. If she wasn't a Wiccan, then what was she exactly? Her words implied that she belonged to something even older, and possibly more powerful. The mystery of this intrigued April. If her magic was somehow more potent, perhaps it was strong enough to finally remove the Dark Man from her life forever—and maybe even reunite her with her departed family members. She had to find out.

"I'd be very honored to learn from you," she said, hoping she didn't sound too eager.

"Splendid!" The old woman smiled broadly, displaying her too-perfect teeth once more. The delight in her face was impossible to fake. "Then we should arrange a regular time for our sessions. I'm free on Saturday afternoons. Would two o'clock be convenient for you?"

April didn't have to think about it for very long. She didn't really have anything resembling a social life. She was involved in a few extracurricular activities, but those all took place right after school on weekdays. There was no good reason why she couldn't come over on Saturdays.

"That sounds perfect to me," she agreed.

"Excellent! Then we shall begin this upcoming weekend. Our sessions should only last about an hour or so. No need to bring anything but yourself. Is there anything you'd like to ask me?"

April began to shake her head in the negative, then stopped herself. "Yes, actually there is. I've been wondering . . . why do they call you Madame Wendigo?"

"I've spent most of my life abroad, on a little island in the Mediterranean. One of the friends I made when I lived there gave me that name."

Maybe that explains that strange accent of hers? April thought.

"It's not very flattering, though. I mean, a Wendigo is an evil spirit that eats people," April said, eager to show off her newfound knowledge.

"True, but it's also a fierce and powerful opponent. Someone with a hunger that can never quite be satisfied. In some ways, that describes me rather well. Besides, I don't think the friend who gave me that name even truly understood what a Wendigo is. He just thought it sounded cool—and so it does."

April wondered what hunger Madame Wendigo might have that is impossible to quell. She wasn't entirely sure that she really wanted to know.

"It's also a useful name to use when advertising my fortune telling services. Much more mysterious and evocative than Helena Hairston, wouldn't you say?"

April nodded. "So do you use that for telling fortunes?" She pointed to the crystal ball.

"Yes, amongst other things," Madame Wendigo answered mysteriously.

"Is that how you make a living?" April wondered if she could learn this skill from Madame Wendigo. If so, maybe she wouldn't have to work so hard at school. It must pay well if she could afford to keep a house this large looking so good. April loved learning, but no particular career really called to her yet. She was equally interested in everything! How did people narrow it down to just one thing? All she knew was that whatever she decided to dedicate her life to had to be something that paid well. Having lots of money was vital to her dream of having a more stable life and someday reuniting with her remaining brother.

Madame Wendigo laughed heartily. "No. The pay isn't bad, but it's something I do more as a way of helping people and keeping myself busy. Both I and my husband were quite fortunate in that we never had to concern ourselves much with not having enough money. We both came from very old, rather well-to-do families." She turned her head away curiously then, almost in embarrassment, as if recalling that discussing her finances was in poor taste.

April could only imagine what it must be like not to have to worry about money like that. She was determined to find out for herself someday.

The rest of the visit to Madame Wendigo's house passed pleasantly. Chris had his fill of cookies and belched loudly at the table, mortifying poor Jo. Madame Wendigo graciously replied that in her travels around the world, she'd discovered that *not* belching after a meal was considered to be an insult in many cultures, which always struck her as being quite sensible. In the end, she put the remaining cookies in a small Tupperware container and gave them to a grateful Chris to bring home with him. "To share with the rest of your family," Madame Wendigo told him gravely. April was glad that she'd added that last bit. She knew she'd want some more of the cookies too. She wondered what the old woman put in them that made them so damned good.

April slept well that night, despite the desperate, buzzing background noise of the Dark Man's bilious words. She'd never before felt so sure that she was on the right path, never before felt like her differences as a person weren't just tolerated, but fully accepted. She smiled as she drifted off to dreamland.

Yes, things are definitely beginning to look up for me.

Part Four : Waiting in the Rain

*T**hings are definitely not looking up for me.* Angela Hogan thought as she examined the grade on her paper in disbelief. As if staring at the "B+" scrawled on the top page would somehow alter it. Lots of students would be quite happy to have a grade like that in a class as demanding as Honors Latin, but for Angela, anything less than an "A" was a catastrophe. Her parents demanded perfection from her: perfect grades, perfect smile, perfect skin, perfect hair, perfect nails, perfect clothes, perfect shoes, and especially perfect piety before God.

She worked hard to avoid disappointing them, and oftentimes it felt impossible. At other times, she felt herself thriving off the challenge of it. But mostly she just felt exhausted from it all. Would it ever end? She was only sixteen years old. She was too young to feel so burned out, yet that's exactly how she felt: like she was all used up and running on fumes.

Despite that unacceptable "B+" on the paper before her, out of the list of perfect things that her parents demanded of her, the one that worried her the most was the perfect piety. She had her own ideas about her faith—ideas that her parents definitely wouldn't approve of. It was getting harder and harder to hide them, to keep her mouth shut and fake it. She knew she could pull up her grades, but how could she get rid of the sinful thoughts that constantly charged through her brain? Thoughts and desires that only grew more intense whenever she looked over at April McKenna, who now stood only a few feet away from her.

It wasn't that Angela didn't like boys at all. There were a *few* that she thought were cute but couldn't date, of course, due to her parents' strict rules. Yet she couldn't deny that she often found herself being just as strongly (if not more so) attracted to other girls. In the case of April, it was particularly powerful and difficult to ignore. She didn't want to ignore it. She didn't want to make these feelings go away, even if she could. But what choice did she have? She knew her parents would toss her out onto the street if they knew what she really was. It was hopeless. What was the point of torturing herself by thinking about it? Even though she'd never seen April show much interest in any guys, she was certain that April didn't reciprocate her feelings. All April seemed to care about was her GPA.

April, who was always so quiet and reserved, yet would occasionally surprise everyone by suddenly saying something hilarious out of left field. April, who was the subject of so much of the gossip at school. There were a million different stories about the mystery of her past. Everyone knew that she was a foster kid, so these stories tended to center on what had become of her real family and parents, each one more tragic and sordid than the last. If April was aware that she was the subject of so much speculation by her classmates, she didn't show it. Instead, she floated through her classes and the few clubs she participated in with a kind of regal, detached grace that Angela couldn't help but admire.

She also admired April's sharp mind and humility. She didn't have any of the nauseating smugness or cutthroat, competitive edge about her that so many of the other kids in the Honors Program had. Instead, she had a very down-to-earth and business-like demeanor. She was someone who was here to get things done without showing off or pumping herself up at the expense of others. These were qualities that Angela sometimes felt she lacked herself, which made her all the more appreciative of those who already seemed to have such things figured out.

Her attraction to April went far beyond these qualities, of course. It was physical, as well. How could she not be attracted to those dark, mysterious eyes? Her smooth, mocha skin? The cute way that part of her hair always flopped over one eye? Angela stole a hungry glance at her now as they waited for their ride to arrive, then quickly returned her gaze back to her disappointing paper.

Angela had stopped beating herself up for feeling such desires. If she had any guilt about it anymore, it was centered only on how angry her parents would be if they knew the truth, how they'd disown her. She was long past believing that such feelings were actually sinful. She wasn't even sure that she believed in the concept of sin anymore. The kind of God she liked to believe in was far too loving to bother obsessing over everyone's faults like Santa with his damned list.

Her parents expected her to be pious (according to *their* understanding of the concept), but it was so difficult. They'd pushed her to excel in school and to learn the Bible inside and out, and it had backfired on them. The classes Angela took as part of the Honors Program had opened up her mind, made her into too much of a critical thinker to take the Bible at face value as the undisputed, literal word of God.

She had no doubt that some of the events in the book had happened in some form or another, only to be heavily mythologized later on. Archeological finds had already proven that in a few cases. However, there were just too many things that were so fantastic that she couldn't take them seriously, although they worked just fine as allegorical stories. The logistics behind the story of Noah was her favorite example of one such story.

To her, it seemed glaringly obvious that the Bible was just someone's idea of what God might be like, as well as an attempt by pre-scientific people to explain how they got here. Then the trouble started when someone realized that they could use it to control how people behave. Telling someone that they have to act a certain way because God says so holds a lot more weight than just saying "Hey everyone, I think this is a really good idea!" She agreed with most of the morals found in the Bible, and didn't really have a problem with what Jesus had to say, but some of the things that were forbidden just seemed so wacky and outdated. Why was eating shellfish a sin?

She felt the same way about the Biblical attitude towards gay people—it was outdated and arbitrary nonsense created by people trying to control other people, and it had nothing to do with God's will. She grudgingly accepted that perhaps it might've made a twisted kind of sense thousands of years ago. If you're a small nation of people who are surrounded by hostile kingdoms, you might want to encourage people to "be fruitful and multiply" since potential invaders might be discouraged if they're hopelessly outnumbered. Maybe the fact that gay people don't tend to make as many babies was what made them so threatening to the Christianss? She didn't know, she just knew that the whole thing was ridiculous. She didn't think that God cared who you loved and was likely instead more concerned that you were someone who is capable of giving love.

Unfortunately, everyone seemed so hung up on these silly little details that had attached themselves to the Holy Book over the millennia like barnacles to a boat that they couldn't see the forest for the trees. That's how her parents were. Like so many people at her church, she felt like they were just there to show off what good Christians they were rather than focusing on what Jesus was actually trying to say. His message of love and acceptance was lost on those who needed to hear it the most, and who felt like they already understood it better than everyone else.

It made her sad to know that she could never trust them with the truth about herself, that it would destroy their carefully constructed picture of who they wanted her to be. She was even more despondent when she allowed herself to realize that it was this false image of her that they loved, and not the real her. She liked to imagine that someday she might be free of them completely. Her grades could get her into a good school and lead to a good career. Then she'd get out of this town, and once she was gone, she'd never look back. That was the great hope that kept her going, kept her so motivated to excel in school. Well, that and not having to listen to her parents complain when she let them down. It was so much easier to just give them what they wanted whenever she could. But she didn't plan to spend her whole life doing that—she couldn't.

That brought her back to the unfortunate "B+" before her. She wasn't looking forward to hearing them whine about it when she showed it to them. Yet she knew there was no point in delaying the inevitable—they'd find out about it in time; they always did. Better to face it now and get it over with.

A fat drop of water suddenly landed on her paper, causing the ink that her grade was written in to smear. Angela grumbled, quickly folded up her paper, and shoved it back into her backpack. The snow from earlier this week had given way to intermittent rain during the past few days as the weather warmed up slightly. Now, more thick, heavy drops rained down on her. She was stuck here after school, waiting for her ride to whisk her back home, but how long would she have to wait in the rain before the car finally showed up? She was about to head back to the steps behind her to take shelter under the roof overhang when a nearby sharp whooshing sound drew her attention.

It was the sound of April opening up an umbrella that she'd produced from somewhere. April must've noticed Angela looking at her, so she waved her over.

"C'mon! There's room enough for two under here!" She shouted to be heard over the rain as it picked up in intensity, becoming monsoon-like in a matter of seconds.

Angela needed little persuasion. She would've jumped at the opportunity to huddle with her under an umbrella even if she didn't have a hopeless crush on April. The only alternative was to get soaked by the freezing rain. She ran over to April, each step spraying cascades of water from the newly formed puddles that separated them.

"Thanks. It's getting crazy out here! When is our ride gonna show up already?" Angela asked in exasperation as she made it to the shelter under the umbrella. It was indeed an impressively big one. It was candy-apple red and shiny from the rain that slicked down its sides. April lowered it once Angela was underneath it so it would better protect them. It now completely covered the tops of their heads.

"Not soon enough, that's for sure," April said sympathetically.

An awkward silence hung in the air for a while as the two girls shivered under the umbrella. April decided to break it.

"I just wanted to let you know that was some really great research you did on the GDP of Brunei. I was just looking it over when the rain started up. Top-notch stuff."

Angela grinned from ear to ear at the compliment, until she decided that it must make her look exceedingly foolish and she reined it in. "Thanks. Hopefully it'll give you plenty to work with for your paper?"

"Oh yeah, definitely lots of good material in there for me to work with," April agreed.

They were both at school so late because of a meeting of the Model UN Club, a school activity that tries to emulate the actual workings of the United Nations. The students in the club pick a country, and then they have to research that country and represent their interests in a mock-up of one of the UN councils. Their school was set to travel clear across the country to Toronto to do that in a few months. April had agreed to write a paper that would outline all of the official positions of the country they were going to pretend to represent on the topic at hand, which in this case was economics. The other students in the class were doing the research, which April would then collate and refine into one (hopefully) coherent document. After the meeting was over, the other students in the club either walked home, which wasn't an option for April or Angela, or left on the activities bus. Jo usually picked up April, and since Angela lived only a block away from them, she always gave her a ride too.

Angela was glowing from April's praise, but was also trying hard not to show it by breaking into another silly smile. Instead, she said, "This is getting nuts! What's taking her so long? I should've just taken the bus."

April bit her lip, and a worried look crossed her face. Angela wondered what was going through April's mind. She had no idea that April desperately trying not to think of the last time a parent had failed to show up, which was the night her parents died. Angela had no way of knowing that as the weather grew worse, April was praying that Jo hadn't gotten into an accident. Angela didn't understand how vulnerable April was. How she wouldn't be able to bear it if something like what happened to her parents happened to Jo, who'd always been so kind and understanding like a real mom was supposed to be.

"I dunno. I hope she's okay." April said softly.

Angela hadn't thought of that. She hoped she hadn't sounded too ungrateful for the ride home Jo provided. The ride technically wasn't something that she needed. She could've just taken the bus. Honestly, the whole thing was just an excuse to spend more time with April, but she truly did appreciate that Jo was always willing to oblige. "I'm sure she's safe. We should see if we can wait inside in the meantime. No point in getting soaked out here."

April nodded. "I think they've already locked us out, but it's worth a try!" She lifted the umbrella high enough that she could see where she was walking and began steering them towards the back entrance. They splashed up the short series of concrete steps and were swiftly under the extra layer of protection offered by the overhang. Even beneath it, the high winds flung the rain towards them.

Angela tugged on the door handle. "No luck. I guess we're stuck out here." She shook her head in exasperation. They lived in a town where most people didn't bother to lock their front doors, yet Harold, the overly paranoid head custodian at their school, always locked the place up like it was Fort Knox at the first opportunity.

April beckoned her back under the umbrella, then lowered it again once Angela was under the comforting dome. They stood there for a while together in silence, until, to her eternal mortification, Angela's teeth began to chatter. She pushed up on the bottom of her chin to stop the embarrassing sound.

April giggled; it was obvious what Angela was feeling from how red her face had become. "It's okay. We all do it sometimes. Let's see if we can't warm each other up." With that said, April threw an arm around Angela, pulled her close, and began rubbing her back.

Angela's eyes widened at this unexpected gesture. She knew April was just doing it so they could keep warm, but she couldn't help but feel a secret thrill of excitement at being this close to her. They were standing so close together now that she could feel the heat of April's body pressed against hers. The warmth of her breath against her face was intoxicating. If the weather wasn't so miserable, this would've been her greatest fantasy come true. She returned the gesture, rubbing April's back. She couldn't believe she was actually touching her.

They were huddled so tightly that the tips of their noses brushed up against each other. Angela looked into April's eyes, and she saw something in them: a pleading kind of hunger that she recognized. Was it just her imagination, or had April started to rub her back more intensely? She took a chance and turned her head ever so slightly until her lips grazed April's. They hung there for a painstakingly long sliver of eternity. April didn't pull away in disgust or confusion. Instead, they each felt the weight of their lips barely pressed up against the other's. Angela chanced taking another look into April's eyes. They still smoldered with what she prayed was unfulfilled desire.

What the hell? You only live once, Angela told herself, then she took the plunge and kissed April. To her unimaginable relief, the kiss was returned with even more passion. Sparks seemed to be exploding in her head before they pulled away, each panting for breath.

"That was nice." April smiled at her.

"I didn't know you were . . ." Angela's voice trailed off. Somehow, she couldn't quite bring herself to say it out loud.

"I am," April assured her.

"I thought I was the only one in this school."

"So did I!" April laughed.

Angela laughed too. It felt so good to be able to finally share this part of herself with someone. It was as if years of tension were being washed away in the relentless downpour.

"Do you think we could try that again?" April asked with a desperate kind of vulnerability that broke Angela's heart. She answered her by pulling the umbrella down even further and kissing her again. This time, their tongues met and explored each other's mouths. April purred in contentment. Angela's legs suddenly buckled and felt weak.

This slice of heaven was interrupted by an insistent blare of a car horn. April pulled back and tilted the umbrella so she could see out into the parking lot where Jo's sensible sedan was idling, its headlights painting the asphalt before it a yellowish white.

"Shit, she's here!" April hissed.

"You don't think she saw us, do you?"

"No way. The umbrella was covering us up. It'll be okay, c'mon!" April replied as she grabbed Angela's hand and began to lead her down the steps and towards the waiting car. As soon as they reached it, April pulled the back door open, and Angela tumbled inside. Once her umbrella was closed, April joined her.

The instant they were inside the warm sanctuary of the vehicle, Jo began apologizing. "Oh, You poor girls must be soaked. I'm sorry I was so late in getting here. The traffic got all backed up from a wreck on the road. I feel terrible that you had to wait outside for so long in this crazy weather."

"It's fine. Don't sweat it," April said. Her fingers sought out Angela's hand and wrapped around it.

Angela squeezed it back. She was doing her silly grin again. This time, she didn't care. She didn't care about her wet hair or her even wetter clothes that she now shuddered in. Her heart pounded in time to the rhythm of the storm raging around outside of the car, yet she felt a calm inside that she'd never felt before. Without a doubt, this had to be the best day of her life—B+ in Latin be damned! The girl she liked, the smartest and most beautiful girl in the whole school, liked her back. Against all odds, they'd found each other.

Despite Jo's overly slow and cautious driving to compensate for the weather, the ride was over far too quickly for Angela's taste. When the car pulled into Angela's driveway, she reluctantly released April's hand.

"Call me later. There's still so much more we need to discuss . . . about Dubai," April said when she popped open the door.

"I will. I promise," Angela swore to her before turning to burst out from the car and sprint to her front door.

Later that night, Angela made good on her pledge. The two girls, who up until then had restricted most of their too brief conversations to school-related matters, began sharing their secrets with one another. April shared that she was Wiccan and would be studying under her neighbor Madame Wendigo soon. Angela in return told her of her own unconventional spiritual speculations. The two spent most of the night just talking and getting to know each other. They agreed to begin a romantic relationship with each other under the cover of a conventional friendship.

Angela was grateful that she had her own phone line; if there had been a possibility of her parents picking up the phone and listening in, there was no way she would've been comfortable discussing any of this. She was taking an awful risk by starting this relationship. But she didn't care, she needed this. She needed to do something for herself for once instead of living her life simply to please others.

***

April slept well that night. The dreadful presence of the Dark Man, hovering on the tip of her awareness, couldn't disturb her. Her optimism for the future was too great to be broken by some cranky old phantom. For the first time in her many years, she truly felt blessed. Blessed to be in this house with the kind family who treated her like one of their own and celebrated her religious differences. She even felt blessed to have been stuck out in such shitty weather. If not for that, she might not have ever had such an intimate encounter with Angela. She felt doubly blessed to have found out today that the girl that she liked, the smartest and prettiest girl in the whole school, liked her back. Against all odds, they'd found each other. She couldn't wait to see her again tomorrow, to call her and spend another few hours just talking. Now that she finally had someone to talk to, she realized she had rather a lot to say on practically every topic.

Is this love? Is this what it feels like? Yes. Surely it must be. What else could it be? She'd never felt this kind of excitement before. Yet she also knew that she couldn't declare these feelings to be what they were to Angela, at least not yet. Doing so too soon would *definitely* scare her off.

She drifted off to sleep. The warmth of her cocoon of blankets couldn't match the warmth she now felt in her heart. The fear that all of her recent good fortunes could be ripped away was still there too, but was soon chased away and reduced to nothing more than a shadow by this new light that burned inside her.

And shadows couldn't hurt her. Not anymore.

Part Five: The Hart Foundation

The rest of the week flew by. April and Angela spoke on the phone every night for hours on end, growing ever closer with each call. They found ways to spend more time together at school too, and began sitting together at lunch. It was difficult to find enough privacy to steal another delicious kiss, but they managed. It was even harder to spend any time together outside of school because of how strict Angela's parents were about letting her go out anywhere on a school night.

It was a miracle that they let her stay on the phone for so long each night, especially considering how much the "B+" had upset them. Angela thought the reason they allowed this was because April was black, and the idea that their daughter had a black best friend made their family appear to be more open minded and less racist than they actually were. All her family truly cared about were appearances. Would they have approved of such a friendship if April hadn't proven herself to be what her parents insultingly called "one of the good ones" because she was a well-behaved honor student, and someone who appeared to have assimilated to white culture? Angela already knew the answer to that question, and she was embarrassed and ashamed by it.

***

Soon, it was Saturday, and time for April to visit Madame Wendigo again. April nervously banged on the front door with its brass ouroboros, which stared at her with its lifeless eyes. The door appeared to swing open of its own accord, and April wondered if it was an automatic door, remotely controlled by Madame Wendigo. It would certainly be a convincing way to persuade her fortune-telling clients that she really possessed some kind of otherworldly powers. April knew it had succeeded in making her feel even more uneasy about this meeting than she already was. Coming to this house by herself, she was more aware of how spooky and imposing the place was.

"Come in, come in!" Madame Wendigo's voice floated to her from somewhere within. April stepped inside, and the door slammed shut behind her. She glanced around the doorframe but could see no mechanism that would open and close it like that. From the parlor to her side, she thought she could make out an eerie sort of chanting sound that sounded absurdly like baby talk. The odd sound abruptly ceased, but not before she wandered off in the direction of it.

Inside the parlor stood Madame Wendigo, dressed in much the same fashion as she had been on the previous occasion, except the colors and pattern of her dress were different. The fire still burned in the fireplace, and again April struggled to recall if there had been any smoke coming out of the chimney. Madame Wendigo was before the fire, its glow making strange shadows dance over her wizened face. She now turned to face her guest and smiled at her with her jarringly too perfect teeth.

"Welcome! Take off your coat and stay awhile. Have a seat," she thundered in her odd pastiche of accents.

April awkwardly pulled out one of the chairs from the table and draped her coat over the back of it before sitting.

Madame Wendigo crossed the room and lowered herself into the chair at the head of the table with a grunt. She put her elbows on the table (April couldn't help but think about how she'd heard once that that was supposed to be some sort of a breach of table etiquette), laced her fingers together, and leaned towards April conspiratorially.

"Well, now you've had a whole week to think about it. Did you have any more questions for me before we get started?"

April almost felt like the old woman was reading her mind. For all she knew, she was. She wasn't quite sure how she felt about that possibility. There was so much that she wanted to ask the old lady— she didn't know where to begin. Could she help her get rid of the Dark Man for good? Could she help her find her lost brother? Communicate with the spirits of her parents and brother? In the end, she asked her none of these things. All those questions were too big, too scary. She took the easy way out. The thing she ended up asking was actually the thing that she was the least curious about.

"You said something the last time I was here that confused me. Something about not being a Wiccan and being part of an older tradition. I was wondering if you could explain that?" April asked hesitantly.

"Ah yes, where to begin? The Wiccans don't have a monopoly on witchcraft, you know. There are many different kinds of witchcraft practiced all around the world by different cultures. The kind of magic that I practice is the oldest, however. It is also the most powerful and is the basis for all the rest. It's older than written history."

April couldn't help but snicker a little at that last statement. It sounded so grandiose and unbelievable. Of course, everyone always thinks that their particular belief system is the oldest and the best. The one big truth that trumps all the others. It made her a little sad that someone who seemed so wise had fallen into that kind of an intellectual trap.

Madame Wendigo sniffed indignantly at her skepticism. "Don't believe me, do you? I suppose it can be difficult to accept if you weren't raised in it like I was. The world wasn't always like this, child. It wasn't always dominated by machines and science. There was a time when humankind used magic to do most of the things we use technology for today. Long-distance travel and communication, building great structures, even storing information. That's one reason why there are no written records from that time. Most information wasn't written down, it was stored in objects." She looked wistfully off into the distance, as if she could actually see this bygone age.

April was intrigued by this unusual idea that appeared to conflict with any version of history she was familiar with. She decided to humor the old woman to learn more. "So, what happened then? Did everyone just forget how to do the magic? Why do we rely on machines now instead?"

"Forget how to use the magic? Don't be ridiculous! That's like forgetting how to breathe.! Magic is all around us. We are made of magic. People do a million little acts of magic a day and don't even realize it. Magic can be suppressed, controlled—but it can never truly be eliminated. No, even back then, most people didn't consciously know how to use the most powerful kinds of magic. There were two main groups that specialized in hoarding that kind of information. All the smaller groups of magic-users were aligned with one of these two factions in one way or another. The leader of one of these major factions was a man who called himself the Celestial Emperor, and he had a dream of uniting the whole world in peace under his banner."

"World peace? That doesn't sound so bad," April commented.

"It doesn't, does it? The problem is that the road to hell is always paved with good intentions, as they say. That's exactly what the Celestial Emperor did: create a kind of hell on Earth. He tried to unite everyone by force, abusing his magic to conquer and pacify the land. In time, he came to enjoy the destruction. He became addicted to the thrill of victory and conquest. Eventually the other major faction of magic-users, my ancestors, were forced to intervene as his conquests brought him ever closer to their borders. At first, their intentions were also noble: to defend their allies and maintain a buffer between the free lands and those of the Emperor. In time, they found themselves going on the offensive, liberating nations from the Emperor only to install their own puppet leaders. They too became caught up in the allure of empire-building. They became obsessed with freeing the whole world. The conflict grew in size. The magic used to fight it became more terrible, and the devastation greater. It was almost as bad as any nuclear war. The entire world, the whole human race, was nearly destroyed. This is why there is little evidence of this time left. The war destroyed all the great cities, scattered the people, reducing them to nomadic tribes."

"So how did the knowledge of how to use the magic survive?" April asked.

"The two factions survived. When the war finally ended, the survivors of these two great factions dedicated themselves to peace. They swore to never use magic in that way again. To ensure something like that could never happen again, they also swore to make sure that nobody else ever discovered the secrets of how to do this kind of magic. Sometimes they used the new religions that were emerging to suppress inquiry into magic. The new world was to be one that would rely on reason and technology to accomplish what magic had once done for mankind."

April's eyes widened. "'Never suffer a witch to live,'" she quoted. "Is that why the Church used to burn witches at the stake?"

Madame Wendigo looked down. A look of shame clouded her features. "Yes," she said quietly. "Your intuition serves you well. It's a dark stain on our people's history, one which we have since abandoned. These days, we are more tolerant. Magical traditions that we feel are not particularly threatening, like Wicca, are allowed to persist. We prefer trying to bring promising young people like yourself into the fold rather than throwing them to the wolves."

"So this is the kind of magic you want to teach me?" April was still a little skeptical, but also a little awed. If what Madame Wendigo was saying had any truth to it whatsoever, she was being entrusted with a potentially tremendous kind of power.

"Yes. If you want to learn, I sense great potential within you. In time, you could become one of our most important assets. However, I also sense that you've seen much and been through a great deal already in your young life. You are holding onto significant pain, and many secrets. If you're not careful, these things can consume you, can make you a danger to yourself and others. There are dark forces swirling around you that are intent on making that happen. Forces which I don't fully understand. It is for that reason that I intend to take things very slowly with you. You must first learn to master yourself, to conquer this darkness, before you can master the most powerful kinds of magic. Otherwise, you might end up like the Celestial Emperor."

"I want to learn. I want to learn how to overcome this ... darkness," April assured her without falling into the trap of telling her what little she knew about the Dark Man. She still wasn't sure she was ready to trust the old woman with that information yet.

The old woman appeared pleased by her answer. "Good! Then we will start with a regimen of meditation. Have you ever meditated before?"

"No," April admitted. It had always sounded like some kind of flaky hippie stuff to her.

"I shall teach you how to do so. It's essential to be able to place yourself into an altered state of consciousness quickly to be able to do the kind of magic you will learn from me, and this will help you do that. It will also have the extra benefit of easing your anxieties and promoting your general mental health, which will help you in dealing with the darkness that surrounds you."

Madame Wendigo led her through a basic meditation and asked her to practice it twice a day, once in the morning and once at night. April found it to be quite a pleasant experience in and of itself. It brought her a kind of inner peace that she hadn't really known before. Yet at the same time, she felt a certain degree of impatience that this was all that her new mentor had bothered to teach her thus far.

The first time April tried it at home in her own bedroom, she was a little frightened that the Dark Man would show up and ruin it. In fact, the notion that he might choose to appear while she was meditating terrified her. What would he be like when she was in that altered state of mind? Would she be able to see and hear him clearly? The thought of seeing him as he truly was was simultaneously tantalizing to her curiosity and something that she wanted to avoid at all costs. Eventually, she was able to overcome her fears and meditate in her room anyway. She found that the actual result was quite the opposite of what she'd feared: She couldn't hear or sense him at all while she was deep in meditation.

She came to enjoy the calm that came with meditation so much that she told Angela all about it, and even tried to walk her through how to do it over the phone one night. It didn't go so well.

"I'll never get the hang of this. I can't help but think of something!" Angela laughed through the receiver.

April didn't mind that Angela wasn't able to do it. he thought it was sweet of her to be open-minded enough to try.

During that first week of meditation, April could barely sense the Dark Man at all when she went to sleep. It was as if he was sulking and losing interest in her. April again began to wonder if he was real. Perhaps she really had seen a ghost as a child, and all of her subsequent encounters with him had been a figment of her imagination. She had only really seen him that one time so many years ago. All the other times, she just heard him in her head and sensed him nearby. But Madame Wendigo seemed to be aware of him too, which suggested that he had some existence independent of her own mind—or did it? If he was just a manifestation of her own dark side, then perhaps that's what Madame Wendigo had been picking up on. April shuddered to think that such dark and violent thoughts as those that the Dark Man muttered to her might've really originated from inside of herself. She liked to think that she was better than that, but was she really?

In either case, the important thing was that his presence seemed to be weakening. If he was just some projection of her own inner darkness, then the meditation regimen was already helping her to master this aspect of herself.

Later on that week, April had a rare visitor to her home. His name was Nathan Shane, but eEveryone just called him "Nate". He was a tall, somewhat husky boy with a tousle of sandy brown hair, a round face, and bright hazel eyes. He was the first person at her school to show any kindness to April when she'd first arrived a few months earlier when he let her sit at the same lunch table as him and his small circle of friends. He had taken her under his wing and showed her how to survive in the school. He was also in the Honors Program and was her lab partner in one of the science classes they shared.

She considered him to be her best friend at school, or at least she had until she'd started talking to Angela so much—though, Angela was so much more than just a friend. However, this friendship hadn't really extended itself much beyond the confines of the school grounds. Nate had suggested hanging out outside of school a few times, but she'd always brushed aside such suggestions. She did this partially because she buried herself in her studies so much that she rarely had time left for anything else, but also because she was a little scared that maybe Nate wanted something more out of the friendship than she was ever prepared to give.

Science was the reason for his visit that day. A science fair was coming up in a few months, and the two lab partners had resolved to team up and enter it. Winning a science fair was the sort of thing that looked great on a college application, so she had decided to let him come over so they could try to brainstorm ideas for the science fair. Jo and Rob were okay with the idea of her having a boy over. Honestly, they were happy for her to have anyone her own age over to the house and that she was showing signs of having something resembling a social life. They just demanded that she leave her bedroom door open.

While Nate was over, April noticed Chris was loitering in the hallway and walking past her bedroom more than usual. It amused her to know that Jo and Rob had likely recruited him to act as their spy. It was the old "use the younger sibling to spy on the older ones" routine. Her own parents had employed her in that capacity plenty of times against her own brothers. If only they knew that they had nothing to worry about. Nate probably was the kind of boy she would've liked if she liked boys at all, but she didn't. Even if she did, she was far too in love with Angela to even think of anyone else.

They couldn't agree on what to do for the fair. April's efforts over the years to figure out what the Dark Man was had led her to read many books on parapsychology. She wanted to do something that might be able to test some of the assumptions that such researchers make about that sort of phenomenon in a more scientific way. Nate thought this was a very intriguing idea, but he was also afraid it would prove to be too difficult to design and demonstrate that kind of experiment.

They decided to take a break from talking about the pros and cons of the different experiments they could do. They went downstairs to the vacant family den to watch some TV, hoping to find inspiration in its randomness. They sat next to each other on the shag carpet in front of the TV. April flipped listlessly through the channels with the remote until she came across something that made her smile with the pleasant glow of nostalgia: pro wrestling was on!

Her father used to watch a local wrestling program called *Stampede Wrestling* when she was younger. She had many pleasant memories of sitting there beside him, cheering on the faces (the heroes) and booing the heels (the villains). Even after he began to succumb to the lure of the bottle, she still had a good time watching wrestling with him. After her father died, she and her brother Ty tried to carry on the tradition whenever they could. She knew it was all fake, naturally. Yet, in an odd way, she thought that the performance aspect of it elevated it into being more of an art form than a mere athletic competition. These guys had to be part athlete, part stuntman, and part actor. Even in these pre-planned fights, the injuries were often quite real and brutal. The set ups might be false, but the danger was all too real.

"Oh, cool! We're watching this," April announced. Then realized she was being a terrible host. She decided that she should probably let her guest have some say in the matter. "Is that okay with you? I mean, we don't *have* to watch this. You probably think it's really silly, because well, frankly, it *is* very silly—but I love it anyway."

Nate laughed. "No, this is fine. I like watching this stuff too."

"What? Really? No way! I'm glad to see that you can appreciate something so . . . unsophisticated."

She meant it, too. Some of the other kids in the Honors program were kind of snobby when it came to things like this. They always wanted to show off how much they liked things like fine art and classic literature. It was like they were trying to show the world how adult they could be, but to such an extent that they were pissing away what little remained of their childhoods. It's like they were all in such an awful rush to grow up that they were already forgetting how to have fun, how to be kids. It was a trap that April was wary of falling into herself. She hadn't detected much of that kind of attitude from Nate in the relatively brief time she'd known him. That was probably part of why they got along so well, but it was always nice to find out that somebody was even cooler than you initially thought they were.

"Oh, but it is sophisticated, just in an unconventional way. It's like an under appreciated art form," He said earnestly.

"Yes! That's exactly how I feel about it too."

"You could even look at it from a sociological standpoint. The different kinds of personas that the wrestlers take on and their storylines reflect different trends going on in the real world," Nate continued.

"Hmmm . . . I never looked at it like that before, but you're right! It just goes to show, you can make anything into something highbrow if you look at it from the right point of view." She was overjoyed to have a friend who not only appreciated this stuff as much as she did, but even found new ways of understanding it.

"Or if you're adept enough at slinging fancy-sounding bullshit to justify your love of something." He laughed again. "The more I think about adulthood, the more I realize that maybe seventy percent of success is just being able to talk a lot of bullshit well. For better or for worse, people seem to respond to hype more than substance. The world the adults have created runs on bullshit. Nobody can handle the truth. They'd rather pay people to lie to them. It's sad, but true."

April chewed on his words. It seemed like a rather cynical way of looking at things, but she could also see truth in it. She just nodded, too busy digesting his ideas to formulate a good response.

He wasn't done with his thesis yet. "Hell, I could even use wrestling to prove this point, too. You know those promos that the wrestlers do before a match, where they just come on and talk lots of smack? Half of the really successful guys aren't even that great at wrestling, but they're so good at talking about themselves that they seem much more badass than they really are in the ring."

"Everything is a microcosm," April added, summing up his ideas with an elegant succinctness.

He smiled. "Right. Like I was saying earlier the wrestling world just reflects the real world around it. Because it's such a caricature of the world, you're actually able to see the world more clearly when looking at it through this medium. Or maybe that's all a bunch of bullshit too, and the five-year-old in me just likes to watch a bunch of dudes pretending to kick the shit out of each other."

April shook her head in astonishment at the way that Nate could go on about something with total conviction, only to then completely cut down his own argument in a self-effacing way. "You shouldn't be so dismissive of yourself. That was some pretty brilliant stuff you just said there."

He winked at her. "Nah. The worst thing you can do is to start believing your own bullshit. That way lies madness! Trust me on that one."

Again, April was left speechless by his words. She wanted to tell him to be more confident in himself, but she could also see the wisdom in what he'd just said. Surely the best approach was a balance of the two extremes. Before she could ponder this any further, she was distracted by what was on the TV.

"Oh, cool. The Hart Foundation is gonna be in the next match," she cried out in delight. The Hart Foundation was a tag team made up of Bret "The Hitman" Hart and his brother-in-law Jim "The Anvil" Neidhart.

"You like them too?" Nate asked, surprised.

"Of course. They're local heroes, aren't they? I used to watch Bret wrestle all the time, ever since I was a little kid."

"Bret Hart, now there's a guy with some substance. If only he was a little better at bullshitting, he'd probably be a bigger star," Nate chimed in as they watched the tag team approach the ring.

April couldn't disagree with his assessment of her wrestling hero. Bret was known for his technical skills at executing difficult holds in the ring, but his promos tended to lack a certain verve.

They had a good time together watching the Hart Foundation wrestle. They were really getting into it. It was almost like being back watching it with her brother Ty. Thinking of Ty made her heart ache. How she missed him. She was still angry at him though, for leaving her alone, but she didn't want to think of that right now. Didn't want to spoil the good time she was having. Then the program cut to a commercial break.

"I'm so glad I asked you over. We might not have made much progress on the science fair thing, but it's been fun. We should spend more time just hanging out outside of school, eh?" she blurted out.

"I'm happy to hear you say so, April," Nate said. A nervous trembling quality had crept into his voice. "I was hoping that we could spend a lot more time together in the future . . . like maybe go out on a date together some time?"

April gasped. "Omigod! Are you . . . are you asking me out?" She was taken aback. Why did everyone suddenly seem to have the hots for her? She was feeling irritated, too. Here she was, having a great time, and now he had to ruin it all by asking for something from her that she wouldn't—*couldn't*—possibly give him. It wasn't fair. Why couldn't they just hang out and have fun together as friends? Why did he have to drag this into it?

"I like you April. I like you a lot. I always have. From the moment I first saw you,." He stammered.

She was getting even angrier. So, was all his kindness just for show? Just part of a strategy to get into her panties? How much did he *really* like her? Then she looked in his eyes and saw the genuineness in them, the vulnerability, and her heart broke. She knew that he meant what he said. She wasn't just some kind of a conquest to him, another notch on his bedpost. He wasn't that kind of guy. He really did seem to like her for who she was, or rather who he thought she was. She was flattered, actually. Had she been heterosexual, he would've been a good match for her. But she wasn't, and there was no getting around that fact.

She realized that she now held his heart in her hand. It didn't make what she had to do next any easier. Even if she wasn't already in a relationship, she would have to turn him down, have to to break his heart. It was bad enough that she had to pretend to be straight and sneak around to see Angela. She wasn't about to compromise herself any more than she already was. She had to live her truth, or as much of it as it was possible to do at this time.

"I'm sorry, Nate. I'm so sorry. A part of me wishes that I could, but I just can't. I really can't."

"Why not? It's me, isn't it? I'm just too much of an uncool goofball," he said petulantly.

"No, not at all! You're brilliant. You're one of my favorite people, you really are.! You're the most wonderfully unpretentious pretentious person I know"

He laughed at that last line. It felt good to hear him laugh. Maybe she could still salvage this horrible situation, and they could still come out of it as friends after all? His laughter gave her hope that it she could.

"It really *is* me. There are things you don't know about me, Nate. Things that make it impossible for us to be together like that."

Nate looked confused. "What kind of things? You can tell me. You can trust me."

April bit her lip. Could she trust him? She'd never told anyone else about this part of her life before, aside from Angela of course. She *wanted* to tell him, but how would he take it? She looked at him again, his eyes like those of a wounded puppy dog. *Fuck it.* She was sick of holding all these secrets inside of herself. It was eating away at her spirit. She decided that she had to take a chance. If she ever wanted to have friends, *real* friends that she could depend on, she would have to learn how to start trusting more people with her true self. Something about Nate told her that she could trust him. Her instincts told her so, and Madame Wendigo told her to always trust in her instincts.

"It's because . . . because I'm gay, Nate. I'm a lesbian," she revealed in a whisper. It felt so strange to actually say it out loud. "You can't tell anyone else, please don't tell anyone."

His eyes bulged in a way that she would've found to be quite comical under other circumstances.

"No way. Are you sure?"

Now she was annoyed with him again. What kind of a stupid question was that? "Of course I'm sure. Are you sure that you're only attracted to girls?" she countered.

"Yeah." he smiled mischievously "While I do enjoy watching sweaty men in tights and underwear grabbing each other, it doesn't excite me on that level."

She couldn't help but grin at that response. "Well, it's exactly like that."

He was quiet for a moment, still mulling over the new information in his mind.

"You're not afraid to be my friend now, are you? You don't think I've got AIDS or anything, do you?" she asked nervously.

"Don't be silly!" He looked vaguely offended by the question.

"Oh, thank the Goddess," she muttered under her breath.

Suddenly Nate's eyes widened. "I'm a big dummy! I should've known. Angela! You like Angela, don't you? That's why you're got her sitting at our lunch table now. That's why you're spending so much time together all of the sudden. You're more than just best friends, aren't you?"

"Shit! Keep it down, will you?" April said in alarm. He was so excited in his new role as amateur detective that he was announcing his leaps of logic at full blast to the whole house.

He covered his mouth in embarrassment. "Sorry! I forgot. Don't worry, your secret's safe with me. But I'm right though, aren't I?"

April looked down. It was one thing to out herself, but was she really about to out Angela too? Still, she didn't have much choice, did she? Nate had already figured it out, and she didn't want to lie to him. She still felt that her instinct to trust him had been correct.

"Yes, but you have to swear not to ever tell anyone else. You don't know how horrible her parents are. If they ever found out, they'd throw her out of the house."

"Hey, I told you that your secret is safe with me, and I meant it," he reassured her. Something in his eyes, in his whole demeanor, told her it was true.

"I . . . I think I might be in love with her, Nate," she confessed. It felt good to be able to tell *someone* that, even if it wasn't the someone who needed to hear it. Maybe having someone else she could confide in, someone that she could talk to about her relationship with Angela was a blessing in and of itself.

"I'm happy for you, April. Happy that you've found somebody you can love." She could tell that he meant it, but she could also detect more than a hint of sadness and self-pity in his tone. She decided that she needed to throw him a bone. She might not be able to date him, but she knew someone who would be happy to.

"I may not be able to return your affections, at least not in the way you'd probably prefer, but I *do* know someone who thinks that you're pretty cute . . ." she said teasingly.

"What? Really? Who?" Clearly he wasn't expecting this.

"Jenny Cronin," April said with a sly smile.

"Jenny Cronin," Nate repeated. Jenny was one of the most talented artists in the school—a fantastic sketch artist and painter. She was also a bit of a hippie.

"She's ... not bad!" Nate grinned. She was, in fact, what he would've typically called " a real cutie."

"I know, right?" April agreed gleefully.

"And so talented. Did you see those posters she made for the fall play?"

April nodded eagerly.

"Well, she's no April McKenna, but I could do worse, eh?"

"You should totally go for it."

"And when did you plan on actually sharing this valuable information with me?" Nate said in a tone of mock irritation.

"Hey, you never asked." April shrugged.

Nate grabbed a pillow from the couch behind him and tossed it at April playfully. She deftly dodged it. She was grateful that Nate was taking this so well, and grateful that he had turned out to be someone that she really could trust.

"We should still hang out though. As friends—if you still want to? I could use more friends," April told him.

"I'd be honored to."

"So you don't think I'm a freak because I'm gay?" she asked.

"Oh no, I know that you're definitely a freak, but only in the best possible way. It's alright, so am I. Only bona fide freaks ban apply to be part of this club," he said with gusto.

April didn't think he was particularly freaky—compared to her, he was positively normal. She also didn't doubt that he saw himself that way, probably because his high intelligence made him feel like he didn't have much in common with most of the other kids at school. She could only speculate. She was just grateful to have a friend that she could be real around.

She picked up her half-empty can of Coke off the floor and raised it high in the air over her head. "Here's to the freaks!"

Nate cast about on the carpet for his own can of Coke, which Jo had dutifully provided earlier (no doubt as a way of keeping tabs on them herself). When he found it, he returned the impromptu toast.

"Here's to the freaks!" he repeated, their cans clinking together with a tinny clang and accompanied by the swish and fizz of the liquid within. They both slurped from the cans, with Nate chugging his. He belched loudly as he slammed it back down. April rolled her eyes. What was it with boys and their love of belching?

"Please excuse me. I needed to vent some bodily gasses," he said in an overly serious tone.

She giggled. "See? You're the most unpretentious pretentious person! This is exactly what I'm talking about."

He raised an eyebrow. "You know, you really suck at giving compliments."

She shrugged her shoulders again. "Guilty as charged."

During their whole recent conversation, the WWF wrestling program they'd been watching had returned from its commercial break and gone off the air. Their conversation had been so intense that they'd hardly noticed. Now the station had switched over to the evening news. Nate was the first one to notice the change in programming.

"Aww man, we missed the rest of the match! Now the boring old local news is on instead."

"Boring? But I thought you liked to keep up with current events. Otherwise, how would you know what societal trends are being mirrored by wrestlers?" April teased.

"I'm more interested in international affairs. All this local stuff seems so pedestrian," he said airily.

"Oh, a real man of the world, are you? Have you ever considered joining the Model UN? We could always use a few more members."

"No offense, but I've got enough extracurricular stuff going on right now. I'm not about to take on something else."

April didn't say anything in response. He watched as a strange look transfixed her features, and her mouth hung agape. She was completely engrossed by something on the news report. For the first time since the news came on, Nate actually looked at what was on the screen, probably trying to figure out what had so utterly captivated her.

The screen was showing mug shots of three different men. Across the bottom of the screen, the words "Armed Robbers Captured" were emblazoned in white pixels. The anchorwoman was speaking over the images in a flat, empty voice.

"Three men were arrested today following a botched bank robbery in Calgary, including the alleged ringleader, Ron McKenna."

"That's my brother!" April cried out as she turned to Nate, tears streaming down her face.

Part Six: The Prodigal Son

Nate gave April an awkward hug after her tearful revelation. She swore him to secrecy. "The last thing I need is for everyone at school to find out that my brother is a bank robber," she exclaimed. Nate needed no further convincing. She was grateful to have found such a good and trustworthy friend.

She now was caught up in a whirlwind of conflicting emotions. On the one hand, she was happy to learn that he was still alive and to finally know what had become of him. On the other hand, she was confused and embarrassed and worried to discover that he had gotten mixed up in a life of crime.

After Nate went home, she told Jo and Rob about it. They were already aware that she had an older brother who had gone missing, and how heavily not knowing his fate weighed upon her. Rob had even toyed with the idea of hiring a private investigator to find out what happened to him. They comforted her as best they could. They decided to look into where he was currently being held for sentencing to see if they could arrange a visit. Rob was even talking about hiring a lawyer for him.

They found out where he was being held and set up a visit on the following Saturday. This would mean that April would have to cancel her session with Madame Wendigo for that day. The old woman was obviously disappointed when April told her during their next Saturday meeting, but she also understood how important it was to the girl to reconnect with her long-lost brother and wished her luck. "I'll be lighting a candle for you and your brother, my child," she said to her in that mysteriously impossible-to-place accent of hers. It warmed April's heart when she called her "my child." The strange old woman was rapidly becoming like the grandmother she'd always wanted. April had never really known her own grandparents. Her father's mother had passed away long before she was born. Her maternal grandmother was tucked away in a nursing home somewhere, forever lost in a fog of dementia; she'd only met her once or twice.

Madame Wendigo's lesson for that week was just building more upon the meditation techniques she'd already taught her. April would've been frustrated with this slow pace if these exercises hadn't proven to be so effective in grounding her during this difficult time. As it turned out, it was precisely what she needed when she needed it.

The rest of that week passed at an agonizing pace. It was lightened somewhat by developments at school. As far as April could tell, Nate was as good as his word. It didn't appear that he had revealed any of the secrets that April had recently shared with him. She had been worried that things might be strange between them now, but thankfully the opposite was true, and they both seemed more comfortable in each other's presence.

Nate hadn't wasted much time in asking out Jenny Cronin. April found his eagerness to do so amusing but was surprised to also find that she was a little offended that he'd gotten over his crush on her so quickly. Hadn't that been the whole point of telling him that Jenny liked him? Jenny had said yes, naturally. So, it wasn't long before they were doing all those cute little things that couples in high school do: holding hands all the time, passing notes, and covering up their hickies. Jenny had joined them as a regular at their lunch table, and her buoyant energy often brightened the periodically too-serious mood at the table.

April sometimes felt a bit of resentment, though—resentment that Jenny and Nate could get away with being so open in displaying their affections for one another. In contrast, she and Angela had to always be so careful about keeping the true depths of their feelings for each other a secret. It wasn't fair, but she didn't like feeling angry about it, either. It wasn't Nate and Jenny's fault that the world was this way. She instead tried to focus on just being happy that two people that she liked had found happiness with each other—a happiness that she had played a major role in facilitating—and that her circle of friends was growing.

All four of the friends agreed to get together at April's house every week to watch wrestling together. It became their new weekly ritual. Even Angela's restrictive parents had relented and allowed her to participate—although they thought she was going to April's house to study. Some adults would've been irritated to find their house suddenly invaded by a gaggle of babbling teenagers, but not the Johnsons. Jo and Rob both seemed quite pleased to see that the girl they were already beginning to think of as their real daughter was starting to build something for herself that resembled a normal social life.

That Thursday morning, April was violently ill—so ill that Jo insisted that she stay home from school. April had a perfect attendance record up until then and was loath to break it, but eventually succumbed to the inescapable logic of the situation. She *did* feel like shit, and would likely end up puking at school, which was infinitely more embarrassing than doing it at home,just to be sent home anyway. Jo spent the day dutifully nursing her, and by the time night rolled around, she felt much better—physically, at least.

Her mind was still a bundle of anxieties over the fate of her brother. She couldn't stop thinking about him while she was sick. In the end, the whole incident was chalked up to being nothing more than a twenty-four hour stomach bug—although April couldn't quite shake the feeling that there was somehow something more to it than that.

Unfortunately, April's nights were becoming quite fraught again. The Dark Man, whom she had hoped was losing interest in her, was back with a vengeance. Although she could shut him out completely with meditation, she couldn't meditate all night long. When she went to sleep, she could hear him more clearly now than she could in years.

His words were as ugly as ever: *You have no real family, and you never will. Your brother is lost to you now, nothing but a common hoodlum who will spend the rest of his days rotting away in a prison cell for his crimes. You think you have friends, a mentor, and a lover now, but they'll all turn on you in the end. The pain you'll feel when they disappoint you and betray the love you have for them will be unbearable. It's better to spare yourself that anguish, to just end it all now. End them or end yourself. Why cling to this wretched life? Why continue to suffer? Pain is inevitable. Break the cycle of pain. The only escape, the only peace is in death. Embrace your death!*

On and on he went, as if drawing strength from her anguish. How did he know what was in her mind so intimately? Could he read her mind? Or did he know because he was a product of her mind? Both possibilities terrified her equally. She instinctively tried to plug her ears with her fingers to stop the flow of his venomous speech, but the vile words were in her head, not the air. Was she losing her mind? Was knowing that her brother was alive, yet possibly facing a long prison sentence worse that not knowing what had happened to him? At least when she had no idea where he was, it was possible to imagine that he'd found success and happiness. Now that dream seemed impossible.

She was only able to get through these nights by focusing on the many positives in her life lately. To think about the joy she got from finally being in a safe and supportive home, the love she felt for Angela, and how good it felt to have a friend like Nate that she could confide in. For the first time in her life, she felt like she was able to share more of her true self with others without fear of rejection. It was a wonderful feeling after keeping so many things hidden deep inside for so long. She concentrated on this feeling and let it sustain her.

The day finally came when the Johnsons were able to drive her out to the jail where her brother was being held. It was what April called a "deceptive day," meaning a day that was bright, sunny, and beautiful to look at through a window, but the minute you stepped outside you realized how bitter and bitingly frigid it truly was. It was warm inside the family car, at least.

They brought Chris along for the trip, and he was unusually quiet and well behaved. She hoped he was okay. She wondered how he was processing all of this. Did he really understand why they were making this trip today? April looked over at him and thought about how much she already saw herself as his big sister, even after only a few months in the house. It was odd to think that she was now riding to visit someone who literally was her older brother. Was this how Ron had felt about her once? Was it still how he felt? But if so, why had he stayed away? Why hadn't he reached out to her? These questions tortured her for the entirety of the ride.

She told Angela all the details of the visit over the phone when she got back home. "The ride to the prison was long and uneventful. When we finally got there, they patted us down and searched us really thoroughly. Even little Chris got the same treatment. I half-expected them to order us to strip down and to shine a flashlight up our asses looking for contraband," April began.

Angela snickered through the phone line. "I'm sorry. There's nothing funny about what you went through today. It's just the way that you describe things sometimes, I can't help it."

"No, go ahead and laugh. I love to hear you laugh. It's true, it wasn't a good day, but I'd rather try to find the humor in any situation than sit around and cry about it endlessly."

"I love that about you. It's such a good attitude."

April's heart soared to hear her say "I love that about you." It was so close to the "I love you" that she longed to hear from Angela, but hadn't been granted yet.

"It's not a good attitude, it's a coping mechanism—a survival skill," April said, appearing to bluntly deflect the praise while she was actually dancing in joy on the inside.

"So what happened next?" Angela prompted.

"Next they brought us into one of those rooms where the prisoners are sitting behind a Plexiglass window, and you have to talk to them through a phone just like you see in the movies."

"Wow. I've never seen anything like that in real life."

April bet she hadn't. She couldn't imagine Angela's family ever visiting a place like that.

"I recognized my brother Ron right away, even though he looked so much older and even more haggard than he had in his mugshots. His expression brightened slightly when he first caught a look at me, but then it clouded up again right away. It was like he'd already decided that he wasn't going to allow himself any pleasure in seeing me, but had momentarily slipped up and was ashamed of that. I sat down and picked up the receiver. Before I knew what was happening, I was already talking to him. I had to ask him the question that had been burning away in my mind for years now.”

***

“It’s so good to finally see you again!”Ron said.

“Yeah, I just wish it was under happier circumstances. Look at you, though! You’re almost all grown up! Almost a woman.”

“What happened? Why did you just disappear like that?”

He looked down and studied his hands, afraid to look me in the eye.

“Those cans of food and the other stuff you and Ty were bringing to me weren’t cutting it. I was always hungry. I started breaking into people’s cars, stealing loose change and anything else valuable that I could find so I could buy myself a few hot meals. I never told you two about any of that. The cops started patrolling more heavily, and one night I almost got caught. They chased me through a bunch of people’s backyards before I finally lost them. After that, I knew I had to get out of there. I’m sorry. I should’ve at least said goodbye, but I didn’t know how to. I guess I was too embarrassed about it all to admit to you two why I really had to go.”

***

Angela inhaled sharply into the phone. “Wow. So that’s why he left? How did it make you feel to finally have an answer?”

April contemplated the question for a minute before speaking. She hadn't even really allowed herself enough time to ask herself that question yet. "Satisfying and yet totally unsatisfying at the same time. Honestly, that's the best way to describe this entire situation. It's good to at long last have some answers . . . but then the answers totally suck. At least he was trying to apologize for just disappearing like that, in his own half-assed kinda way. I could understand his reasons for it to . . . to an extent. He was the oldest. He was our role model, and he didn't want us to know that he was involved in any criminal stuff."

"How did he go from breaking into a few cars to trying to rob a bank?" Angela wondered aloud.

"I'm getting to that. Basically, he next told me that he hitchhiked into the city. Once he was there, he lived on the streets for a while before eventually getting hooked up with a street gang. From there, things just kept on escalating. He really didn't want to talk about it in much detail., he's pretty ashamed of it all, the sorts of things he had to do to survive."

"What did he have to say about the robbery itself?" Angela asked.

Something about the way she said it annoyed April a little. There was a certain hunger in her voice, as if begging for the latest juicy gossip. A part of April wanted to scream at her that this wasn't just some salacious true crime story to dig into to pass the time—this was her life. Her *real* and incredibly fucked up real life.

April took a deep breath, as if beginning a meditation, and fought down these feelings. Perhaps she was reading far too much into Angela's tone. Maybe she was just trying to show that she was fully interested and engaged in her story, and it had just come off wrong. She decided to give her the benefit of the doubt. That's what you're supposed to do for the ones you love, isn't it?

"He didn't have much to say about it. Like I already said, he's really very embarrassed and humiliated to admit that he's involved in any of this sort of stuff. That's also why he never tried to find me or Ty. The main thing that he wanted me to know about it was that he never planned to hurt anyone. He said that the guns they had weren't even real. They were really realistic looking BB guns."

"BB guns? *Jesus!*" Angela said in surprise. Unbeknownst to April, she covered her mouth and glanced around nervously hoping that her parents hadn't heard her taking the Lord's name in vain like that—or there would be hell to pay. Satisfied that her blasphemous outburst hadn't been overheard, she continued.

"So if, like, the guns weren't even real then, how can he be charged with armed robbery? He wasn't armed with anything but toys."

"That's just the thing, it doesn't matter. If the people being held up believe that your weapons are real, the fear or mental anguish that they experience is the same as if it was the real deal. So the law treats it like it's the same thing," April explained.

"Whoa, I never knew that. That's messed up. I mean, I guess I can sort of understand it, but it feels like it's bullshit, too."

"Bullshit, eh? I see that our hanging out with Nate has been rubbing off on you," April teased.

Angela tittered gleefully into the phone at that remark. "Never before has one man been so obsessed with the concept of bullshit," she agreed, her voice noticeably lowering a few octaves each time she said "bullshit." Her parents might consider her casual use of the dreaded "s-word" to be a crime almost on par with that of taking the Lord's name in vain.

"He is the self-appointed prophet of the Gospel of Never-Ending Bullshit." April smiled.

"I guess it makes sense that your brother wants you to know that even though he's gotten mixed up in criminal stuff, he's no killer. That he draws the line at hurting people like that," Angela said, probably trying to steer the conversation back on course and be supportive at the same time.

April start sobbing into the phone almost as soon as the words were out of her mouth.

"What is it? What's wrong? Are you okay? Was it something I said?" she asked desperately.

April fought hard to get her emotions under control long enough to explain herself. "That's just the problem, he did kill somebody! Not during the robbery. It happened after he was caught and was put in jail. He got into a fight with one of the other prisoners over something stupid. He said the other guy started it, that the other guy had a kind of homemade knife on him and attacked him with it. He was scared for his own life, so when he fought back and got the knife off of the other guy . . . he felt like he had no choice but to use it on him," April revealed in between hitching breaths as she fought down her tears. What she didn't tell Angela was that the day all of this happened, the day when her brother killed a man, was this past Thursday, the same day that she'd felt incredibly sick, as if she'd somehow sensed his distress.

"Holeee shit," Angela replied. She must have been too swept up in the emotion of the moment to worry about her double whammy of a sin of using the accursed s-word and equating such malodorous bodily byproducts with something holy.

"Oh, Angela, I don't know what to do! Even though it sounds like it was in self-defense, he's still looking at a possible murder charge on top of the one for armed robbery. He told me to forget about him, that he's a lost cause. He told me that he thinks he's never gonna get out of there. Rob told him that he wanted to hire a better lawyer for him, that he'd pay for the whole thing, but he refused! He said he's a lost cause and they shouldn't waste their money on him. He doesn't even want to see me again. he says it's too painful for him. It's like I've finally found him, only to lose him all over again.!" April started crying again, letting all of her pent-up misery out full blast.

Angela was speechless, . April couldn't have imagined how difficult it was for her, just sitting there listening to the person she cared the most about in the whole world crying uncontrollably into the receiver. Angela was unable to even put her arm around her, to comfort her the way that she longed to. She'd never felt so awfully powerless before in her life. Then in a flash she realized that she did have some power in this situation.

"April, I'm so sorry! I just want you to know that I love you. I truly do I want to always be here for you, whenever you need me. I'm all yours, always and forever."

Now it was April's turn to go silent, except for the occasional sound of her sniffling. "What? Do you really, really mean it?"

"I do, I really do! You may have lost him, but you'll never lose me." She swore.

"I love you too! I've just been too afraid to say it. But please, don't make promises like that, promises you can't possibly keep. Who knows what the future holds for us? It never seems to go the way you hope it will."

"I don't care what the future holds. My intention is to continue loving you, no matter what."

"Thank you. Thank you for that." April should've been overjoyed by Angela's admission of love, but she couldn't help but wonder if she was just saying it because she felt sorry for her. She always felt like she was some kind of a pathetic charity case that had been foisted upon everyone, and it made her sick. Why couldn't she just enjoy this moment? Why did every sweet thing in her life have to be chased by something sour?

"What I told you wasn't even the worst part of the visit," April said sadly.

"Wait, What? It gets worse?"

"He asked me if I knew where Ty was, and if he was okay. Angela, he didn't know. He didn't know that our brother killed himself. I had to be the one to tell him. It was the hardest thing that I've ever had to do. But I had to do it, he deserves to know the truth. Hearing it just about destroyed him. A big, tough guy like him, and he just crumpled at the news. I hated to see him like that, looking so miserable. Now I'm afraid for him, afraid that he might try the same thing. He probably feels like he has nothing left to live for. And he won't let me in, he won't let me help him. He just wants to push me away." April started crying again, hating every fresh tear that stung her cheeks. She couldn't help but feel that each one represented her weaknesses and inability to control the hopeless situation.

"Omigod, my love, I'm so sorry. I can't begin to understand how hard it must've been to tell him something like that. But he's still alive now and that's the important thing to focus on. Where there's still life there's always hope. Hope that he'll change his mind and reach out to you again, hope that he'll find the strength to go on living just like you do."

"Strength? I don't feel very strong right now. Right now, I feel all used up," April confessed as she wiped the tears from her eyes with her sleeve.

"Get out of town! April McKenna, you're the strongest person I've ever met. I mean, holy shit, 1! Look at all the stuff you've been through - all the stuff you're *still* going through. You're also the smartest, funniest, and prettiest person I've ever met, and I'm completely in love with you." The sincerity in her voice dispelled all of April's earlier doubts. Angela's love for her was definitely real.

"Hmmm. I could get used to that kind of praise." April laughed.

"I promise you, we'll get through this together. I'll always be here if you need to talk, always just a phone call away," Angela assured her.

April yawned. "Thanks, I'm so glad that I found you. You're definitely the best thing that's ever happened to me, but I'm totally beat, and I really should start getting ready for bed. Talk to you tomorrow?"

"Sure. I'll give you a call after church, okay?"

"Sounds like a master plan. See ya."

"Good night, I love you," Angela whispered.

It was so good for April to finally hear those long hoped- for words - and to believe in them.

"Love you too." April replied, but she was talking to the sound of the dial tone. Angela had already hung up.

That night was one of the worst ones she'd had in years when it came to dealing with the Dark Man. The rituals she used to keep him at bay barely seemed to be working anymore. His words were more powerful and awful as ever.

"Your dreams are all dead now. You have no real family left. Soon your brother will join all the others in death. You will always be alone. These friends and lovers of yours won't last. Soon they'll tire of you and move on. They won't even remember you. Don't believe their sweet words, you're nothing to them. They know that you're just another pathetic foster child that'll be gone when your foster parents get bored with you, too. Do you think your little spells and meditations will ever bring you any true peace of mind? Forget it! The only real peace lies in eternity—in death! Embrace your death! It's the only way you will ever be free of this endless pain. It would be so easy . . .

On and on like that, he droned. She wanted to scream at him that none of what he said was true. She never dared to speak back to him, but that night, wasn't the reason she didn't shout at him.

That night, she was silent simply because she was too exhausted to fight back.

Part Seven: A Spreading Evil

The next week was a difficult one for April. She was consumed by a deep depression over the fate of Ron. She also couldn't help but feel like the words of the Dark Man were slowly trickling into her being and eating away at the edges of her sanity like some kind of a weak acid. She found herself to be more irritable and short-tempered than usual. Everything around her seemed to piss her off in one way or another, and it was all she could do to reign in this pounding tide of negativity that endlessly assailed her. The meditation regimen helped, but for the most part she did what she always did to cope with her trauma: he buried herself in her studies, distracting herself with the work.

She doubted she would've been able to get through it at all if it wasn't for Angela, Nate, and even Jenny, who was fast becoming one of her best friends too. It felt great to spend time with them, to finally feel a little less like an outsider, to know what it was like to belong to something. She began to think of them as being her surrogate family. But thinking of them in such a light was dangerous. It exposed her to the possible pain of what it might be like to lose them too someday. However, she felt that the risk was well worth it. What else did she have without them?

The four friends got together again for wrestling night to watch WWF. Earlier, Angela had explained to April that although she wasn't a fan of the sport, she considered the gathering to be a rare opportunity to spend some with her beloved beyond the confines of school. She'd said she only wished they could do so in a more intimate setting. They could hardly make out in the Johnson's den, especially not with Jenny around, who didn't know their secret.

***

Jenny wasn't all that into wrestling either, but she was more open to it than Angela, and with each passing week, she appeared to be getting sucked into it a little deeper. As the consummate artist of the group, she had gotten into the habit of bringing her sketchbook and colored pencils over with her so she could draw some of the wrestlers. That particular week, she was working on a portrait of the wrestler Rowdy Roddy Piper. She was furiously scrawling away with her pencil as they watched "Piper's Pit," his segment of the show.

Nate leaned over to cast a critical eye over her shoulder as she lay planted on her stomach, far too close to the TV.

"Damn, That's really good! Looks just like him," he commented.

Jenny felt like she had to take his compliments with a grain of salt. The guy seemed to think that everything she did was nothing short of amazing. It was sweet, but she also longed for a bit of some more objective, constructive criticism sometimes.

"Thanks. I'm not so sure that I've nailed the likeness. I really wish they'd do a few more close-ups."

Angela, who was sitting cross-legged on the floor nearby, now threw her hat into the ring. "I'd say you nailed it, alright. It looks just like him. I don't know how you do it, it's like magic to me. I can barely draw a stick figure."

Jenny sighed. The stick figure remark was a common one she got. People often thought she was some sort of a great artist just because she had moved a little beyond the stick figure phase. She'd like to be a great artist someday, but she sure didn't feel like one. What she usually felt like was what her dad would've, with his typical blunt and earthy charm, called a "big shit in a little pond". She might be one of the best artists in school, but she knew that there were thousands, maybe even millions of other people out there in the wider world that were far more talented. How could she ever hope to compete with them, especially if most of the people around her weren't able to give her any meaningful insights into how she could improve?

***

"Don't you think it's great, April?" Angela asked.

"Uh, sure. It looks fine. Your work is always so rad, Jenny. Don't be so hard on yourself. We're always our own worst critics, aren't we?" she said vacantly, barely taking her eyes off the TV screen long enough to look at the drawing.

"*That's* certainly true," Jenny agreed.

"I think it's totally awesome," Chris said enthusiastically. The kid loved wrestling and had started joining them for these weekly meetings once he got wind of what they were watching. April also suspected that he was there as a spy for the Johnsons to make sure that Nate and Jenny, who they knew were now a couple, didn't get too "handsy" with each other, as they called it. None of them really minded him being there; he was a pretty charming little guy. He loved to have this opportunity to hang out with "the big kids"—April knew it made him feel cool. If only he'd understood that this particular group of big kids wasn't considered to be very cool by most of their own peers.

"You think it's so great? I'll tell you what, kiddo—it's yours, you can have it," Jenny told him with a grin as she tore it from her sketchbook. Honestly, she wasn't very happy with it at all and could barely stand to look at it anymore.

"Really? Cool! He's my favorite wrestler!" Chris said.

"He is? What about Hulk Hogan? I thought you were one of his little 'Hulkamaniacs"?" April asked, genuinely surprised.

"No way, Hogan's just a big nerd. Always telling people to eat their vegetables and say their prayers what a total geek. Piper is way more badass," Chris replied.

Everyone laughed to hear him cussing, except for April.

"Careful with the curse words, Chris. If Rob and Jo hear you talking like that, they might blame it on you hanging with us and won't let you down here when we're around," she warned.

"No way! I'll just tell them that I heard it from them first. It's true, they curse way more than you guys do," hHe countered.

"The kid's got a point. I've only been over here a few times, and even I know that." Jenny laughed. It was true; Jo in particular could be quite foul-mouthed when confronted with the slightest bit of adversity, yet she tried to impress upon the kids the importance of keeping their speech clean.

"Yeah, but April's right too. Never underestimate the hypocrisy of adults," Nate chimed in.

"Adults? What does that even mean anymore? We'll be adults in just a couple of years. I already feel like one now, it's just not official," Jenny said philosophically.

"Shit! Adulthood can't come soon enough. I can't wait to get out of my parents' house," Angela exclaimed.

"Yeah, and you also get to start paying all those bills on your own. Sounds like a good time. I'm not always sure that the freedom of adulthood is quite what it's cracked up to be. I feel like we're just trading one kind of slavery for another. Is anyone ever truly free? I feel like it's all an illusion," Nate added cynically.

"Slavery? That's a little melodramatic don't you think?" April snapped. As a decedent of actual slaves, she was frequently peeved by how casually whites made these comparisons between slavery and relatively trivial annoyances.

The others must've sensed her mood, because an awkward silence settled over them, only interrupted by Nate's mumbled response of "Yeah, you're right."

"Hey! You didn't sign it!" Chris suddenly said, waving his picture in front of Jenny.

Jenny blushed, clearly flattered by the fact that he wanted her to sign the picture.

"Okay, I'll sign it. It's not like it matters, though. I'm not famous or anything." She took the sketch back from him and placed it back on her sketchbook long enough to scrawl out a large signature that conveyed far more confidence in her abilities than April knew she felt.

"But you might be someday," Chris told her as he took back his picture. "When I get older, I think I might want to become a good drawer too, like you."

Jenny's face flushed even brighter until she was sure that she was literally glowing. None of them could've understood how great it made her feel to inspire someone else to create something.

"Well, maybe you will be if you keep on practicing. I didn't know that you liked to draw too."

"Are you kidding? This guy makes his own complete comic books. True, the stories don't make any sense half the time . . ." April started to say.

"My stories make sense! You're just not cool enough to understand them," Chris interrupted her defensively.

"Whatever As I was saying before I was so rudely interrupted, the drawings are all pretty good—for something made by a bratty little kid." As she said that last part she stuck her tongue out at Chris playfully. He just smiled back at her coolly and gave her the finger by miming cranking it up into position with his other hand. Everyone laughed.

"You should show me some of those comics, Chris. I'd really love to see them," Jenny confessed.

"I can't right now. My teacher caught me passing them around in class, so she took them all and locked them up in her desk. But I can make some new ones to show you!"

"That sounds great. It really gives me something to look forward to next time I come over." Jenny smiled back at him.

April looked around the room at her small yet tightly knit group of friends. She was grateful for them all, for this time they could spend together. When they were around, she didn't think about all the things that were troubling her lately. most of her negative thoughts felt so far away, like a half-remembered nightmare. She wished she could feel this way all the time, but she knew it wasn't possible.

Soon they'd head back to their homes, and she'd be left to deal with the spreading darkness inside of her all on her own. She was increasingly certain that the Dark Man was a creation of her own tortured psyche. How else would he know all of her fears and anxieties so well? Even though in many ways she felt more loved, accepted, and supported now than ever before in her life, she also had never felt like she was so close to the verge of snapping and losing control completely. The last thing she ever wanted to do was to hurt herself, or even worse, someone else, but it was becoming so difficult to resist the Dark Man's suggestions.

She was contemplating asking for some kind of psychological counseling, but she didn't know how to ask. She was afraid to do so, afraid of the stigma that was attached to people who were diagnosed with such conditions and what effect that might have on her future. Would anyone want to hire her for a well-paying job if they thought that she was mentally unstable? She felt so helpless now, like all her hopes for the future were evaporating away before her eyes and there was nothing she could do to prevent it.

Nothing more of significance happened that week, and soon it was Saturday again. That meant another visit to Madame Wendigo's house.By this time, April was almost getting used to the peculiar home, with the front door that opened for her on its own and the perpetually burning fire that seemed to produce no smoke, despite that old saying. This time around, Madame Wendigo did not meet April in her parlor, but instead met her in the foyer and wasted no time in ushering her into a room a little deeper into the house that she called her "Turkish cozy corner."

It was certainly cozy, but it was hardly a corner, as it consisted of an entire room. As to how authentically Turkish it was—well you'd have to consult with someone who was native to that part of the world to tell for sure, and April was not. It was definitely filled with all manner of ornate Oriental-style decorations. The walls and ceilings were covered with red and gold patterns. A delicate chandelier dangled from the ceiling. The colored glass of its lamps was bulbous and sensuously curved. Oriental rugs covered the floor, and an elaborately patterned large couch situated under a window dominated the room; it was covered with throw pillows and blankets. April had been here before—it was where they had meditated on her previous visit. It never failed to impress her with its excess, or its comfort.

Madame Wendigo motioned for her to sit on the couch, which was really more like a bed. April sank into the soft surface, and it almost threatened to swallow her with its decadent softness. The elder woman was soon sitting opposite her on the couch in a cross-legged position.

"How was your visit with your brother, my child?" the old woman inquired innocently.

April frowned. "I'm not sure I feel like discussing that," he said honestly.

"That bad, eh? I'm sorry to hear that it did not go well. You mustn't lose hope that a successful outcome might be possible someday. Hope and intentions are very important to working magic successfully."

April brightened slightly at the mention of magic. "Are you finally going to teach me some magic this week?"

"Finally?" Madame Wendigo looked offended by the statement. "Have you not found the meditation I asked you to practice helpful in regulating your mood and improving your concentration?"

"Oh, it's very helpful! It's just that I thought you were going to show me how to work some magic, and so far you haven't really done that . . ." Her voice trailed off as she saw a stern look flash in the matriarch's eyes.

Madame Wendigo stared at her for some time. April withered slightly under the imagined disapproval she perceived in that gaze.

"I will not teach you any magic today. Instead, we will continue to work on mastering the meditative state so that you may more quickly and effortlessly slip into it at any time. That's why we're here in this criminally comfortable room again, *duh*."

April was taken aback by the immaturity of that last sentence. She would've expected it more from one of her classmates than from this supposedly sophisticated woman.

"However," Madame Wendigo said suddenly, pointing dramatically with one bony, ring-encrusted finger. "I may have to demonstrate a bit of magic for you today, just so that you develop a proper appreciation of how serious this is and what is at stake. Perhaps then you won't trouble me with this impatient attitude any further."

April had never seen her act so solemnly before. She must've really upset her somehow. "I'm sorry, I didn't mean any offense!"

"*Hush*," Madame Wendigo snapped at her. "Watch and listen," she said slowly in a more kind, inviting tone.

The old woman's eyes rolled back up into her skull until only the whites of them were visible. She produced an odd sound from deep within her chest that reminded April of Tibetan throat singing that she'd heard once in a documentary. This oddly resonant sound turned into words, yet they were incredibly peculiar words which were not from any language that April recognized. It sounded more like baby talk than a real dialect. It also felt strangely familiar, giving her an eerie feeling of déjà vu just from hearing it. Madame Wendigo's arms and hands now swayed back and forth in a rhythmic pattern.

April looked on in amazement as one of the smaller pillows littering the couch whooshed up into the air above her until it was hovering near the ceiling. April gasped. This was nothing like the magic she practiced from her handful of books on Wicca. This was more like something out of a Spielberg movie. How was this possible? Was she dreaming?

The pitch of Madame Wendigo's words and the rhythm of her movements intensified. What looked for all the world like a miniature sun suddenly sprang into existence beside the flying pillow. The churning ball of flame dwarfed the fluffy decoration. April could feel the intense heat it was put out. It edged closer to the pillow, and as it did so, the pillow started to burn, but it happened so quickly that the entire thing was reduced to ashes before the flaming pieces of it could had fall to the ground. Those ashes now rained down upon April. She looked at them in wonder. Just as quickly, the small sun disappeared into nothingness. The unsettling chanting abruptly stopped, and the old woman sat still.

Madame Wendigo's eyes closed, then flew open. "The magic I command is very real and potentially very dangerous. These are no mere parlor tricks. This is *real* power. A power that nearly tore this world apart once. Do you see now? That is why we must proceed so cautiously. I sense a great darkness constantly swirling around you. I can't tell if it is purely internal or not. It is most peculiar. It must be dealt with before I can teach you any of the really cool stuff."

"The really cool stuff?" April echoed with an arched eyebrow.

"Yes, like what I just showed you. Wasn't that cool?"

"Yeah, it sure was! It was *beyond* cool. Was that an actual miniature nuclear fusion reaction that you just generated with *words*? Do you realize that you could end the world's energy problems with something like that? Scientists have been trying to figure out how to create that for decades, and you're just casually doing it to destroy perfectly good pillows," April babbled.

Madame Wendigo sighed and waved her gnarled hands in exasperation. "The powers that be have no interest in ending the world's energy problems. They like things just fine the way that they are, believe me. Anyhow, I wonder if you're missing the point of my little demonstration? Perhaps I should've chosen something different. Did you understand the point of what I was saying? Or are you still too busy looking at the trees to see the forest?"

April thought about it for a moment. Despite being distracted by the implications of what she'd just witnessed, she did indeed understand the point of it. Honestly, she wasn't sure that she *should* be entrusted with such knowledge. Not if her mind really was capable of producing something as twisted as the Dark Man - , or entertaining, if only ever so briefly, some of his nastier ideas. Yet she also longed to be able to do what Madame Wendigo could do, even if she had no idea how she'd use such a power. In the end, she knew that the old woman was right—she had to get her dark side under control before they could progress further, and the only way she was comfortable doing that with was with more meditation. Perhaps mastering these meditation techniques could be her ultimate salvation, Her one real hope for managing this increasingly irresistible darkness that threatened to destroy her future

"I understand. And I apologize. I understand that you are trying to build a strong foundation before moving on to the really cool stuff. It's like when Mr. Miyagi made Daniel-san do all those chores around his house before teaching him karate. He was really teaching him karate the whole time," April answered.

Madame Wendigo blinked at her in confusion. "Honey, who the hell is Mr. Miyagi?"

"You know, the old guy from *The Karate Kid*?"

This was met with another vacant stare. "Never heard of it."

"No way, really? Where have you been? It's a very popular movie."

"*Bah*. You kids watch too many movies. I lost interest in all that nonsense after Valentino died," Madame Wendigo said dismissively.

In a way, April wasn't terribly surprised by this response. She didn't think that the woman even owned a TV. She'd never seen one in any of the rooms she'd been in.

"At any rate, you're right. I am trying to build a solid foundation for you. You must become expert in the fundamentals before you can tear apart and stitch back together the fundamental forces of the universe itself. So today we shall meditate again, but we shall go even deeper this time."

April nodded her understanding. "I'm ready."

Madame Wendigo raised a questioning eyebrow. "Are you? We shall see, my child."

***

After her latest lesson with Madame Wendigo, April's issues with the Dark Man improved considerably. She could still sense him hovering around the edges of her bedroom, but he barely bothered to speak. When he did, she couldn't quite make out what he was saying anymore. As had happened before in the past, she got the distinct impression that he was sulking. Not having to hear his bloody-minded diatribes every night lifted April's spirits considerably, although, of course, she was still very upset about the situation with her brother Ron. She dared to hope that things were improving for her.

It was to be a short-lived hope.

A few days later, she was walking by Chris's room and noticed him hard at work at his little desk, doing some drawings. Impulsively, she poked her head into the room.

"Hey there! Whatcha drawing? Some new comics to impress Jenny with?"

Chris quickly moved his elbow to cover up the paper he'd been drawing on. "No! It's nothing like that," he exclaimed.

April was confused by this. Normally the kid was all too eager to share his work. In fact, sometimes you couldn't get him to shut up when he tried to explain the significance of each picture. She usually found it either incredibly endearing or annoying depending upon her mood.

She walked fully into the room. "C'mon, you can show me. What is it? Naked ladies? I'll bet you're drawing bare naked ladies, aren't you?" she teased. "Maybe even naked pictures of Jenny."

"It's not naked ladies!" Chris replied angrily.

April laughed. It was fun to irritate him sometimes. She was really starting to get this big sister thing down pretty well.

"C'mon, show me!"

"No!"

She knocked his arm out of the way so she could see what he was drawing. Then she fell backwards right onto her ass with a heavy thump. She couldn't believe what she'd just seen. Chris had drawn an astonishingly accurate picture of the Dark Man himself.

"Where did you see that . . . that *thing* in your drawing?"

"He's a ghost. He comes into my room at night when I'm trying to sleep sometimes and talks to me. He says mean things. He's always telling me to hurt other people. Don't worry, I don't listen to him. I wouldn't ever really hurt you or Mom and Dad," Chris told her hesitantly.

April just sat there in shock. Chris was seeing the Dark Man, too. That meant he was real. He wasn't just some aspect of her own mind. While the fact that this meant that she wasn't crazy was a great comfort, the fact that he was targeting other members of her family, targeting a *child* like he had with her, filled her with a fury so deep it was indescribable.

April was struck by a sudden insight. If the Dark Man was talking to Chris, how many others had he talked to over the years? Had he encouraged her father to drink? Had he convinced Ty to commit suicide? Convinced Ron to rob that bank? How much of the ruin of her life was he responsible for?

"You probably think I'm nuts now," Chris said as he looked down sadly.

"What? No! Not at all. I've seen him too," April assured him as she rose to her feet. She massaged her butt a little; she really had hit the floor pretty hard.

"You have?" asked Chris in amazement.

"Yes. He's been bugging me ever since I was a little girl. That's why I got into witchcraft in the first place, to try to protect myself from him. It worked for a while, but lately . . . not so much. I was starting to think that *I* was the crazy one, that he was all in my head. But if you've seen him too, then that means that we're both sane and he's totally real."

"No way."

"Way," April asserted.

"But who is he? Why is he bothering us?" Chris asked. April had to admit that was a very good question.

"I don't know. I don't even have a clue as to why he's been haunting me like this for my entire life," she admitted earnestly.

Chris's eyes grew wide. "Do you think he's here now? That he can hear us talking about him?"

"I don't think so. Normally, he only comes around when I'm trying to fall asleep. I can usually tell when he's around. It's a feeling I get, a terrible feeling like, um . . . like . . ." April struggled to find the right words to describe it.

"Like all the love went out of the world," Chris finished for her.

"Yes, Exactly! Just like that." Then she looked extremely forlorn. She hated the fact that Chris had experienced that awful feeling too. She gave him a quick hug.

"I'm so sorry that I got you into this. This is all my fault. I'm the one that he really wants, I can feel it. He's probably only messing with you as a way of getting at me."

"It's not your fault. He's just . . . *wrong*. Evil. Evil isn't your fault," Chris told her as she released him.

April smiled. "Thanks for that. I needed to hear that."

Jo walked into the room. "What was all that racket? I was afraid that someone got hurt up here."

"We're fine. I just, uh, tripped on something in here. I fell on my butt," April explained.

"Are you hurt?" a concerned Jo asked.

"Only my pride." April knew that she couldn't go wrong giving the time-honored standard response for such embarrassing situations.

Jo glanced around at the untidy floor of Chris's room. "How many times have I told you to clean up this room? It's no wonder she tripped in this pigsty!"

"Hey, is it okay if we go next door to see Mrs. Hairston for a minute?" April suddenly asked, hoping to distract Jo from making Chris clean his room. She didn't want to get the boy in trouble.

"Huh? Oh sure, I guess so. Just be back home before dinner," she answered absentmindedly as she wandered out of the room.

"Why're we going to see Madame Wendigo?" Chris asked as soon as she was gone.

"Because she's a really powerful witch. Like, you wouldn't believe how powerful. If anyone can help us get rid of the Dark Man, it's her."

"The dark what?"

"It's what I call it."

"Oh. Why haven't you asked her for help before?" Chris wondered.

"Because I thought he was all in my head. C'mon, grab your jacket. Let's go!"

***

The two rushed over to the house next door, and soon April was rapping frantically

on the door with its curious knocker.

"I don't believe today is Saturday," Madame Wendigo's disembodied voice called from seemingly nowhere.

"I know, I'm sorry, but this is an emergency! Please let us in!" April shouted.

The door swung open with its characteristic groan of protest, only to slam shut behind them as soon as they were inside. The sound of heavy footfalls and creaking wood altered them to the presence of the house's owner coming down the spiraling staircase towards them. She was wearing a bonnet on her head and tying a robe around herself, looking as if she'd just been roused from a deep slumber despite the fact that it was still quite early in the afternoon.

"This had better be good. A woman my age needs all the beauty sleep she can get," she complained as she reached the bottom of the stairs and faced them.

"We're both being visited at night by an evil spirit that's telling us to hurt people," April blurred out excitedly.

Madame Wendigo's eyebrows shot up. "Ah, so perhaps that's the source of the darkness I always sense clinging to you."

"I think it might be. It's been with me ever since I was a little girl, following me whenever I've moved. I thought it was all in my head, but now Chris is seeing it too! He drew a picture of it," April explained breathlessly and held up the drawing.

Madame Wendigo fished out a pair of glasses from her robe, then perched them on the end of her nose. Her eyes squinted appraisingly as she studied the paper. She snatched it from April, then folded it up and placed it in the pocket of her robe.

"Hmm. Quite literally a dark entity. This is an urgent matter indeed. You were quite right to come to me with it. I only wish you'd entrusted me with this secret sooner."

"I . . . I didn't want anyone to think I was some kind of a nut case," April said apologetically.

Madame Wendigo barked out a laugh at the remark and placed a comforting arm around her shoulder as she steered her towards her parlor. "With all the strange things that I've seen in my life, and all the even more peculiar things that I know are possible, it would take rather a lot for me to dismiss anyone as insane."

"Do you have any cookies?" Chris asked. He'd surely been patiently holding in this request since he'd first seen the old woman hobbling down her staircase and could no longer contain it.

Madame Wendigo whirled to face the boy, her robe swirling out dramatically like a cape. "Cookies? What do I look like, a cookie vending machine? This is no time for cookies. Perhaps in the interest of cordiality I would've prepared some if I'd known you were coming over, but alas, that was not the case."

"So, that's a no?" Chris tried to clarify.

Madame Wendigo didn't bother to dignify that remark with a reply. She just grunted as she walked over to the table in the parlor. She carefully removed the crystal ball from its center, placing it on a side table that held a Tiffany lamp. She then pulled off the table cover with a flourish like a magician doing a tablecloth trick. In the center of the table, a large, inverted pentagram was painted in gold inside of a circle. Next, the old woman grabbed a candelabra from a built-in bookcase on the wall. With a single word, all the candles blazed to life. She carefully set a candle on each point of the star.

"How did she do that?" a shocked Chris whispered to April.

"I told you she was a powerful witch, didn't I?" she whispered back. Madame Wendigo must've overheard her remark, as she smiled slightly at it.

Next, the old woman took a small sack that was secured by a drawstring down from near the same spot she had taken the candelabra. She opened it up and began pulling what looked like salt out of it and sprinkling it on the ground until she had made a complete circle around the table. With one spoken word, she made all of the electric lights in the house switch off.

Madame Wendigo sat down at the head of the table. "You two, please do not break that circle. Sit, and take the seats on either side of me," she instructed.

The two youngsters did as they were told. They watched with a mixture of awe and confusion as the witch unfolded Chris's drawing and placed it on the table before her. From somewhere beneath her robe, she produced a silver dagger with tiny rubies and emeralds set into the blade.. She did some of her odd chanting and gesticulated wildly with her dagger. Then she slashed the palm of her hand lightly, letting the blood drip onto the back of the paper. April and Chris both winced as she cut herself. She drew a spiral on the paper in her own blood. Next, she set down the dagger before her, aligning it with the center of the star on the table.

She slid the paper over to April.

"Pass this around and concentrate your entire mind on the image," she instructed. They each took turns staring at it. When the paper was returned to her, she stood up and burnt it using one of the candles. She then sprinkled the ashes into the center of the star before sitting down again.

"Now I would like us to all join hands and concentrate on this dark entity. Envision what it looks like in your mind and call it forth to materialize here in this very room. Whatever happens, do not let go of each other's hands."

They all linked hands, and Madame Wendigo began chanting her unearthly words again. And she chanted. And she chanted some more. She chanted with ever-increasing and decreasing levels of intensity. Finally, a look of frustration fixed itself over her features.

"This simply isn't working. You can release your hands now," she declared in disappointment.

"What exactly were you hoping to do?" April wanted to know.

"To call the entity here, to try to find out who he is and send him far, far away. The trouble is that I think he's already far away. This is no ordinary ghost that's stuck roaming this plane of existence—otherwise, my spell would've worked. He's someone who comes and goes as he pleases. In fact, I'm not certain that it's a ghost at all. Perhaps it's a rogue wizard that's astrally projecting. It's odd, because I get some faint impressions of him from the psychic residue he's left on you both. He seems too old to still be a living wizard. It's all quite puzzling!"

"So there's nothing you can do to help us? Are we stuck with him?" April asked despairingly. She had been so certain that Madame Wendigo could help her.

"No, not at all. There's still hope! For whatever reason, I may not be able to summon him here to banish him from this plane as I had hoped, but there *are* alternatives." With that statement, she rose from her seat. She said one of her strange words, snapped her fingers, and the candles all blew out.

The only illumination in the room was now coming from the fireplace that perpetually roared away. She walked over to it and bent over an old-fashioned chest that sat beside it. She threw the lid open and was greeted by a choking plume of dust. She waved it away with her hands and began throwing out an unusual variety of items from within the chest, many of which didn't look as though they could have fit inside. April and Chris spied a beach ball, a taxidermic beaver, a top hat, a staff with a crystal set into its top that gave off an eerie green glow, a broadsword, a battle axe, and a saxophone.

Finally, the old woman cried "Aha!" and came back to the table carrying a jewelry box made of cherry wood. She set it down and opened it. From inside, she pulled out two necklaces. Each one had a white crystal dangling from it.

"I would like each of you to take one of these and always wear them. An old friend of mine, a wizard much more powerful than myself, makes these. My husband and I used to work for him. He's retired now, like I am, and has a little occult shop down at the Jersey Shore in the States. He sells some like these there, but these are much more potent versions that he gifted to me. They will keep this dark entity from getting near you. You'll be quite safe from his influence so long as you keep them on."

Chris took his and slipped it around his neck with a smile. "Cool, thanks!"

April looked a bit more skeptical as she put hers on. As she studied the crystal, she thought she could detect a faint blue glow from somewhere deep inside it. "Will these really work?"

"Of course they will. In the meantime, I will mess around with my Tarot cards, consult my books, and maybe even make a few calls to some of my old associates. I will find out who this dark being is and get rid of him for good, but it may take some time to do so. Until then, you'll both be perfectly safe so long as you wear these necklaces. I guarantee it."

"Thank you for your help," April said, feeling slightly more confident now.

"It's nothing, my child, nothing at all. Now, you'd both better run along. I sense that Jo will be calling you back home soon for dinner."

"Wow! You can tell that because you're psychic, right?" Chris asked.

She pointed to an ormolu clock sitting on the mantelpiece above her fireplace. "No, I can tell because I own a clock. Not every problem in the world requires magic to solve. Don't either one of you fret—I believe that we have this situation under control now, and this entity can no longer harm you. Now, good evening to you both I will see you again on Saturday, April. We may be able to move to more *advanced* exercises now that this darkness is behind us."

April smiled at that last remark. Was the Dark Man finally out of her life now, despite the failure of the ritual? Would this rock around her neck really drive him away? It sounded too good to be true. If it was true, then why did Madame Wendigo feel the need to do more research on him?

She wanted to believe the old woman, but she'd just been burned too many times over the years by adults and their promises to take her claims seriously.

Part Eight: A Killer is Born (Early 1987)

Somewhere across town, the winter winds gradually gave way to the flowers of early spring. The man continued to stare out of his window, feeling trapped by the circumstances of his life. The frame of the window was boxing him in; he had his freedom, yet he still felt like a prisoner—a prisoner to this world. What good was freedom if you didn't feel free? If you didn't feel like you had the means to do anything that you really wanted to do?

He was stuck on a constant cycle of sleep, work, eat. Rinse and repeat. He was sleepwalking through what was left of his life. It all felt so empty, so utterly meaningless. He wanted to change it, but he didn't know how to, didn't believe that it was still possible to do anything to change it, not at his age. No, he'd blown it. Whatever greater potential he'd once had was wasted and would never manifest. This was his life now. There was no escape. He was utterly stuck.

It hadn't always been like this, but this is what it was now and for the foreseeable future: endless grey days stretched out before him in a monotonous procession. Each day was just as unremarkable as the next. Was it Tuesday? Was it Friday? Who knew, and what did it really matter? What was the difference anyway? Just another day older and another day poorer. It hadn't always been like this. Once there had been love and color and hope in his life, but he didn't like to think of that. All that brought was pain. He had nothing left to him now but regrets.

He had nothing of value. Not even a house—that bitch had taken everything in the divorce. This window that he looked out of wasn't even his, it was just a part of someone else's house in a pathetic little room that he rented there. He had been reduced to a mere shell of himself, with nothing to call his own or to take pride in.

On his days off from the mill, he would just sit there in a shitty, wobbly, uncomfortable wooden chair beside a tiny window—the only one in this chokingly small room. He'd sit there and look at them down below. There were more of them out there lately, and they were out more frequently now that the weather was a little warmer. They were the neighborhood kids. Those damned kids.

God, how he hated them!

Always running around and playing. Not a care in the world. As if they had all the *time* in the world. Didn't they know? Didn't they know that their lives were ticking time bombs? Tick tock. Tick tock. You can't stop the clock. The relentless push of time. They only had so much time to do something to make sure that their lives went right, to make sure that they didn't end up like him. They still had opportunities, a chance to do it right. But all they did was fuck around. They'd blow it too. They were on the same path he'd been on. All headed towards this never-ending gloom, this living death. The little fools didn't deserve what they had.

What he wouldn't do for a sliver of the time they had before them. Time to do it right. Time when people still looked at you like you were the future, like you were worth fighting and sacrificing for. Time when people put all their hopes into you and believed that you would help lead everyone into a brighter tomorrow. Times when it was still so easy to believe in yourself. To believe in this world. To believe that a brighter tomorrow was even possible.

What these children had was so different from what other people saw when they bothered to even look at him. So different from what he saw when he caught an accursed glimpse of his own reflection in the window. All anyone ever saw in him—all that he saw in himself—was someone who was dead inside. Someone who had wasted away their life and was just waiting for the inevitable coming of the physical death must always follow the death of the spirit. He disgusted other people; he could see it on their faces. He was a living reminder of the worst parts of themselves, of all the ugly truths they tried to hide from with their stupid jokes and their vapid music, with their alcohol and drugs and sex.

That was okay. They disgusted him, too.

Especially the teenagers. They were the worst. The clock ticked the loudest for them, yet they blithely ignored it. The fools! He would see them walking hand in hand, stealing kisses. Wasting their precious time with their meaningless puppy-dog romances. They'd find out someday. They'd find out that love didn't even exist. That it was all just a lie. A trick of biology. An impulse implanted in our DNA so we'll make more babies. So the race won't die out. And for what? What was the point of it all? It was an endless chain of heartless beings spreading around the planet, all fighting over the increasingly limited resources, bashing each other over the head with bigger and bigger rocks so they can have the biggest house or drive the best car. As if that would bring them happiness. As if everything wasn't just a distraction. A distraction from the fact that love was a lie and happiness was a lie. All just pretty little lies that they tell us so we'll all run ourselves ragged chasing our own tails until we drop dead from exhaustion.

The only reality was pain. The only truth was suffering. And the only freedom came from embracing that reality, not hiding from it like all the weaklings, all the intellectual cowards that surrounded him.

At least this is what his friend told him. His only true friend, his Dark Companion.

At first, he'd been terrified when he'd started visiting him a few weeks ago. When he first saw him, when he first heard that voice, he had feared that the years of isolation and loneliness had finally driven him insane. He begged him to go away, to shut up, to stop bedeviling him. But once he actually started listening, once he really heard what his Dark Companion had to say, he came to see how much sense it made. He saw how much his words echoed the conclusion he himself had been coming to, but was afraid to fully embrace. He didn't know who or what had sent this Dark Angel to him, and he didn't care. He was simply grateful that he was always here with him now. Always here to show him the truth. The truth that had set him free.

And now he had a purpose. His life was filled with meaning again. The time was coming for him to lift the veil from the eyes of them all. He would show them the truth behind the lies. He would show them the truth; he would set the whole world free. He would save them all, save them from the endless years of toil, misery, and disappointment that awaited them. He was special. He was their savior. They would die before they could be crushed by the grinding wheel of life, die when they still had that pure glimmer of hope in their eyes. It was an act of mercy, really.

And he, in his infinite wisdom, was a being of infinite mercy.

He also had infinite patience. He'd watched this one from his window for days now, but now the time had come. The blessed day of her deliverance. He knew her rhythms and her patterns. He knew when she was out and about outside. Waiting for the school bus, checking the mail, taking out the trash, sitting on her front porch reading her magazines. He knew the best time to strike. His Dark Companion had given him many helpful tips and suggestions. He was never really alone anymore. His friend was always there to help.

So it was with little fear of discovery from the unenlightened fools who surrounded him that he crept through the alleyway between the houses as she dropped a trash bag into the can. He was next to her in a flash, the handkerchief soaked in chloroform covering her nose and her mouth. Her warm little body struggled and lashed against his own, and he felt a thrill of excitement that he hadn't felt in years. He felt more alive in this moment than he could ever recall feeling before.

"Hush, now. Hush now, child," he whispered softly into her ear. Her eyes fluttered as her body went limp. He set her down on the ground and began wrapping his calloused fingers around her smooth, delicate little neck. He squeezed and squeezed with ever more ferocity. Her eyes flew open once more before the light faded from them completely. "Do you see it? Do you see the truth? You do! You do, don't you?" he whispered.

It was then that he went to work on her with his knife. It was then when the fun *really* began. He'd make a display of her. His friend had told him how. A display that would show them all the truth.

The only real beauty lies in the truth. And beauty was his gift to the world.

Part Nine: In the Grip of Terror

For April, the past few weeks were some of the best she could remember. The plight of her brother Ron still weighed heavily upon her, but she hadn't heard any bad news about him from the jail, so she assumed he hadn't harmed himself. Everything else in her life was moving in the right direction. Madame Wendigo's crystal necklaces worked amazingly well—for the first time in her memory, she couldn't sense even a hint of the Dark Man around her. At long last, he seemed to be completely gone from her life. It felt like having a heavy stone removed from her back that she hadn't even been aware she'd been carrying. Free of this burden, she felt lighter and more alive.

Her love for Angela continued to grow and deepen. Her friendships with Nate and Jenny also grew more comfortable. She felt as though Chris, Jo, and Rob were her real family. Madame Wendigo had started to show her some of "the really cool stuff," as well. She could now astrally project, which basically meant that she could induce an out-of-body experience any time she wanted to do so. It was an amazing sensation. She loved the feeling of freedom when she was unshackled from the bonds of her physical body and could float and fly around. However, Madame Wendigo had cautioned her against doing it when she wasn't accompanied by the old woman.

"In your astral form, you won't have the amulet I gave you to protect your spirit. You could come under attack from this 'Dark Man' of yours if you stray too far away from your body. It's best to only practice this when I am present, at least until I have figured out how to banish him completely or taught you more about how you can defend yourself from such an assault," she had told her.

She had already taught her one way she could protect her physical form. "The first thing that all young magic-users must learn is how to protect themselves," her wizened mentor had proclaimed. April could now cast a spell that would create a glowing green shield of energy in front of herself. Madame Wendigo was teaching her ways that she could expand the size of it, shrinking it down to only a few inches, blowing it up to the size of a wall, or wrapping it around herself completely to form a bubble. The old witch claimed that with practice, it was possible to even make one big enough to cover a large house like hers. She claimed that such barriers were strong enough to stop bullets, or to flatten a speeding car, but of course April had no opportunities to test that out. Unfortunately, these shields only lasted for about twenty minutes or so before they had to be conjured up once more. April still couldn't believe that she was capable of making such a thing. It made her feel more secure than ever before—invincible, even.

The old woman had warned her about using it in front of "mundanes," as she called non-magic-users. "You must only ever use it in an emergency to save your life or that of someone else. The mundanes must never see you do it." She explained that her people had ways of covering up such things, of keeping their secrets, but in order to do so, they had to call upon another secret organization that was aligned with them. "It's a huge pain in the ass, believe me," Madame Wendigo complained. "And you wouldn't believe all the paperwork you have to fill out! No, it's best to avoid calling *them* if you can manage it."

April had sighed. *Secrets! I can never seem to get away from them,* she'd thought bitterly. It felt like she was just trading in one set of secrets for a different one. Would she ever be free of them? Would she ever be able to share her complete being with anyone? She couldn't even tell Angela about the magic Madame Wendigo taught her. Angela wouldn't believe her and would think she was delusional without a demonstration, but they were never alone long enough for her to risk such a thing. Still, she hoped that someday she could share this increasingly important aspect of herself with the one person she loved the most.

This relatively idyllic period of April's youth soon came grinding to a tragic halt. It began with the grisly discovery of the mutilated body of one of her classmates in an alleyway right outside of her home. The girl wasn't anyone that April had really known personally. She hadn't even known her name until it was insensitively splashed all over the local news. She did recognize her, though. How many times had she passed her in the hallways at school? It seemed surreal to think that she'd never see her face in the crowd again.

The whole school closed for a day after the body was discovered, and the town started to go into something of a panic. A murder in this town was unheard of—especially the murder of a child, and especially one that was so horrific. If you weren't safe right outside of your own home, where were you safe? The local constables had never had to deal with anything like this before and were obviously out of their depth. There was even talk of calling in the Mounties.

April and her friends were trying to put a brave face on through it all. Trying to act like they weren't that bothered, even though they were all really quite frightened. They even made jokes about the killer sometimes, which might have seemed insensitive, but it's sometimes how people cope with the unknown. They all were trying their best to distract themselves with their usual weekly gathering to watch wrestling. By now, even Angela was starting to get into the sport.

So it was a genuine groan of frustration that Angela let out as a particularly exciting match was interrupted by a breaking news bulletin. They all watched with mounting discomfort as the discovery of another corpse was announced. This time it was a boy. A picture of him flashed onto the screen.

"Does anybody know that guy?" April asked to break the awful silence. They all shook their heads except for Nate.

"Not really. I've seen him around, though. I think he's a freshman."

"They found the body on this side of town this time," Angela noted, her voice trembling slightly. April took her hand and gave it a reassuring squeeze, not caring how the gesture may have been perceived by Jenny at that moment.

"Great. I had a hard enough time convincing my mom to let me come over here today. Now that this has happened, she's totally going to freak. There's no way she's gonna let me out of the house again until they catch this psycho," Jenny grumbled.

"Two murders in a week. Both bodies all cut up. You know what this means, don't you? Our little town has its very own serial killer—and we're all targets. The victims are always teenagers. *Jesus Christ.*" April knew Angela felt a slight thrill at being able to take the Lord's name in vain so openly. "I feel like I woke up in a Friday the 13th movie!" Angela seemed to be almost on the verge of a nervous breakdown.

"Hopefully they'll catch him soon," April said reassuringly and squeezed her hand again. "I hear they're calling in the Mounties."

Nate barked out a hollow laugh. "Oh yeah! The good old Mounties to the rescue!"

"Hey, do you think we'll get another day off from school tomorrow?" Jenny wondered aloud.

"I sure hope so," Chris chimed in.

They all heard the phone ring. There was an extension in the den with them,sitting on the side table next to the couch. Before April could answer it, it stopped. A moment later, Jo walked into the room, an apologetic look on her face.

"Jenny, your mother just called. I'm sorry, but she wants you to come home right away. Go ahead and gather up your things, and I'll give you a ride over there."

"Okay, Mrs. Johnson," Jenny said as she began putting away her colored pencils. She looked at the others. "See—what did I tell you? It's already begun. She's totally freaking!"

Nate frowned. "Do you think she'll still let us go out on any dates?"

"Not anytime soon. You don't know how paranoid she can get. She probably won't let me go anywhere but school until all this shit is over with."

"Don't worry. We'll find a way to be together," Nate asserted.

"All we can do is hope that they catch this freakazoid soon," April added, and then looked at Angela. "I'm surprised your parents aren't clamoring for your immediate return home yet. Aren't you supposed to be the one with super strict parental units?"

Angela shook her head. "Forget it. When it comes to this kind of thing, their attitude is that it's all in God's hands. Our faith is supposed to be our armor. They probably think those kids that died deserved it somehow. That they were sinners, or their faith wasn't strong enough to protect them. The killer is just an instrument of the

Lord's judgment. They wouldn't even think that their perfect little girl could ever be a target of God's divine fury."

"Shit! That's harsh." April was astounded by the callousness of their beliefs.

Angela shrugged. "Yeah, that's my parents for ya."

Once the last of April's friends had left the house, Chris came into April's room.

He shut the door behind him and had an unusually serious look on his face.

"What's up, squirt?" April inquired, although she was sure she already knew.

"April, I'm . . . I'm . . . *scared.* What if this killer is doing what he's doing because of us? What if he decides to come after us next?"

April's heart went out to the kid. She wanted to give him a big hug and never let him go, but she could also tell from his expression that such a gesture from her right now would only piss him off.

"Whoa. Back up there for a minute. How is he *our* fault?"

"I've been thinking maybe when we made the Dark Man go away with our necklaces, he didn't go that far. Maybe he just found someone else in town to bother. Someone who was easier to drive crazy. And maybe he wants revenge on us for making him go away. Maybe he just wants us to be really, really scared first. What if he wants to scare the shit out of us before he finally sends his new friend to finish us off?"

April let out a long breath to calm herself. She had to admit that what the kid had to say all made a certain kind of sense. In fact, she'd been having similar thoughts herself, but had been trying to rationalize them away. She wasn't about to admit that to him though. As the big sister here, it was her responsibility to calm him down and make him feel better about everything.

"Number one: remember what you told me once? 'Evil isn't our fault.' You were totally right about that. If there's any truth to what you're saying, we didn't cause it to happen. We never asked for it. We had a right to protect ourselves from that monster. We weren't wrong to do what we did, and we're not responsible for anything that the Dark Man decides to do. Number two: Madame Wendigo is finally starting to teach me some really awesome witch stuff. I can use my magic to protect you, to protect our whole family. I won't let anything bad happen to you, I promise."

Chris was looking down at his feet, but he nodded his head in agreement. She got up from the desk where she'd been working on one of her endless extra credit assignments and gave him a hug, sensing that he was ready for it now. She wasn't wrong.

"Do you really mean it?" He asked once she released him.

"About using my new powers to protect us? Of course I do."

"No, I mean when you said 'our family.' Do you really feel like we're a family now?"

She almost cried right then and there, but she managed to keep herself composed long enough to say "I sure do. We *are* a family now.

I'll always be your big sister, no matter what." She suspected that the Dark Man might've had a hand in the destruction of her birth family, but she'd be damned if she'd let him destroy her new family too.

As soon as Chris left her room, his spirits somewhat lifted, she picked up the phone in her room and dialed Madame Wendigo's number.

"Hello, my child. What can I do for you?" the old woman answered. She always seemed to know when it was April who was calling her. It always kind of spooked April a little.

"I assume you've seen what's going on in the news lately," April began.

"Only what I've read in the paper. Such a terrible way to die. I do hope they catch the monster responsible soon."

"Did you know there's been another one? Another dead teenager was found today. And a lot closer to this side of the tracks, too."

"Oh dear! It wasn't anyone you knew, was it?" The old woman sounded genuinely surprised.

"No, fortunately it wasn't. But it's still pretty awful. My friends and I, we're all really freaked out by it."

"Quite understandable under the circumstances. I do wonder though, what does any of this ghastly business have to do with me?"

Not the most encouraging of responses. April sighed as she worked up the courage to try to make her understand what it had to do with her. *Fuck it, I just need to dive in and go for broke.*

"I was hoping that maybe there was something we could do about it. Some way that we could use our magic to help catch the killer before he strikes again."

"*What?*" The old woman sounded uncharacteristically furious. "Absolutely not! That's completely out of the question. We do not use our abilities to interfere in such pedestrian affairs. This is a matter for the police," she said firmly.

"But I don't understand why. What's the point of having all of this awesome power if we never use it to make the world a better place?" April asked.

"We use it to take care of ourselves and our own. To further our own spiritual and material wealth," the matriarch declared loftily.

"That sounds incredibly selfish. Do you even have any idea how selfish that sounds? Don't you care about anyone who doesn't use magic?"

"Of course I care, but we simply cannot run about trying to save everyone who needs help. Not everything can or *should* be solved using magic. The mundanes must learn to sort out their own problems without depending on us to do everything for them. Over-dependence on magic is what nearly destroyed the world the last time." April heard Madame Wendigo let out a long sigh before she continued.

"Perhaps it is somewhat selfish. If it is any comfort for you to know, sometimes, very rarely, extraordinary threats do arise—

threats to the entire world. When that happens, we have always done our part to eliminate such threats.”

“Okay, well my friends and I feel extraordinarily threatened right now,” April countered.

“My child, I’m very sorry that you all feel that way, but the current situation isn’t of the magnitude that warrants our intervention, and you’re smart enough to understand that.”

“All I understand is that someone I trusted won’t help me when I need it. It’s like . . . living next door to Wonder Woman, but she won’t help you catch the bad guys that are coming after you,” April said in exasperation.

The old woman bristled at that comment. “Haven’t helped you? My dear, have I not given you the knowledge to protect yourself and others from attack? Didn’t I remove that vile Dark Man from your life?”

“That’s just the thing. I think he might be the one who’s really behind this. Maybe he’s driven someone else in town crazy? Maybe the killer is working his way up to coming after us as revenge for kicking the Dark Man out?”

“There’s no evidence of that. Not everything in life has a supernatural cause behind it. Sometimes bad things just happen. Sometimes people are just insane and murderous without some devil whispering in their ears. That people are capable of doing evil all on their own is one of the hardest things for us to accept. What I do *not* want you doing is putting yourself at real risk by trying to play amateur detective. What is happening right now is tragic, it's frightening, it's horrific, but it's a matter for the proper authorities to deal with, not us. If I ever find that you've been using any of the knowledge I've shared with you to interfere in this matter, I will wipe all of it from your mind!"

April was speechless for a moment. She couldn't believe what her mentor had just threatened to do. "You can really do that?"

Madame Wendigo laughed a hollow, dark laugh and replied, "My child, I was an Inquisitor for over twenty years, I could do something like that in my sleep." Then she added, in a softer, kinder tone: "But I pray that I never have to. You are a most gifted student, and I have greatly enjoyed our time together. I would hate to see it all come to such an unfortunate end. It would break my heart. So please, promise me that you'll stay out of it. If you actually do come under attack, use what I have taught you to defend yourself or to save those you care about if there is no other way, but leave it at that."

"Okay, I promise," April said reluctantly. "See you Saturday?"

"Yes. See you then. Goodnight, my child." With that, the line went dead.

She couldn't believe that she was on her own in dealing with this. But maybe the old witch was right. Maybe this had nothing whatsoever to do with the Dark Man. And maybe the killer would be captured soon, and life could return to normal again.

All she could do was hope.

Part Ten: I Just Died in Your Arms Tonight

Another week crawled by, this time without any new murders. The Mounties did indeed show up and wasted no time in arresting a suspect. The suspect was a transient they found camping out in the woods on the edge of town. He had a history of rape (although none of the victims in town had been violated in that particular way), but steadfastly refused to confess to the murders—yet. The arrest of a suspect and the lack of new murders had lulled some of the town into a false sense of security. Many parents that had forbidden their children to go anywhere outside of school started to loosen such restrictions again, confident that the Mounties had gotten their man.

Jenny's mother, however, was not one of those parents. Nate and Jenny could only see each other at school, and her mother still wouldn't allow her to hang out at April's house to watch wrestling. They both found it infuriating, especially because their relationship was beginning to really heat up physically right around the time when the murders started. They'd explored each other's bodies as much as they could possibly get away with doing in darkened theaters and were eager to move on to the next phase. As kids in the eighties say, they wanted to "go all the way," but there was little opportunity to do so. Having a serial killer running loose in your town can really complicate your love life.

It was Nate, in his eagerness to consummate the relationship, who came up with a possible solution. A few years earlier, back when he'd been in his more rebellious, "punk rock phase" (as he called it), he'd perfected the art of slipping out of his house undetected in the dead of the night. Now he intended to put those skills to the test again for a late-night rendezvous with his beloved.

Back then, he snuck out to join a group of like-minded friends who had temporarily become obsessed with painting graffiti on the box cars of the cargo trains that wound through town. He'd gotten quite good at it too, before he eventually got bored and gave it up. Fear of his impending adulthood had caused him to buckle down and work harder in school. He still thought that most of adult life consisted of empty, unfulfilling bullshit, yet he'd succumbed to the inescapable inevitability of it. He was going to grow up whether he wanted to or not. If he had to grow up, it was better to be an adult who could at least provide for his own material needs and maintain a comfortable standard of living than one who couldn't. So that meant getting serious about school and college and all that stuff. The compromise he'd made with himself was that once he had made sure his future needs would be satisfied, that he'd try to find something more meaningful in life than mere survival to keep him going. Something that didn't seem like it was just so much bullshit.

Now he thought that maybe he'd found that something in Jenny. Love for someone else. That was something that was worth living for, worth fighting for, wasn't it? The more cynical side of him told himself that he was confusing love for lust. That his raging hormones were getting the better of him. In a way, that is part of why he was so eager to go all the way with her. How else could he be certain? Would his feelings for her suddenly fade away once they'd done it? Would it start to feel old after a while? Just part of a tired routine? He couldn't imagine that something as exciting as sex could ever become like that, yet he'd heard that's how it is sometimes for adults. He wanted to hold on to the excitement of it forever. If sex could become boring and tiresome, that meant potentially *anything* in life could. That idea truly terrified him. He never wanted to become one of those jaded adults that was completely worn out by life—one of the walking dead.

He had to find out. He had to find out if the thrill he felt around her was lust, or if there was really something deeper to it. Was he a young man in love, or simply another guy who was just thinking with his dick? He certainly felt like he was in love; he certainly wanted to be in love. He liked to think of himself as something of an intellectual and not just some shallow person driven purely by animalistic instincts. He believed with all his heart that he appreciated Jenny for who she was and not just how her body could arouse him. He loved her humor, her compassion, her talent, and her intelligence. When he wasn't with her or talking to her on the phone, he always wondered what she was doing, what she was feeling. He always longed to be with her. He burned for her.

But doubts still assailed him. He had to be sure it wasn't all some delusion on his part, that all the things he loved about her weren't mere justifications to satisfy his own self-image as a sophisticated person by actually going all the way with her and seeing if he suddenly lost interest afterwards. He had to know that he wasn't just exaggerating her charms in his mind to rationalize his desire to get in her pants as being something nobler, as an expression of their love for one another. And if he was wrong and it was lust? He'd let her down gently. He didn't want to lead her on, to live a lie. In the end, that would only destroy them both. He didn't want to ever lie to her, to use her. She deserved better than that. If they were going to be together, he wanted it to be real. He wanted it to mean something.

For her part, Jenny seemed eager to do it too, so long as they took the right precautions. She didn't want to wind up pregnant any time soon. Nate didn't want that either; he was all too aware of how much that could derail both their bright futures. Not that he didn't want kids someday with her. He even fantasized sometimes about how his and Jenny's kids might look like. He just didn't want them *now*. So Nate had procured a few condoms that were now carefully tucked away in his wallet. He'd actually shoplifted them from a local drug store, too embarrassed to buy them. Sure, he'd heard that sex felt better without them, but he couldn't imagine that it still wouldn't feel great with one on. Honestly, he'd be far too anxious about getting her pregnant or catching a VD (not that he really thought she had any, but you never know) to actually enjoy the act without one.

Now he was running through the night towards Jenny's house. He wasn't terribly concerned about the situation with the killer. Despite his initial skepticism, he was confident that the Mounties had caught him. There hadn't been any new murders, had there? It was only a matter of time before the suspect confessed. Either way, even if the real killer was still on the loose, both he and Jenny lived in the safest neighborhood in town—a gated community with the (rather nonsensical, in Nate's option) name of Woodmere. It had its own twenty-four-hour private security force. This security force was hardly fool proof. Nate and some of his former associates were quite adept at eluding their patrols. But that's because, as residents, they were intimately familiar with their routines. They knew what routes they took and when they patrolled. Outsiders wouldn't know such things. Nate was fairly certain that whoever the killer was, they didn't live in Woodmere.

Nate's lungs burned as he ran through the night's crisp, chilly air. But it was a good burn, the kind of burn that made him feel alive. He was jogging along the shoreline of a smallish man-made lake at the heart of Woodmere. It was one of his tricks for getting around the place late at night without being detected. There were no streetlights around the lake, and the patrols never went there at night. Plenty of homes circled the lake, but nobody had a backyard that was directly on it. From this central location, you could reach any part of the community fairly quickly. Nate marveled at how brilliantly the stars and the moon shone over the lake as he circled it, away from the harsh glare and light pollution of the streetlights.

Finally, he reached the part of the lake near Jenny's house and veered off from the shore, back up onto the aptly named Lakeside Drive—the road that orbited the lake. Within minutes, he was on Jenny's road. He jogged off the road when he was able to, traveling through the woods that ran parallel to it, and sticking to hedgerows when he wasn't. When he got to her house, he walked up to her window, which fortunately was rather low to the ground, and tapped on it lightly a few times.

The curtains parted, and he could barely make out Jenny's form in the darkness. She slowly and carefully pulled up the window so as not to make a lot of noise. "I wasn't sure you were really coming," she whispered.

"I wouldn't miss this for the world," he assured her in a hushed voice.

"You're a nut!" She smiled and helped him crawl inside.

Once he was inside and the window was closed, Jenny turned to him. "Do you think that April and Angela ever do anything like this?" she asked him. Yes, Nate had eventually told Jenny about April and Angela's relationship, but only once he was sure that she was the sort of person who wouldn't care or hold it against them.

"Are you kidding me? Not with how strict Angela's parents are, and especially not now that there's a killer on the loose."

"Yeah, they're not as crazy or desperate or whatever as we are. I can't believe you really came here with everything that's going on."

"Hey, can I help it if I believe that you're worth the risk? Besides . . . how do you know that *I'm* not the killer?" he joked, and then, in a more serious tone, added, "Anyhow, it's probably not really all that dangerous. That bum that the Mounties picked up is probably the killer. There haven't been any more deaths since they caught him."

"The only thing you're killing right now is the mood with all this morbid talk." She grinned and pulled him in for a long kiss. He wanted to remind her that *she* was actually the one who first brought up the murders, but the sweet sensation of her tongue in his mouth somehow made him forget all about such petty things. Then she began to steer him towards her bed, and they both dropped onto it.

"Did you bring some rubbers?" she asked in a husky voice, the heat of her breath tickling his ear.

"Got 'em right here!" he said, patting his pants pocket where his wallet was.

"Oh, is *this* it?" she asked innocently as her hands found a distinctly non-wallet shaped bulge in the front of his jeans and began running her hand up and down it.

"You've definitely found it!" He gulped. Who was he to argue the facts at a time like now?

Within moments clothes were being stripped off and they were moving through the various bases until a home run was all but inevitable. And what a home run it was! They both lost their virginity that night—unless you count all the things they'd already tried out in the movie theater, which many people would consider to be sex, but this was their first time doing the kind of sex that can make babies. It went surprisingly well for both of them. They'd both been a little anxious about it. They'd all heard the horror stories: guys who blew their load right away, girls who found the whole experience to be more painful than pleasurable. But somehow, none of these problems had plagued them. They'd dodged that bullet and had a wonderful time.

The only downside was that they both had to try to keep things quiet so they wouldn't get caught. This concern was a bit of an unwelcome distraction, yet also added to the thrill at the same time. Fortunately for them, the odds of getting caught were relatively low. Jenny's recently-divorced Mom's bedroom was located some distance down the hall, and her Valium prescription usually kept her well-sedated throughout the night. In any case, Jenny had locked her bedroom door and calculated that Nate could throw on some clothes and get out the window in no time. Still, it was hard to stop from crying out when he brought her to orgasm like he was an expert rather than a novice.

They lay together for some time, covered in sweat and other assorted fluids, their bodies intertwined. Nate was quite pleased with himself. He didn't find that his feelings for Jenny had diminished in the slightest. In fact, if anything, he wanted more. Could she really be *the one* who he was meant to be with? His equal half he'd always longed to meet? To join with? It seemed too good to be true, yet there was no denying how he felt at that moment. So many people spend their whole lives looking for someone like Jenny, yet here he was. He had barely just turned seventeen and he had already found her. Then a sudden fear gripped him. A fear of the future. Surely, when they both went off to (more than likely) different colleges, they'd drift apart, become interested in new people? He'd heard of things like that happening a million times. How could he hold onto this? How could he keep it forever? The odds were against them. He literally shuddered at the thought.

"Are you okay?" Jenny whispered to him as she felt his body trembling against hers.

"Me? I'm great! Never been better. It's just that . . . I don't want this moment to ever end. I don't want *us* to ever end," he confessed.

"Me too. I'm so glad you're, well . . . *you*. I'm glad that my first time was special and not with some icky dirtbag. I'm grateful that you've given me a memory that I'll treasure forever, no matter what the future holds for us."

And with that tender exchange of feelings, it wasn't too much longer before they were back at it again, working on filling up condom number two. The second time was almost, but not quite, as sweet as the first, as is often the case.

Having worn themselves out, the time came that the Bard once described as being "such sweet sorrow." It was time for him to go back home. Besides, tonight *was* a school night. Yet our Juliet couldn't quite bear to see her Romeo disappear out her window and vanish back into the night that spawned him. Jenny insisted on walking back with him for part of the way. Nate was in no position to argue, and he was grateful for the company. After all, he never wanted her to leave his side.

***

So it was that they were soon both slipping out the window. Jenny herself was an old pro at this. She had once snuck out regularly to participate in neighborhood games of "manhunt," conducted in the dead of the night during the summer. Unfortunately, unlike Nate, she had been caught by the neighborhood security goons and escorted back home to face her angry parents. She'd gotten in so much trouble from that incident that she'd never dared to sneak out again—until now. The memory made her smile. Things had seemed so innocent back then. Kids could run around at night without any real fear of being brutally killed. It seemed so far away now. As she walked with Nate, every shadow seemed to loom menacingly towards her. She had agreed to walk him back to Lakeside Drive, but now she was beginning to regret her decision, to regret the lonely walk back to her house that lay before her. She was fearful of facing these shadows alone, and whatever terrors lurked within them.

Get a grip, she told herself. *There's nothing to be scared of anymore. Like Nate said, they already caught the killer. If you keep this up, you'll be worse than Mom!* She tried to forget all these new fears and just bask in the warm afterglow of her recent lovemaking.

***

The man could hear footsteps crunching on the asphalt near the car he sat crouched behind. He risked looking over the edge of the car and smiled at what he saw. He wasn't smiling at the heartwarming sight of two young people who were clearly deeply in love walking hand in hand. No, he was smiling because he couldn't wait to bash their fucking brains in with his sledgehammer.

His friend, his Dark Angel, had not steered him wrong. The boy was indeed headed this way. Better yet, so was his little whore. He knew what they'd just been doing. It was obvious. The stench of it was all over them, carried on the crisp night breeze. He shook his head. Didn't these young fools know that there was a virus out there killing people who were loose? But he already knew the answer. These idiot kids today were all the same—they never thought about the future, never thought about the consequences of their actions.

That's why they had to die.

He wasn't sure exactly why his friend had chosen this particular boy to die. It had something to do with someone this kid was friends with, someone the Dark Companion wanted to break. He didn't care about all the petty details; killing the boy fit well into his own agenda, and he was happy to help out his only friend. The two of them had grown closer over the past week—literally. The man had let his friend enter his body, and now it was sometimes hard to tell where one of them started and the other began. He could feel him there, looking out through his eyes, content to just watch for now. Sometimes this strange state, the cohabitation of the same body, brought him images that he couldn't explain. He supposed they must be memories of his friend. He caught glimpses of a scorching desert under a starry sky, being led to the gallows, and flashes of various rotting corpses dressed in nineteenth-century garb, posed like mannequins. None of it made any sense to him, and he didn't care much to ask what it all meant. He had his mission, his Great Purpose, and it was all that he cared about anymore.

This past week had felt excruciatingly long while he laid low and took a break from his Great Purpose at the suggestion of his friend. But now . . . now the moment was upon him, the moment of blessed release that he'd been waiting for. *Two for the price of one!* he thought as he licked his lips in anticipation, feeling the reassuring weight of his new weapon in his hand. The weapon had been the Dark Angel's idea. He had suggested that changing his modus operandi would confuse the authorities. The weapon had been "borrowed" from his job and inspired by a recent hit song by Peter Gabriel. One of the few pleasures left to the man was music. He enjoyed singing along to this particular tune in his car. It played through his head as he moved from the side of the car to the back and lay waiting for his targets to get a little closer.

Oh yes, he wanted to be their sledgehammer. He wanted them to call his name. He wanted them to beg for mercy, not understanding that the death he was bringing to them was the highest kind of mercy. He was sparing them the pain of discovering that their childish infatuation with each other was just an illusion. Letting them hold onto this pleasant delusion of love before the cruelty of the world inevitably tore it from them.

As the two teenagers began to reach his hiding spot, he wound himself up like a batter about to hit a home run. He swung out into the space before him, the sledgehammer connecting with the rib cage of the boy, who happened to be the closest to him. He heard the satisfying crunch of breaking bones as the boy went tumbling backwards. The swing, which he had made from an awkward crouching position, also threw him off balance for a moment. He shot out his hand to catch himself as the asphalt rushed towards him.

As he rose to his feet, he was vaguely aware of the girl letting out a scream.

You have to shut that one up before she draws attention to us, his friend told him, although he hardly needed such a reminder. However, his attention was now focused on the boy, and the strange way his body twitched and jerked on the ground. He stepped forward to put him out of his misery, raising his sledgehammer high over his head.

Watch out behind you! the Dark Companion warned suddenly. Without bothering to look, the man simply stepped to the side. He whipped around just in time to see that the girl had been trying to charge at him. Now that she found herself plowing through empty space instead of running into him, she quickly lost her footing and crashed down into the street, landing right on top of her lover.

***

Jenny moaned in horror as she landed atop Nate. Horror at the spreading wetness that stained his shirt, the blood that looked like ebon ichor in the darkness. She could feel something sharp poking into her side, she quickly processed it as probably being a broken rib. Worst of all was the fact that she couldn't feel the rise and fall of his chest. She looked up at his face, permanently frozen into an expression of shock, his eyes already taking on a glazed expression. They were dead eyes. He was already gone. She began sobbing at the realization. Then she started struggling to try to get back up. The palms of her hands stung from where the skin had been scraped from them when she fell. She managed to flip herself over, but the killer was already upon her, standing right over her. His hammer raised high, silhouetted by the moon.

"No! Please, no!" she cried out instinctively. But he was not to be swayed. With terrible finality, he brought the sledgehammer barreling into her skull. Warm, wet fragments of it went flying in a million different directions, peppering him with the contents of her head.

***

The man looked down upon his works and trembled slightly. Something about the position of the bodies before him inspired him. He quickly bent over and moved the arms of the two lovers so that it

156

looked like they were locked in an eternal embrace. The Dark Companion encouraged such displays. He could hear him purring his approval inside his head now .

Yes, nicely done! What a touching little tableau. A tribute to the folly of young love. Now, you'd better get off the street, my friend. The little bitch's cries may've attracted some unwanted attention. It wouldn't do to be seen, now, would it?

The man grunted in disappointment. There was so much more that he longed to do to these bodies. Mutilating the corpses had become one of his favorite parts of this process, and he was eager to study in more detail the damage that a blunt instrument could do to a body as opposed to a blade. Yet there was no escaping the logic of his friend. If he lingered too long, he risked getting caught, and then his Great Purpose would come to an end. Besides, he knew that if he didn't obey the suggestion of his friend soon, the Dark Angel would just seize control of his body, reducing him to nothing but a helpless passenger until his friend grew bored with pulling his strings directly. It was an unpleasant sensation, not being in control of one's own body, and one that he wasn't keen to repeat. The man ran into the nearby cluster of woods and began making his way through them towards his vehicle, which was parked on the other side of the ineffectual fence that the people who lived here dared to dream kept them safe from the outside world.

Yes, that's it. Good! But don't forget to dispose of the weapon in the lake when you get closer to it, like we planned, his friend reminded him. So, when the man could see the silvery pool of water through the trees, he crossed Lakeside Drive in a run, not stopping until he reached the shore. He then, with a bit of reluctance, spun around and tossed the sledgehammer as far as he could throw it towards the center of the lake. He hated to see it go. He felt that his work with it wasn't quite done, that he had yet to unlock the full potential of using such a tool in this way. But his friend had already explained to him how disastrous it would be to be caught with the murder weapon if the police happened to stop him before he could reach his room.

There are a million different ways of killing left for us to explore. A whole universe of inflicting pain awaits us. No need to be so sentimental over that old thing. Now clean yourself up a bit while you're here. I can feel the bits of her brains still clinging to your face.

With that, the man edged closer to the lake and scooped up some of the frigid water in his cupped hands. He let it drop over his head and rubbed his face with his wet hands. He looked down at himself— even in the moonlight, he could make out some blood splatter on his shirt. It was a good thing that he had brought a change of clothes in his car. If he could only reach it. He turned and ran back to the road, and once he was certain that no cars were approaching, he crossed back into the safe haven of the woods. The tangle of trees and brush swallowed his hulking form until all that could be glimpsed between their grasping, tangled branches was an all-pervasive darkness.

Eleven : Stages of Grief

About a week had gone by since she first got the news, but it still felt impossible to her. Even now, as she finished doing her hair for the second funeral she'd be attending in as many days, none of it felt real. April McKenna looked back at her own reflection in the bathroom mirror and felt no connection to the person in the glass. She felt nothing but a total detachment from the crushing reality of everything.

Jenny's funeral yesterday had been a closed-casket affair. That had only enhanced April's general sense of how unreal it all was. How could anyone expect her to believe that Jenny was truly gone for good and never coming back if she couldn't even see the body? How was she supposed to believe that this whole thing wasn't just some impossibly elaborate and tasteless prank? That Jenny and Nate wouldn't pop out from behind a curtain at any moment?

"See? I told you it's all bullshit!" Nate would say, laughing, as he stepped out from behind the curtain. She kept on scanning the curtains for a tell-tale pair of sneakers poking out from behind them during the entire ceremony. But there were no sneakers. Of course there weren't, it had been a formal affair.

She was forced to entertain the terrible idea that they were really gone. Her friends were really gone, and they weren't coming back.

At Jenny's funeral, she had found herself wondering how much Jenny had truly liked and accepted her. Sure, they'd always seemed to get along really well, but was that only because Jenny didn't know the real her? Would she have felt differently about her if she had known the truth about her and Angela? Had Jenny ever really been her friend?

Just as soon as these thoughts entered her mind, she felt ashamed of them. Of course Jenny had been a true friend. She knew in her heart that Jenny wouldn't have cared about her secret. Such bigotry was incompatible with everything April knew about her. She only wished she'd trusted her enough to share it with her while she was still alive. A fresh pang of guilt pierced her heart all over again. Why hadn't she thought enough of Jenny to trust her with her true self? Worst of all, she couldn't blame the Dark Man for these unpleasant thoughts and feelings, wherever he was now—he was too far away to influence her. No, this were all her own special brand of dysfunction.

Jenny's death had hit Chris particularly hard. It was obvious the kid had a crush on her. Now April regretted all the times she had teased him over it. She tried to comfort him as best she could, but it was difficult. He wasn't just grieving Jenny—he was also more scared now than ever before. He told April he was now completely sure that the Dark Man was behind this, and it was only a matter of time before he would send the killer after them. In the end, the only thing that had actually calmed him down was when April showed him the energy shield she was now able to conjure up at will. "I told you I can protect us with my magic. You've got nothing to worry about, I promise," she'd told him with a confidence that she didn't really have. The truth was that, despite her new abilities, she was just as scared as Chris was.

"Are you okay in there, April?" Jo's voice called from the other side of the bathroom door. "We have to leave soon, or we'll be late."

"Yeah, I'll be out in a sec. I was just finishing up," she lied. She'd been done for minutes now. She'd become fascinated with the oddity of her own reflection, with the thought that the thing staring back at her was actually her. How could this animated hunk of meat encapsulate all of her thoughts and experiences? She'd lost track of time and been as untethered from the passage of one moment into the next as she had been from her own identity.

Now it was time to shake herself out of this strange funk. Time to leave behind this eternal now and merge back into the normal flow of time. She wouldn't want to be late for Nate's funeral, would she? This time, she'd actually get to see the body. Maybe it would make all of this finally seem real. But is that what she really wanted? Wasn't it more comforting to go on feeling like this was all some illusion? She sighed. She supposed that sooner or later, she had to face the reality of it, but she was scared to do that, too. Scared that she couldn't handle it, that this latest loss would be the straw that finally broke the camel's back.

Of course, she knew that the spirit was a real thing from her experiences with the Dark Man and all the times that she had astrally projected recently. She knew it was something which survives the death of the body, yet this knowledge brought her little comfort. When she was outside of her body, she'd never encountered the spirits of anyone she knew. Although a part of her was pleased to know some part of them still survived somewhere, it didn't change the fact that she was alone. That there was no guarantee that she'd see them again any time soon.

As it turned out, seeing Nate's body at the viewing didn't really help at all. So much makeup had been caked onto him that he barely looked like himself. The thing in the casket looked more like a poorly constructed wax dummy of him. It was so generic-looking that it could almost be anyone. Seeing it gave her no sense of closure; it hadn't grounded her in the slightest from the surreality of it all. As she looked upon it, she found herself getting increasingly angry.

How could you go and leave me to do this science fair project all by myself, without a partner? she caught herself thinking, then flushed with embarrassment at the absurdity of her fury, at the selfishness of it. What did science fair projects matter now?

As she turned to walk away from the casket, she caught sight of Angela walking up behind her. She looked stunning all dressed in black, even more gorgeous than she had been at Jenny's funeral. Again, April chastised herself for her thoughts. She was supposed to be thinking about Nate, not getting horny! But she was desperate *not* to think of Nate, to think of anything but him. Angela threw her arms around her when she got near enough, sobbing into her shoulder.

"I still can't believe it! I can't believe that he's gone," Angela managed to get out between heaves.

"None of it feels real to me either. It feels like just the other day that we were all sitting around the den, laughing and watching wrestling . . ."

April's voice trailed off, then she completely lost it. The floodgates of emotions that she'd been suppressing for days suddenly burst open. She wailed and cried, not just for Nate, but for Jenny too. For the unfairness of it all. Here were two people who had forever been frozen in time, who would never get to experience growing up, who would never get to see the future. What she wouldn't do to be able to change things for them, to give them back their shot at life. Yet despite all the amazing things she could do now, such things were still beyond her powers. What good was all this magic if it couldn't bring her friends back to her? What was the point of it at all?

Throughout her breakdown, Angela held her, anchoring her. Eventually, Angela must have realized that they were making a scene and holding up the line, so she gently steered April back to where the Johnsons were all sitting. April barely knew what was happening anymore. Tears stung her eyes and blurred her vision as she sat down numbly. She had to force herself to let go of Angela's arm.

"At least I still have you," April told her, meeting her eyes.

Angela leaned in and whispered into her ear. "And you always will, my love. You always will." She squeezed her hand and started moving back towards her own seat.

April sat through the rest of the ceremony as if she was in a trance. Soon enough, they were all being whisked away to the graveside. The wake soon followed. The only thing that penetrated the daze she was in was a snippet of conversation that she overheard between Nate's father and someone else. Nate's father was telling them that they'd already picked out a headstone and was describing what would be engraved upon it. It was to be a Biblical verse: "Whosoever believeth in Him should not perish, but have eternal life."

April found the anger rising within her once more, because she felt like this just illustrated how little Nate's parents actually knew him. The guy was agnostic. If he'd actually believed what that verse had to say, she would've been fine with it, but it just underscored how divorced his folks were from his life. Or at least how little he had felt comfortable confiding in them how he really felt about such things. How many other kids were there out there that felt like they had to keep their real thoughts and feelings a secret from their own parents? Even with as much as she had come to love the Johnsons, April still didn't trust them with the secret of her sexuality.

The thought just depressed her. That his parents' real loss—that they may have never known the real Nate. Did they understand what a kind person he was? How genuine he was in his desire to find the things in life that held real substance, real meaning? Did they know how funny he could be? If they had known the real Nate, they'd know that he'd probably want his gravestone to read something like "I'm dead now? This is total bullshit!" That thought made her actually giggle out loud. Nate's mother heard the sound and shot her an ugly look. She fought to regain her composure, then found the part of the room where her foster family were sitting. "I think it's time we left," she told them. There was no argument from any of them; they were just there to support her and pay their respects. After two funerals in a row, everyone was pretty sick of it all.

A few more days went by. There were no new murders. There hadn't been any in nearly two whole weeks now, but this no longer made anyone feel more secure. The only suspect in the case had been released once it was obvious he couldn't possibly be the one to blame. There had been a little resistance to this at first. The unusual weapon used in the latest murders made the authorities question whether they were dealing with a different killer, but in the end they had to concede that, while the choice of murder weapon had changed radically, everything else about the killer's M.O. still fit.

April sunk into a deep depression during this time. Even meditation brought her little peace. She didn't go to school for a few days, ruining her perfect attendance record. She mostly stayed in bed sulking. Sometimes she would astrally project and just hover over herself, looking down upon her inert form.

Is this what it's like to be dead? To be a ghost? she wondered. She couldn't imagine that it was all that different. So far as she could tell, the only difference between herself and a spirit at this moment was the golden umbilicus of energy connecting the astral version of her body to the physical one still lying in the bed. She thought about disobeying her promise to Madame Wendigo, of flying out into the night to confront the Dark Man. Two things were stopping her. The first was a fear that once she was out of range of the protective effect of her magic amulet her spirit form would be vulnerable to attack from the Dark Man. The other was a fear that the old woman would somehow know she had broken her promise. Sometimes she swore that Madame Wendigo was able to read her mind. Also, for all she knew, she had her house under some form of magical surveillance, and all kinds of alarms would go off if her astral body left it. She called out to Nate and Jenny in her mind. She called out to all the people she had lost in her life that were precious to her, figuring that if they answered her summons, they could communicate openly while she was out of her body. She tried this every night, but they never came, which just added to her great melancholy and her sense of powerlessness.

The Johnsons were disturbed by April's behavior. They were talking about getting her some grief counseling but had yet to actually do so. Even Angela couldn't shake her out of her torpor. Truthfully, she was ill-equipped to do so, as she was dealing with her own deep sadness. It was quite a thing to finally feel like you've found your people, your own little tribe of friends, only to have most of them ripped away from you in the worst possible way.

They had tried to hang out to watch wrestling like they always did, but it just wasn't the same without the other two. There was no Nate to crack sarcastic jokes, no Jenny scribbling away on her sketch pad. Their absence just reminded them all the more of everything they'd lost. In retrospect, it had been idiotic to try to bring back their weekly tradition so soon, but at least it still gave them a rare opportunity to spend some time together outside of the confines of school. Unfortunately, most of that time was spent in an uncomfortable silence, as they were both too lost in their own gloomy thoughts to enjoy anything around them.

Even their nightly phone calls offered little comfort to April. April was so scared of losing Angela now that she was all that was left of her circle of friends, that, quite ironically, she was starting to shut her out and push her away, sharing less and less of her feelings with her. She wasn't even aware she was doing it. She told herself that Angela didn't want to hear all of her depressing thoughts, that telling her about them would just bring her down as well. So it became the elephant in the room that nobody would ever talk about. Their conversations now took on a routine, superficial quality, like office small talk. She wanted things to go back to how they used to be between them, but she had no idea how to make this happen. Again, she was gripped by an overwhelming sense of helplessness over the direction of her own life.

April had resolved that she had to do something about this whole situation. Something had to give. She couldn't bear to go on like this any longer. She couldn't shake the feeling that she was the next one on the killer's list, and she'd be damned if she was going to just be another victim. True, she had her magic to defend herself with, but it wouldn't do her any good if he surprised her before she even learned to cast a spell.

She had made up her mind to ask Madame Wendigo for help again, even though that hadn't gone particularly well the last time. With the latest murders having struck so close to home, she didn't see how the elderly witch could still maintain that this was all just a coincidence. She was hoping that Madame Wendigo could help her contact the spirits of Nate or Jenny so they could find out from them what the killer look like. That was the rationale she'd give the old woman. The truth was that she just desperately needed to see her friends again to properly say goodbye. If she could learn how to contact the spirits of the dead, then perhaps she could even reach her dead parents and brother. She still hadn't given up hope of using magic to contact them someday. Somehow, she had to convince the old witch to teach her how to do it, or to do it for her.

Finally, Saturday came. April and Madame Wendigo were sitting at the table in her parlor. April was demonstrating her ability to control the shape and size of her energy shield. It hovered above the table and was only the size of a small plate.

"Good, good! Now increase the size so it matches this table," the elderly matron urged her.

April chanted the odd words that would make this happen. She now understood these words to be in a language called *M'bogish*, which Madame Wendigo claimed to be the original language of the human race. As strange as the words were, they were easy to learn.

In fact, it almost felt more like remembering something long-forgotten than learning something new. Madame Wendigo claimed that many people carried ancestral memories of the language, which made it easier for them to grasp than other tongues. "*M'bogish* comes naturally to those who have learned how to listen to their instincts," she had told her.

In no time, April had done as the old woman commanded. The energy shield hung above the entire table.

"Excellent! Your practice is really paying off." She clapped her hands together in delight, the various bracelets she wore jingling musically together.

"Yeah, great. But I wish you'd teach me something a bit more offensive than defensive, considering a killer might be coming after me any day now," she complained.

"What is all this talk of the killer coming after you?" Madame Wendigo asked in alarm.

"Oh, come on! He just killed two of my best friends. Do you honestly still think this has nothing to do with the Dark Man?"

The old woman sighed loudly. "I am sincerely sorry for what happened to your friends. I want you to know that I have been going out every night in my astral body to search for your Dark Man so that I might banish him forever from this plane. But I can find only vestigial traces of his presence, like the ones that used to cling to you and Chris. They could be many months old for all I know. This kind of spiritual pollution can linger for quite some time. This has led me to conclude that he has probably moved on from this town. Otherwise, I'm sure my magic would've flushed him out by now."

"Unbelievable! So you're still saying this was just a coincidence."

Madame Wendigo pointedly ignored the barb. "Also, I have already given you an offensive weapon, you just haven't used your imagination well enough to recognize it."

"Huh? What are you talking about?" April asked in confusion.

"Allow me to demonstrate," Madame Wendigo replied, then began chanting. With a wave of her hand, she sent the energy shield careening across the room towards the fireplace until it smashed into an old Chinese vase that stood in front of it, instantly pulverizing it into dust.

"Whoa!" April was impressed, to say the least.

"Unfortunately, most offensive spells involve firing forms of energy that can easily cause a fire if used indoors. I can't teach you how to do anything like that until your aim is spot on. However, you *can* create and move around a wall that's strong enough to repel virtually anything. It can also be used to smash things quite nicely, as you can see. That's a pretty good offensive weapon, if you ask me."

"You didn't have to destroy that vase just to convince me of that."

"That old thing? Don't worry about that, it's a fake. Besides, it's nothing I can't undo with a little localized time reversal." She started casting a new spell, and before April's watched as the vase flew back together before her astonished eyes. With another few chanted words, Madame Wendigo also made the energy shield disappear.

"You can alter time, too?" April really couldn't believe it. Much like it had when she had seen her mentor create a miniature sun, her mind was abuzz with the myriad possible implications of such an awesome power.

"To a certain extent, yes. But it can be extremely dangerous to do so on a larger scale, or with something living. It's very advanced stuff."

As soon as April got over her shock at Madame Wendigo's latest display of power, she decided to take a chance and tell her what was really on her mind. "Even if you really don't think that the Dark Man is involved in these murders. I still think there's a lot more we could do to bring the killer to justice."

"I understand that you want to see your friends' murderer brought to justice very badly, my child, but I've already explained why we must leave this to the police. Besides, I'm really not sure *what* we could do even if we wanted to."

Says the woman who can reverse the flow of time, April thought bitterly. "Why couldn't you use that ceremony you did when you tried to summon the Dark Man to conjure up the spirits of some of the victims? Get them to tell us who the killer is, what he looks like."

Madame Wendigo shook her head. "That ceremony only really works on spirits that are stuck on this plane of existence, except at certain times of the year, such as Samhain. Even if it did work, what would we tell the police? 'Do you have a sketch artist on hand? I have a description of the killer that was given to me by a ghost.' They'd laugh us out of the station."

"It's not the silliest idea. You know that the police sometimes work with psychics. Everyone thinks that you're just a fortune teller! just tell them that it came to you in a psychic vision or something!"

Madame Wendigo frowned as she continued to shake her head. "There are no spirits to ask! I've already been to all the crime scenes in my astral body, trying to verify if your Dark Man really was involved. I've yet to run into the ghosts of any of the victims. They've all moved on, beyond the veil of death and into the Aether where we cannot so easily reach them. This is a good thing! The silver lining of this dark cloud! You should rejoice at this news, my child! Your friends are at peace now, in a better place. The victims of such brutal crimes are not always so lucky. That's what this is really about isn't it? Wanting to see your friends again one last time? And maybe not just them, eh? Perhaps you're hoping to learn how to see all those you've lost who are precious to you? Maybe you've even been dreaming of such a thing since the moment you first walked through my doors?"

April's head was swimming. The old lady could really see right through her! And beyond that, she was also surprised to learn how thorough her hunt for the Dark Man had been, and been heartened to learn that she had bothered to investigate the possibility that he was involved in the murders. Here she had been, thinking all this time that she had dismissed her concerns out of hand and was doing nothing to address them, when exactly the opposite was true.

"Yes. Yes, I want to see them again! I miss them so much!" She confessed before devolving into a blubbering heap. Finally saying it out loud proved to be as powerful as any magical spell when it came to unlocking the depths of her hidden sorrows. Madame Wendigo rose from her seat and tenderly cast an arm around the inconsolable girl.

"There, there my child. I don't blame you at all. It's only natural to want to see our loved ones again once they've moved on. Don't you think I long to use my great powers to reunite with my husband? I think about it all the time! You have no idea how greatly I miss that man."

April was floored. Madame Wendigo almost never mentioned her late husband, or what had become of him.

"So why don't you?" She sniffled out the question as her sobs subsided.

"It's best to let the dead rest, if you spend too much time with them, you stop living life yourself. Your relatives and friends that have passed on are still a part of you. So long as you can remember them, they'll never really be gone. They live on inside of you - always. Hold onto that truth and it should be enough."

April was silent, still contemplating her words. Madame Wendigo might've mistaken this quiet for confusion, as she apparently felt the need to elaborate further.

She pointed to her fireplace. "Do you see my fireplace? By now I'm sure that someone as intelligent as you suspects that it's no ordinary fire that burns within that hearth. Yes, it's of a mystical nature. It's a tribute to my late husband, who used to enjoy curling up in front of that fire with a cup of hot tea and his favorite book. That flame will endure so long as our love for one another remains alive. It is fed by my love for him, and his love for me. Even though he is on the other side now, his love for me still continues to feed the flames. So you see, our loved ones are never really gone. They still think of us and we still think of them, and this shared love sustains us all, no matter where we may be in the universe."

April was quite shocked that the fireplace held such a deep meaning for her teacher. No wonder that she spent so much time in this room! She'd always just assumed that it was because old people are always complaining about being cold.

"I think I understand what you're trying to tell me," she began, but then her curiosity got the better of her, as it often did. "What happened to him? To err...Mr. Wendigo I mean, if you don't mind me asking?"

Madame Wendigo chuckled at her calling her husband "Mr. Wendigo. It wasn't his actual name, of course, but she had once enjoyed such a fierce reputation amongst her fellow magic users that it's often what other witches and wizards really did call her considerably more mild mannered husband.

"No, I don't mind at all. It feels good to talk about him. We *should* talk about those we've lost. It's an important part of honoring them. I'm afraid it isn't much of an exciting tale. Even though he was once an Inquisitor like myself, he didn't meet his end at the hands of a rogue magic-user as we sometimes do. He had the very best kind of death—here in his home, surrounded by those whom he loved the best. He was about a decade older than me, and he simply passed away of old age. My people have ways of using magic to hold onto our youth, which can extend our lives considerably. My husband was a man of great integrity and idealism. He rejected such ideas as being unnatural and narcissistic. He knew that death is just a natural part of life, that you can't have one without the other. When his time came, he met it without fear, like greeting an old friend. We should all be so graceful in the face of death."

Madame Wendigo gave her much to think about that day. As it started to sink in, she did begin to slowly feel a little better about everything.

Part Twelve: In the Light of Day

Angela felt the constant thrumming of the school bus's engine beneath her as she stared out her window. The rows of trees that rolled by were occasionally broken up by rows of nearly identical houses.

Is the killer living in one of those boring, innocent-looking little houses? she wondered. *Or maybe his next victim?*

It had been almost a month since Jenny and Nate met their end. There had been no new murders, but nobody really believed that it was over. A ghastly pall still hung over everything in town, clung to every interaction between neighbors, and every conversation had an unspoken subtext of fear and suspicion.

This general malaise had started to take its toll on her relationship with April. She still loved her just as strongly as she ever did, yet she couldn't deny that something was missing from their relationship lately. When they were together or talking on the phone, it felt like April was only ever half there. Like there was some remote part of her that Angela could never reach. They were beginning to drift apart; the intimacy she'd felt with her when their relationship was just starting up was beginning to fade away. It didn't feel as special anymore.

She hated it. She didn't know what to do about it, or if April had noticed the same things. She didn't even begin to know how to explain it or bring it up. She was afraid to even try, afraid that April would misunderstand what she was trying to say and think that she wanted to break up with her, when what she *really* wanted was to turn back the clock so they were back to where they had once been. If that was even still possible. April seemed so distant and distracted lately that sometimes Angela felt like she didn't even know who she was anymore.

She got it. They had both been through a lot lately, both lost so much. She missed Jenny and Nate too. But life *had* to go on. They needed to get through this together, to dare to talk about all the things that they were so afraid to talk about. Now was not the time to push each other away, but the time to lean on each other, to draw strength from one another. She wasn't about to give up on their love, to let it become another casualty of this killing spree. If this love wasn't worth fighting for, then what was worth fighting for?

The bus finally reached her stop and lurched to a halt, the grinding groan of the protesting brakes screeched in her ears. As she walked off the bus, she made up her mind that she would do her best to find a way to bring up all of her concerns with April when she called her tonight. She would do it, no matter how scary it was.

Cold eyes watched the girl climb off the bus. Two minds saw through those eyes now, but the man that they physically belonged to licked his lips in anticipation. He'd waited too long since the last time he'd done this, and he hadn't even found the previous occasion to be quite as fulfilling as he'd hoped for. He was excited. He'd never done anything like this in broad daylight before. The cloak of night had always helped conceal him, protect him. Trying something like this during the day was extremely risky, but that added element of danger to himself thrilled him.

His Dark Companion had chosen this victim, just as he had the last. Chosen because of their her relationship to some girl that his friend was obsessed with tormenting. He didn't understand why he was so focused on that one particular person. He got the impression that he saw trying to break her mind as being some sort of a challenge. He had to admit that he didn't really care very much. The girl who he now watched walking up the street from where he was parked was exactly the type that he was interested in making an example of, of freeing from this miserable life before it spiraled into a perpetual living hell. His friend had told him exactly where to park his car, and what time she'd get off the bus, information he'd gathered during one of the times when he left the man's body and went wandering.

The man turned the key in his ignition and the car roared to life. He pulled away from the curb and began slowly rolling down the road towards the approaching girl. There were no sidewalks on this block, and she was walking on the side of the street. There were few houses on this block, with undeveloped lots filled with trees separating many of the homes. It was the perfect spot to do what he planned to do next.

Angela barely registered what was happening before it was already too late. Some unfamiliar car that had been sitting at the end of the block started driving towards the end of the street, then suddenly accelerated and swerved towards her as it got closer. It had all happened so quickly that she had barely formed the thought that she had to dodge it before it was already upon her, slamming into her side. Her book bag went flying into the air. She felt her bones snapping in her hip as she tumbled to the ground. Pain exploded all throughout her body as she made contact with the road. She was lying on her back now, staring up at the clear cerulean skies. She tried to get up, but a fresh stab of agony from the effort swiftly dissuaded her from that course of action.

She was aware of the car backing up towards her until the driver's door was parallel from to where she was lying. The door swung open, and she saw a large, older man with a wisp of thinning, graying hair look down upon her with a strange, unreadable expression on his meaty, ruddy face. It was as if he was assessing the situation, taking stock of it in an almost inhumanly remote way. Yet behind the cool façade, there also seemed to be an animalistic fury flickering there.

"Please . . . please help me . . ." she croaked out, alarmed at how weak she sounded, by how much effort it took to get those words out.

"Don't worry, I'll take care of you," he replied flatly. Something about the way he said it filled her with dread.

***

The man reached over and felt around under his passenger seat until his fingers felt the handle of the small axe he had concealed beneath it. He was looking forward to this. He recalled reading once

180

how difficult it was to chop someone's head off in one blow. It often took several blows to completely separate it from the body. It's the reason why the guillotine was considered to be humane when it was invented.

He wasn't interested in being humane.

His Dark Angel wasn't the only one who enjoyed a good challenge sometimes. The man was very interested to see how quickly he could separate this girl's head from her body. Surely it couldn't really be all *that* difficult to do. Not for a man of his size and strength.

No! I want this to look like it could've been an accident. I want them to wonder if it was a murder or just bad luck. I want to sow confusion. Not knowing will drive this town crazy, the Dark Companion said.

"That wasn't part of the plan," the man complained furiously. He hated the ambiguity of this idea. He *wanted* them to know that this was his work! He wanted to put his signature on it.

OBEY ME!

"No!" he shouted.

The man felt his self-control slipping away. Before he knew it, he was just a mere passenger in his own body. He felt his fingers release the axe handle and watched helplessly as his hands slammed the door shut and the car pulled forwards a little bit. He saw the reflection of his eyes, which were not his eyes, in the rearview mirror as the car maneuvered so it was lined up with the prone form of the girl lying helplessly in the street. He felt the car accelerating backwards and felt it jump up slightly as it ran over her, and he heard the crunching of bones. He saw his hand shift into drive and felt his foot as it pressed down on the accelerator. Inside his head, he howled in rage at being denied the sweet release of doing the killing himself.

For the first time, he wondered just what kind of a being he had invited into his life, and what it would ultimately cost him.

Part Thirteen: To Be or Not to Be?

April McKenna became violently ill at the exact same moment that her beloved Angela lost her life, spewing vomit all over the desk in her bedroom. She didn't know why she suddenly felt so sick, and it would be a few more days before she connected the two events in her mind.

Angela's death had indeed caused much confusion in town. Nobody actually witnessed it. Angela was the only one who got off at her stop, and there were few houses on her block. The even fewer of the occupants of those houses had been at home when the High School kids got back home. However, by now April wasn't the only one wondering if this was simply a terrible hit and run accident or a deliberate killing linked to the other recent deaths. The death of another teenager who was known to be a friend of some of the previous victims seemed to be too great of a coincidence. The authorities knew that this particular killer was not only growing bolder in the scale of his crimes, but also that his M.O. was not fixed. It seemed to be constantly evolving.

A Mountie had even come to April's home to interview her. A part of her was disappointed that he was in plainclothes rather than their bright red, signature dress uniform. It was obvious they were beginning to suspect that perhaps someone had a vendetta against her ever-shrinking group of friends. As badly as April wanted to tell him everything, she kept quiet about the Dark Man. She was convinced that they'd send her to the looney bin and throw away the key if she told them she believed that a mysterious evil spirit was using someone to kill her friends. Or worse yet, maybe they'd try to blame it all on her somehow? Maybe they'd interpret all her talk of the Dark Man as simply being a way to externalize her own dark side, to absolve herself of the evil things that happened when it took control.

She didn't give them enough information for them to solidify their suspicions that her friends had been deliberately targeted, and Angela's death remained classified as an accidental death. A more scrupulous look at the evidence might have revealed that she'd been struck twice by the car, but they weren't as careful as they probably should've been with this aspect of the case. Internally, the idea that this was anything beyond just a run of the mill vehicular homicide wasn't very popular amongst most of the investigators.

As for April herself, she was quickly losing the will to live. The loss of her first true love on top of the still-too-fresh losses she'd already suffered was almost unbearable. She constantly struggled with suicidal thoughts. She wasn't sure that she wanted to go on living if living meant being cursed to be all alone. If she died, then she'd be reunited with everyone she'd ever lost that she'd loved. She'd be with her Angela again. Wasn't that better than what life had to offer her now? She could escape all this constant pain and misery. It would be so easy.

Then she realized that this was exactly what the Dark Man wanted. She wasn't about to let him win. She'd never give him what he wanted after all the evil he'd done. So she was staying alive out of what? Spite? *Yes*. Why not? She'd live out her life for a thousand years just to prevent that monster from ever claiming his reward.

So perhaps she wouldn't kill herself, but she couldn't help but torment herself with guilt. The Mounties might not blame her, but it was hard for her not to blame herself. As much as she had once taken Chris's words to heart about not being responsible for evil, she still couldn't shake the feeling that if she hadn't befriended Nate, Jenny and Angela, they might all still be alive. Whether she'd intended for any of this to happen or not didn't change the fact that it had still happened because of her proximity to these people.

She wasn't the only one who blamed her for it, either. She was soon to discover that Angela's mother blamed her too.

At the funeral, yet another closed-casket affair, she tried to offer her condolences to Angela's mother only to be met with an unbelievably harsh rebuttal.

"I don't want your sympathy! It's you and your kind that are to blame for this!" the woman hissed at her. It was especially hard on April to be spoken to like this by her, because she resembled her daughter so closely. It was almost like being yelled at by an older version of her lost love.

"My *kind*?" April echoed in astonishment. Was the woman really making a racial slur towards her at her own daughter's funeral?

"I should've never let my baby spend any time with kids from outside of our church." She spat the words out. "You corrupted her with your loose morals. You and your other friends, sleeping with each other before marriage and doing Lord knows what else! You've all brought the Lord's judgment raining down upon us with your sinful ways. She wasn't pure enough in her faith because of you! That's why the Lord wouldn't protect her from that car."

"How can you be so cruel?" April shot back. *And how can she want to believe in a God who can be so cruel?* Even with all that she'd been through, even with the loss of Angela, April still couldn't bring herself to seriously entertain the notion that whatever powers might be behind this universe were deliberately so mean, petty, and judgmental. She didn't believe for a minute that anything Angela had done had brought this fate upon her.

April ran from the room, tears streaming down her face. The Johnsons witnessed her abrupt exit and were soon on her heels, chasing after her. Rob was the first one to reach her; she was crouching into a ball huddling up against the side of the building.

"April!" He called to her between heavy breaths, his lungs were burning—this was far more running than his middle-aged body was used to. "Are you alright? What's wrong?"

"That woman, Angela's mother! She's horrible! You wouldn't believe what she just said to me."

"Erm . . . well, don't forget that she's also in mourning. Mourning for an unimaginable loss. People who are grieving often say terrible things that they don't really mean."

"Oh, she meant it alright," April replied as she stood up to face him. The whole family had caught up with them by now. She told them all what the woman had said.

"Holy crow! That is pretty terrible, honey. She had no right to talk to you like that, no right at all How can she call herself a Christian?" Rob said in disbelief.

Jo gave her a long hug, then looked at her sympathetically. "Maybe we should go? It's obvious that we're not very welcome here. Unless you still need to say your goodbyes to Angela?"

"Say goodbye? To what? A sealed wooden box? That's not her inside there, it's just an empty shell. I've had enough of funerals. Let's get out of this awful place."

"Are you sure? I know you two were really close," Rob double-checked.

"Really close? I *loved* her," April confessed, it felt so good to say it out loud.

"Of course you did," said Jo.

"No, you don't understand. Nobody is left anymore who really understands. Nobody knows exactly what I'm really going through. I didn't just love her, I was *in* love with her, and she was in love with me," she clarified, her voice thick with long pent-up emotions. She didn't quite understand exactly *why* she was revealing this profound

187

truth about herself right now, in front of a damned funeral home of all places, but there it was—the secret was out now.

And so was she.

"Oh. *Oh!*" Jo said in shock. She clearly hadn't seen this one coming.

"I . . . I'll understand if you don't want me anymore, if you just want to send me away now." She looked down, she couldn't meet their eyes.

Now Rob spoke up. "*What?* No way. None of that matters to us! In fact, Jo and I have been talking about this a whole lot lately, but we were going to wait until after the funeral to tell you, because we thought you might need a little cheering up after such an ordeal . . . and well, what I'm trying to say is that we'd like to properly adopt you." His voice now became choked up with deep feelings. "April, we'd be so honored if you would let us become your parents, you know, like for real?"

April was flabbergasted. "What? Really? Even *after* what I just told you about myself?"

Jo laid a reassuring hand on her shoulder, gently pushed up her head from underneath her chin with one finger and met her square in the eyes. "It changes absolutely *nothing.* Nothing, do you understand me? We don't care about that at all. We all know what a good person you are. It doesn't matter who you love, just that you *do* love. And I want you to know that Rob and Chris and I have all come to love you very, very much, and we always will, no matter what.

We're a family now, and we always will be. Please, let's just make it official now, okay?"

She still couldn't believe what she was hearing. It was too good to be true. "You . . . you're not just doing this because you feel sorry for me, are you? I don't want to be some kind of a charity case."

"Oh, April! You don't *really* believe that, do you? Not after all the time you've spent with us? We know your heart, and we love you for it," Rob said.

"You're right. I do know that. I guess that I'm just scared. I *do* want to be adopted by you, to really have a family again, but I'm terrified. Terrified that I don't deserve it, or that it's all just a dream that will end too soon. It feels like I'm never allowed to ever get anything that I really want anymore, or to keep it. I'm afraid that if we become a family that I'll lose all of you too."

"You'll never lose us, April. We'll always be there for you, if you'll just allow us to be," Jo told her firmly.

"Yes! Yes, it's what I want more than anything," she told them and immediately began crying again. This time they were tears of joy, although that didn't make them any less embarrassing. "Jeez, here I go again with the sobbing. I'm so sick of crying. I think I've done enough of it lately to last me a lifetime."

"It's alright, honey. We're all doing it too. Just let it all out!" Rob laughed.

It was true, all four of them were crying and smiling. Rob motioned them all to come closer, and he wrapped his big arms around them in a group hug.

"We'll get started on the paperwork next week. We're finally going to be a family!" he told them.

"We always have been, dear. We always have been," Jo corrected him as she pecked him on the cheek.

April reveled in the feeling of that group hug. Surrounded by both the emotional and literal warmth of her new family. She wanted to be engulfed by it, to let it consume her completely and never leave it. She'd never felt so completely accepted in her life.

A real family of my own—at last! she thought joyfully.

Now *that* was a reason to live, wasn't it?

***

Another Saturday arrived, and that meant another visit to Madame Wendigo's house. This was her first time back since losing Angela, and she was eager to discuss these latest developments with her mentor.

"My child, I'm so sorry to hear that another one of your friends has passed away," the old woman told her as soon as she walked through her door.

"Angela's death was no accident. There's nobody else left now. I'm certain that I'm next on his list. What I want to know is what *you* plan to do about it." She just came out and asked her.

190

Madame Wendigo made a face. "Yes, despite what the police may have to say regarding the matter, I fear that you're probably right. I've been very concerned about your safety too. I've decided to call in a few favors. Some people will be coming to town soon from a secret group called the ABC, which is allied with my people. They have many resources at their disposal which the mundane authorities lack. They will watch over you, protect you, and help me find this Dark Man. Yes, unfortunately it will mean that I'll be up to my neck in paperwork for the foreseeable future—but paperwork be damned! Bringing this to an end before anyone else gets hurt is what's important."

"I'm glad to hear it. When will they get here?"

Madame Wendigo looked down in embarrassment. "Soon. Perhaps as early as Monday night."

April couldn't believe it. "Monday night? That's two days from now! You call that soon? We could all be dead by then!"

"I'm doing the best I can do. I'm lucky I was able to convince them to come at all," the old woman protested. "Unfortunately, most of my closest friends and connections within my organization are also retired now—or worse. And my own children have thus far failed to distinguish themselves within it. I'm afraid that my family name simply doesn't carry the same weight that it once did. This is the best I could do, and it will have to be enough."

April couldn't wait around for Madame Wendigo's friends to arrive. She knew that she had to take matters into her own hands.

That night, she defied Madame Wendigo's wishes and went out in her astral form, hunting for some sign of the killer or the Dark Man lurking around her home. She didn't know exactly what she would do if she found what she was looking for, aside from alerting Madame Wendigo or her friends when they showed up. All she knew was that she had to do *something*, especially after what had happened to Angela.

Not seeing or sensing anything unusual, she took a page out of Madame Wendigo's playbook and visited the scene of the last crime. It wasn't very far away—Angela only lived one street behind her. Her bus rumbled past this same street everyday (there was no longer any need to stop on the corner now that Angela was gone), and April had to remember to avert her eyes, to stop herself from gazing up the road to the spot where her first true love had left this world.

It was difficult to stand there in that spot now. She could still see some of Angela's blood soaked into the asphalt. In her astral form, this lingering remnant of Angela's very life force glowed slightly, but it was a faint, sickly yellowish glow. April found herself crying, which was odd considering that this wasn't her physical body, but it still responded to her presence as if it were at the scene of such a sorrowful event. Things hadn't been great between her and Angela before her death, and she'd had a hard time connecting to her like she used to. That it was probably her fault, that she'd been closing herself off to her. She just wished that she'd had a chance to fix it before it was too late. She just wished that she could tell her how sorry she was.

Enough, she thought. *You'll never accomplish anything if you keep on wallowing in regret Focus on the task at hand.!*

With that, she took control of her emotions and closed her eyes. She *could* sense some of that dark aura of dread that she associated with the Dark Man around here f she concentrated hard enough, she could even see it hanging in the air like floating rivulets of black oil, but it was so faint, so scattered and diffuse, that it didn't form into any kind of a coherent trail that she could follow. Now she could better understand Madame Wendigo's frustration and inability to find the Dark Man. She hoped she hadn't been too hard on the old woman earlier that day. All she could do was hope that these ABC people (*what kind of a stupid name was that?*) could really get some results.

There was no more point in being out here away from her physical body and the amulet that was on her neck. She was vulnerable. She floated off back towards her house feeling somewhat helpless, feeling like a failure who was powerless to protect herself or her new family.

As she flew through the night, she thought about running away from home. Not that she really wanted to, especially now that she was so close to being adopted. However, if the Dark Man really was primarily after her, it might be the only way to guarantee the safety of the Johnsons. In the end, though, she decided not to run away. She knew that doing so would hurt Jo, Rob, and Chris very badly, and she couldn't bear to do that to them. All she could do was hope that the ABC would show up in time. It sounded like they intended to monitor the Johnsons' house with a security detail. The Dark Man might be some kind of a supernatural threat, but the killer he was controlling was likely all too human, and therefore as vulnerable as the next person. Hopefully, the ABC would be more than enough to deal with him.

She was about to float down through the section of her roof that was directly above her bedroom when she was startled by the sound of someone outside calling her name. How could that be? Nobody could see her in this form! She must be imagining it—

"April!" the voice called again. This time it sounded closer and therefore was clearer. She recognized it now.

Oh shit. Now I'm in real trouble.

She looked over her spectral shoulder to see the form of Madame Wendigo floating towards her, a cross expression on her face.

"What have I told you about how dangerous it is for you to be astrally projecting so far away from your body right now? You made a promise to me. Explain yourself!" she barked out.

"I wanted to see if I could find the Dark Man or the killer. I can't just sit around and do nothing while I wait for your friends to show up. Not when me and my family are in danger! I can't do that after what they did to Angela. I won't be just another victim," April shot back hotly.

"I'm curious as to what your plan was? What would happen if you actually ran into the Dark Man? I haven't taught you how to banish him. It's too complicated of a spell to perform at your level. What would you do if he tried to possess you?"

"What? He can do that?" April hadn't considered that possibility.

"Yes, quite possibly. I suspect that's why I can't find him. That's what I'm doing out here. I'm still searching for him. I look every night, for all the good that it does I think that he might be spending most of his time hiding inside the body of whoever is actually doing the killing. Some poor fool who was stupid enough to open their mind to him and let him in."

April looked down. " I suppose you're going to wipe my memory now? For breaking my promise?"

"And leave you completely defenseless? I couldn't do that to you! I . . . I couldn't do it to you now even if you weren't in danger. The truth is, my child, that I've simply grown too fond of you. I'm fully committed to seeing you reach your true potential as a witch. And I can't blame you for trying to find the killer, not after all that's been taken away from you. I would've done the same thing at your age." She laughed "Hell, I would've done far worse!"

A wave of relief washed over April at those words. "So, we're good then?"

"Yes, but please, no more late-night astral projecting outside of your house. The ABC will be here soon enough, and then we'll have this whole thing sorted out. I promise."

April agreed, but she still couldn't shake the nagging feeling that it wouldn't prove to be quite that simple. Nothing ever was.

Part Fourteen: The Final Countdown

School, which had once been her sanctuary, was a particularly difficult place for April to be these days. Everything reminded her of her lost friends. After all, this is where they spent most of their time together. Her fellow classmates, many of whom had never bothered to speak to her before were now all coming out of the woodwork to offer their condolences and a hug. Everyone who walked past her had a sympathetic smile playing around their lips or worse, a look of pity in their eyes.

Despite all this kindness to her face, she could feel them talking about her behind her back. They must all think she was like the Grim Reaper. To know her, to get too close to her, was the same thing as courting death. The worst part was that she really couldn't blame them for feeling that way.

That Monday was particularly difficult because they had an assembly in the gym about how to remain safe during this dangerous time. It basically boiled down to obvious things like not going anywhere outside by yourself, especially late at night. Never mind that not being alone hadn't saved Nate or Jenny. Never mind that Angela had been killed in broad daylight. Of course, in the case of Angela, nobody was officially considering her to be a victim of anything worse than rotten luck. April couldn't help but feel as if the people conducting the meeting were vaguely blaming the victims for not taking the proper precautions. What would they say about her if she became the next victim? How would they subtly hint that she had in some way brought her own death upon herself? It all sickened her.

She couldn't wait to get back home that day. Rob had left work early and was supposed to take her over to his lawyer's office to sign some papers that would get the adoption process started. She was also curious to see if the ABC had shown up earlier than expected. To that end, she kept a careful look out as she walked home from her bus stop. Not only because she was wary of becoming another hit-and-run victim like Angela, but because the presence of any unfamiliar vehicles on her street could also indicate the arrival of the ABC's security detail. Madame Wendigo had mentioned that they had a particular fondness for black Cadillacs.

But there were no black Cadillacs to be found on April's street that day. Had there been, perhaps what was about to unfold next would've ended up considerably different.

The first indication that something was wrong was that the front door was hanging almost completely open. She cautiously entered the living room and couldn't help but see that certain things were in a disarray. A lamp had been knocked off of a side table. The coffee table was flipped over, the books that sat on top of it splayed all over the floor. She almost tripped over a cushion that belonged on the couch. A feeling of panic gripped her heart. Everything inside of her screamed to run out of the house now and call the police, yet she moved deeper into the house. There was still a possibility that the Johnsons were alive, that she could use her magic to protect them.

She'd never be able to live with herself if she just cut and ran now while there was still a possibility that she could help them. She clung to this hope as she carefully moved through the room, mindful to make as little noise as possible. All of her senses were alert for the slightest indication that someone else was around.

All that met her ears was a stony silence.

She moved from the living room into the kitchen, and her heart sank as she came around the corner and caught sight of a pair of legs lying on the tile floor. A familiar pair of legs—Jo's legs. They weren't moving, and the blue jeans that covered them were darker at the top as if covered in blood. April forced herself to fully enter the room; she had to see it, she had to *know*. There, lying on her back, was Jo. A large blood stain was turning her white top red. It looked as though she'd been stabbed multiple times. Rob was lying beside her at a different angle. He was facing up—it looked as if he had died trying to defend them. His face was frozen in a terrible grimace, his unseeing eyes staring vacantly ahead. April almost slipped on a pool of blood that was still spreading from out of the bodies. There was blood splattered everywhere, like a macabre Jackson Pollock painting.

April felt dizzy and rushed to the sink, where she threw up. *Where's Chris? Oh Goddess, please let him be alive!*

She turned from the sink, and that's when she saw him, a man standing in the threshold that separated the kitchen from the dining room, just smiling at her—a blood-slicked machete almost listlessly dangling from one hand.

He was a massive mountain of a man. He had a small face for such a big head, with a high forehead and wispy greying hair that was thinning on top. Aside from his size, the most remarkable thing about him was how unremarkable he was. He was the sort of person that someone might see on the street a dozen times and never remember.

"Hello, April. Admiring my handiwork? Poor old April. Every time she starts to trust someone, to love someone, they have an irritating habit of dying, don't they?" He leered at her hungrily, rReminding him her of a wolf. She knew exactly who and what he was as soon as he'd opened his mouth.

"It's you in there, isn't it?"

"Of course it is! Your oldest and dearest friend. Your "Dark Man." Although, my Christian name is Benjamin Crooke. You may have abandoned me, but I'll never abandon you. He didn't want to do it, you know. This vessel that I've poured myself into. He only really enjoys killing children like you. He suffers from the delusion that he's actually doing them a favor, snuffing them out before life can destroy their dreams. Just because his own life didn't turn out the way that he wanted, he assumes that nobody's ever does, that happiness is impossible, and everyone is just pretending. What a pessimist. And people call *me* dark." He chuckled to himself. "Of course, I may have played some small part in helping to encourage him in this unique line of reasoning. You want to know what I think? I think he's jealous of you lot. Jealous of all your potential—potential that he never really had or fulfilled. He hates you for it. All this bother about 'mercy killing' is just his way of rationalizing the fact that he just likes to see you bleed and suffer. He just wants to see what you look like on the inside. The guy really should've simply been a surgeon—oh, that's right. He didn't really have the brains for that, did he?"

She watched the Dark Man's new body suddenly jerk violently in a way that seemed involuntary. He giggled like a little girl as it happened. "He's actually trying to fight me right now. I can hear him screaming in my mind. He doesn't like what I have to say about him. Some of the things I've made him do. We have a few *creative differences*, if you will. But it doesn't matter what he thinks anymore, he is my creature now. Once you let me in, I never really let you go. If only you had let me in, April, then we could've enjoyed this kind of . . . intimacy. But you're a stubborn one, aren't you? You'd never let me in. And now, because of that stubbornness, you've made me have to go and do all of *this* . . ." He waved his hands grandly around the scene of carnage in the room.

"I never wanted it to end like this. Really, I didn't. I've watched you all your life. I'm actually quite fond of you, in my own special way. But all games have to come to an end at some point, and this one has sadly run its course. If you won't join me here on the wild side, then I'm afraid you're just going to have to die writhing in agony like all the others. You've been my greatest challenge and my greatest failure. I don't like to be reminded of my failures. Goodbye,

April. " He advanced towards her, his knife still slick with the Johnson's blood gleaming in the light as he stepped over Jo's body.

"Stay away from me!" April screamed, then cast the spell that brought her energy shield into existence and sent it hurling into into the Dark Man. He went flying through the doorframe and into the next room. His back slammed into the wall so hard that his head left a bloody smear on the wall behind him as he slid down to the floor. He looked as if he'd been knocked out. Suddenly, April felt a hand tugging on her shirt from behind. She screamed and jumped, only to turn around and see that it was Chris. She saw the pantry door was ajar behind him and realized that he'd been hiding in there the whole time.

"Chris! Omigod, I'm so happy that he didn't get you!"

"Where were you? You promised that you'd protect us! You promised!" Chris yelled, his small fists pounding against her legs. Her heart was breaking into a thousand pieces at the sight of seeing him like this.

"I'm so sorry! I'm so sorry! I tried! But we don't have time for this right now. We have to get out. We have to get out *now*!"

Out of the corner of her eye, she saw an intense flash of light and whirled around in time to see the Dark Man standing right next to them, his knife raised and poised to strike. With practiced ease, she cast the spell that created a new energy shield around her and Chris just in time to stop his blade. This new shield wrapped around them completely, like a bubble.

"Very nice. That old bat has taught you well." He laughed as he scraped his knife against the shield.

April chanted and gestured with her hand, and the first shield she'd created, which still glimmered and buzzed with magical energy near the doorway, began moving back in her direction. She intended to trap the Dark Man between the two shields, to squash him like a bug, but he cast his own spell and created his own energy shield to protect him just before it struck. There was a sizzling sound as the two enchanted barriers met.

"Nicely played, but you're not the only one here who knows a little magic, my dear."

"Why me? Why can't you just leave me alone?" she yelled at him.

"Why you?" He laughed. "Oh, that would be telling! No, I won't give you the satisfaction of knowing that. You should just give up, April. It would be so easy. I'll never give up until I win. In a way, the pathetic fool that this body belongs to is right. Perhaps it is a mercy to die here in 19'87? For all its problems, this time seems positively innocent compared to what's in store for this world. I've been there—endless wars on terror, children shooting each other in schools so often that it becomes routine, and everyone is always glued to their goddamned phones all the time. Perhaps I'm actually doing you a favor. Let me in, April. Just do it! We can have so much fun together, you and I. What else do you have left to live for? I know that there's a part of you that wants to. Remember, I know you better than anyone else; perhaps even better than you know yourself. Let me in, and we can let the boy live. You can't hide inside that bubble forever! Sooner or later, you're going to have to come out and play."

"Don't listen to him, April! He doesn't know shit about you. He's nothing but a liar!" Chris shouted.

She grabbed Chris's hand. "When I say run, you run," she whispered to him. He nodded his understanding.

"Run!" she shouted.

They turned to run out of the house. The bubble of energy surrounding them remained them, protected them as they dashed through the still open front door and out onto the front lawn.

There was another quick flash of light and the Dark Man was suddenly standing right in front of them, blocking their escape.

"How?" she sputtered in amazement.

"I keep telling you, girl! You're not the only one who knows magic! My mastery of it far outstrips your own! But if you join with me, all that knowledge can be yours too. All that power. My power is far greater than that old crone's. Yes, I know how you secretly long for her power! I am here because I believe in your potential, April. Your potential to create havoc and destruction. Your potential to punish this whole stinking, rotten world that has never really accepted you, that has done nothing but hurt you. I'm here to help you make them pay. I offer you all my knowledge and power to help you punish them all. All you have to do is join with me, to finally let me in."

She shook her head. How wrong he was about her! It wasn't the world that had hurt her. It wasn't some random quirk of fate. It was *him*! Yes, she had suffered at the hands of others, felt the sting of rejection and worse because of her race, her gender, her creed, and her sexuality—but she'd also known acceptance and love from people who knew the real her, people like Angela, Nate, Jenny, and the Johnsons.

People who he had murdered. Joining him would be like spitting on their graves. She wasn't even remotely tempted by his words.

"GET OUT OF MY WAY!" April snarled, years of pent-up rage surging through her. Here he was, right in front of her—the monster that had haunted her for her entire life. The monster who was still doing his best to destroy it. Who had destroyed three of her families. She'd be damned if she was going to let that happen again.

Before she knew it, a brilliant blue light emanated from the crystals around her Chris's necks. The two lights connected and formed one beam of light that blasted through the energy bubble and seared into the Dark Man. April could smell his clothes and the flesh below them smoking and burning before he was thrown backwards several feet into the air. He screamed until he went tumbling back down to the ground with a thump.

"How did you do that?" Chris asked.

"I don't know."

"Do you think it's over? Do you think he's . . ."

"No. It's never that easy. Let's get the fuck out of here while we still can!"

"Where? Where can we run to? Where can we go that's safe?"

April's eyes fell upon the roofline of Madame Wendigo's house as she gazed skyward for inspiration. Of course, there was only one real alternative. There had only ever been one.

Inside her home, Madame Wendigo was meditating in her Turkish cozy corner when her eyes suddenly flew open. She knew in a flash that April needed her. The evil was practically on her doorstep now. With the agility of a woman a quarter of her age, she sprinted from the room. With an arcane word and a wave of her hand, she made her door swing open as she came skidding to a stop in her foyer. April's hand was already raised as if to grab the door knocker. Her momentary look of confusion was replaced by one of dawning realization. April wasted no time in pulling Chis by the shoulders and rushed him inside.

"He's here! He's after us!" she shouted as she ran inside.

"I know, I can feel him! His darkness is palpable," her teacher answered, and with another magic word and wave of her hand, the door slammed shut behind them.

"I left him on my front lawn. Somehow I zapped him with energy that came out of our necklaces! But I don't buy that he's really dead. You were right about him, he is a wizard or something—he knows magic too!" April said breathlessly.

The older woman was surprised by April's report. "You say you zapped him with energy from your amulet? Amazing.!"

"We both did," Chris added.

The old witch looked as if she was deep in thought, but her pensive look was broken by a pounding on the door. The entire door began shaking, violently vibrating.

"He's here! Get behind me, you two," Madame Wendigo commanded. April and Chris were still within their energy bubble, but now Madame Wendigo created one of her own around them all that was much larger. Just as she completed it, the front door shattered into a thousand pieces, splinters of wood blasting into the foyer and pelting the magical barrier surrounding them.

The Dark Man walked into the house in his stolen body. He was gripping his stomach with one blood-soaked hand. He was clearly hurt but doing his best to ignore it.

"This old crone can't save you, April. I told you, I'm more powerful than she is," he bragged.

"We'll see about that!" Madame Wendigo snarled. She chanted a quick spell, and April and Chris looked on in amazement as a column of fire shot out of her parlor and engulfed the Dark Man, setting him ablaze. April realized that it was the magical fire from her fireplace. Even in death, Madame Wendigo's husband was helping to protect her.

The Dark Man didn't scream as his flesh blackened and flaked. Instead, he looked down and studied his melting hands, turning them over as if fascinated by the process of burning. Within seconds, he was little more than a charred skeleton, and the flames retreated back into the fireplace.

Yet the skeleton didn't fall over or collapse. Instead, it took a step towards them, making April and Chris jump. The walking collection of bones still gripped a machete in one hand. They could see the ebon outline of the Dark Man's astral body superimposed over the skeleton.

"Do you think this will stop me?" He laughed, the his words seemed to be coming from inside their heads now. "I can always find another vessel. I'll never stop! I'll kill you all!"

"You're wrong. This stops right now," Madame Wendigo promised gravely, then began chanting a spell. The Dark Man looked down to see that he was now standing in a luminous circle of pure, white light. The skeleton tried to run out of it, but as he reached the edge, the bones clattered to the ground, some of them shattering as they hit the hard, wooden floor. Now only the shadowy outline of the Dark Man's spirit remained standing within the circle. He looked just as April remembered him from that first time when she was a little girl, although she was struck by how small and pathetic he seemed now.

Madame Wendigo said the words to a new spell, her rich voice rising and falling rhythmically. It was the banishment spell. As it went on and on, her chanting became more intense. Inside their minds, the Dark Man laughed hollowly.

"It's going to take more than that, you old fool," he mocked.

Madame Wendigo looked down in defeat. "He's right. He's too powerful, I can't do this alone," she muttered.

"No! We can't let him win! We can do this! We *have* to do this—together! Join forces. Combine our powers," April insisted.

The old woman's eyes brightened. "Yes, yes it *could* work. It *must* work! Okay. Everyone, concentrate on him. Think of all the harm he's done and how much you want him to leave this world and never return. You must want that, want it with all of your heart. Now, link hands and try to repeat after me." She began repeating the spell, only this time she said the words more slowly and deliberately so that the others could duplicate the sounds.

As the words became more intense, the glow of blue energy appeared around April and Chris's amulets once again. As they did before, the auras joined into one beam of energy that shot forth and struck the Dark Man. He staggered backwards inside the circle that contained him.

Inside their minds, they could all hear him screaming. The blue energy completely surrounded him. April looked on as the darkness dissolved from him. She caught sight of a small, thin, wiry-looking pale man with a curiously bent neck dressed in worn sack cloth. In his light blue eyes was an unmistakable look of fear. "How? How can this be? How?" He howled.

Then, as quickly as he had said the words, he was gone.

Elsewhere, a man sat upon a sandy dune, eyes closed, his mouth twisted into a terrible expression of rage. The very air before him was suddenly rent open, and his astral body came hurtling towards him. It slammed into him, knocking him backwards. Through the same hole in the fabric of reality that his spirit had come through now came a brilliantly burning column of blue energy. It hit him with such force that he was thrown up into the sky. The beam continued to propel him up, up until he wasn't even on that small, sandy world he had been sitting mere moments earlier. He was thrown off of it completely, left to drift in a strange kaleidoscope *place between places*, perhaps forever.

Back in our world, Madame Wendigo hugged April and Chris. "It's over! We've won."

April looked at the spot where the Dark Man had been standing only a few seconds earlier. Was it truly over at long last? She was almost afraid to believe it.

"What's going to happen to us now?" Chris asked sadly. "He killed my parents."

"Don't worry, child. I will take care of you both." She hugged them again.

Their attention was suddenly drawn by a sound from the front door. A pair of men now stood in the shattered door frame. They wore dark sunglasses and were dressed in smart black business suits. They reminded April of The Blues Brothers, if The Blues Brothers were armed with weird silver guns that looked like props from a cheap sci-fi movie instead of harmonicas.

"Mrs. Hairston? Agent Tiny, ABC. Are you alright? What happened here?"

Madame Wendigo sighed.

"Cops. Never one around when you actually need one, eh?" She frowned, thinking of all the paperwork that was laying in her future.

Epilogue: A New Hope (Thanksgiving Day, 2018)

April Hairston Sommardahl stood out on the balcony of her home in New Hope, Pennsylvania. It was raining outside; the cool drops trickled down her face, but that never bothered her. The rain always reminded her of her first real kiss—of one of the happiest moments of her life. Still, it wouldn't do to stay out here for too long and get soaked. Her wife, Wendy, would be irritated if she got their new hardwood floors all wet. With a sigh, she took in a deep breath of the cool air and stole one last look at the forest spread out in front of the deck before opening the French doors that led back into the house.

Inside, a fire blazed away in the fireplace. One that was fueled by the love she still held in her heart not only for Angela, but for all those that she had loved and lost in her younger years. It was as much fed by their love for her on the other side as it was by her own affectionate remembrances.

Her life was good now. So good that it was sometimes difficult for her to believe she had really suffered through all that she had in the earlier part of her life.

Madame Wendigo had made good on her pledge to adopt her and Chris. True, it was unusual for a woman of her advanced years to be allowed to adopt, but April would soon learn that few things were impossible for her new mother. Madame Wendigo was part of a secret society of magic-users called the Temple of the Old Gods, whose history stretched all the way back to the age of the Great Magic War. They were part of a larger organization, a sort of United Nations of secret societies called the Guilds. The Guilds had been the architects of modern human civilization in the aftermath of the Great Magic War. Although the power and influence of the Guilds had been waning for the last few centuries as they grew more insular and disinterested in the outside world, they still wielded considerable clout. They were certainly still influential enough to get an unconventional adoption or two approved.

They were also powerful enough to hush up most of the events of the Dark Man's killing spree, wiping the details from most public records. The Guilds liked to keep their secrets. Even though in time she would come to understand the necessity of that, it always bothered April, because covering up the murders also meant that most of the proof that her friends had ever even been alive was also wiped away, erased as if they'd never existed. It was up to her to remember them, to keep them close to her heart—hence the fireplace. The town still remembered too. The murders left a deep scar on the community, the kind that never really heals.

Madame Wendigo had even eventually taught Chris how to do magic, and he went on to become one of the most powerful shamans in the Temple of the Old Gods. He still lived in Madame Wendigo's home, having inherited it when the old woman quietly passed away of natural causes in the early 2000s at the ripe old age of 103. April was happy to leave the old mansion to Chris; it was too full of the bittersweet memories of that difficult time in her life.

April had then gone on to study at Berkeley in America, then later did some studying in Europe. She went to the finest schools in the world. She wasn't studying to earn a degree in any particular field so she could land a high paying job, as had once been her goal. Once she became a full-fledged member of the Temple of the Old Gods, she received a large monthly stipend that took care of all her financial needs. No, she just spent years learning about a wide variety of subjects simply for the sheer pleasure of acquiring knowledge. She had always been a very curious person, and now she was finally free to explore the wider world of human knowledge. As the years spent abroad wore on, she found herself starting to acquire an accent that was difficult to place, just like her adopted mother before her, although it never became quite as dramatic as Madame Wendigo's had been.

In time, April came to settle down on the hidden Mediterranean island of Elysium, which was the ancestral home of the Temple of the Old Gods. She followed in her mother's footsteps, working as an Inquisitor, searching the world for potential threats of a magical nature. It seemed like the most responsible way to use her new powers. She also wanted to make sure that nobody else like the Dark Man was still out there, hurting people like he had hurt her and her friends.

Her specialty was internal affairs, investigating members of the Temple who might be abusing their powers. In 1995, a small but powerful group that called itself the Knights of the New Order was exposed after they tried to set up a false messiah as the Second Coming of Christ in a bid to take over the world. In the end, it took the combined might of all the Guilds to defeat them. April had been instrumental in seeking out the surviving wizards and witches that were secretly members of the group and bringing them to justice. In that capacity, she had worked closely with the new leader of the Temple—a beautiful, idealistic witch named Wendy Sommardahl. Their professional relationship eventually crossed over into something far more intimate, and in less than a year, the two women would find themselves married. While much of the outside world wouldn't recognize such a union at that time, the Guilds had their own standards and rules that superseded those of the rest of society.

The two of them adopted a child—their daughter, Celine. As a child of adoption herself, April was more than happy to adopt, to be the sort of mother for someone else that she'd so often longed for in her youth. It completed her. Wendy's duties as leader of the Temple of the Old Gods often meant that April was the one who ended up doing most of the parenting. Sometimes she resented that, but usually she enjoyed it far too much to hold it against her wife. Celine was a grown woman now, at the age of twenty-two, but in April's mind, she'd always be her little girl. She was away from home most of the time, studying at Rutgers University, but she was back home now for Thanksgiving break. April shook her head. Even after all these years living in America, she still found it odd to be celebrating Thanksgiving in November.

It felt good to have her daughter back home, but she wasn't the only one who would be here to share this day with her. Her "baby brother" Chris would be here soon, as would her biological brother, Ron. April had used the power of the Guilds to get him released from prison early many years ago and took him in, helping him to adjust to things on the outside and rebuild his life. In time, he had a new career as a successful contractor and started a family of his own. April was now blessed with many nieces and nephews. It turned out that she hadn't been the last of the McKennas, as she had long feared. There were now enough of them to ensure that their family would survive far, far into the future. Ron's family lived nearby, and she saw them often these days, but she never tired of it and was looking forward to having them over.

Even Madame Wendigo's once-estranged biological children, April's stepbrother and stepsister, would be coming to the celebration. They had mended their fractured relationship with their mother before she passed. They were also both powerful magic-users in the Temple of the Old Gods. April wasn't particularly close to them, but they all got along well enough.

Yes, things were definitely better now. Eventually, Wendy had given up her position as the leader of the Temple and April had retired from her job as the Temple's Representative to the Guilds, turning her job over to a trusted old friend. She had so much more time now. Time to spend with her wife, and time to reflect on her life and her journey.

She still didn't really understand who the Dark Man had been, or why he was so obsessed with tormenting her. Perhaps he knew that someday she'd grow up to be an important witch within the Temple of the Old Gods, or perhaps he wanted to destroy her potential, or co-opt it for his own twisted purposes. Who knew? A few years ago, the name he had given her for himself, Benjamin Crooke, came up in conversation with her friend Matt. Matt was a private eye who was associated with the Guilds. Back in 2003, he was involved in a search for a missing child that eventually led him to a serial killer—a serial killer who claimed to have been inspired by the spirit of a man named Benjamin Crooke. Further investigation showed that Crooke had been one of the first documented cases of what we would now describe as a serial killer. He was an artist who had gone insane and murdered several people before he was captured and hanged.Or at least, he was supposed to have been hanged. According to legend, his body disappeared from the gallows just as the hangman's noose lifted him aloft. People at the time said that the Devil simply couldn't wait to take him to hell.

April didn't think that the Devil was to blame, but in a way, she suspected that something or someone else had whisked him away to use him to sow discord in the world. There had been other instances of Crooke's name coming up in connection to murders. "Benjamin

Crooke made me do it" became the new "the Devil made me do it" for a while. There was even a case of an old man who had killed another resident in a nursing home and tried to blame his actions on Crooke's evil influence. It all chilled April to the bone at first. She'd always feared that they hadn't really defeated him. She spent much of her career as an Inquisitor searching for traces of him, only for references to him to start popping up years afterwards. However, she'd never felt any trace of him around her and her family or friends—thank goodness.

She didn't truly believe that he was back. She recalled that he'd once spoken to her of visiting the future, which meant that he'd been some kind of time traveler. Her theory was that her life was just now catching up to some of the things he'd done before he traveled back to the 1970s and '80s and decided to try ruin her life, only to meet with his own final end. And yet, there was a part of her that would forever remain slightly on guard, always vigilant for his possible return.

As she was mulling over all these things on Thanksgiving Day, there was a burst of radiance to her right. She turned around quickly, her thoughts of the Dark Man having put her slightly on edge, only to see Chris standing there. He dropped the suitcases he carried in either hand to the floor and immediately made a beeline for the nearest garbage can, which in this case, was located in the kitchen. She hoped dropping those suitcases hadn't scratched the new floors, or there'd be hell to pay from Wendy. She now heard the unsettling sound of Chris retching and vomiting into the garage can.

"How many times do I need to tell you to take a long enough break between teleportation spells? I don't know why you can't just charter a private jet like the rest of us do," April complained.

"Jets . . . terrible for . . . the environment!" he managed to get out before he vomited again.

"I hate to say it, but the guy's got a point. Jets aren't particularly green," Wendy said nonchalantly as she strolled into the kitchen, completely unfazed by the sight of the wizard throwing up in her trash. "That's why I tasked the TOTOG Foundation with trying to locate one of the portals our ancestors used in ancient times to travel around the world. If we could study one and learn how to make new ones, it would solve so many of the Guild's transportation problems."

The TOTOG Foundation was the public arm of the Temple of the Old Gods. It funded archeological expeditions around the world with the secret goal of recovering powerful lost magical artifacts from the distant past. Wendy might've retired as leader of the Temple, but she was still quite active on the Foundation's board.

"You're going to take that bag outside, by the way," she added looking at Chris pointedly.

"Sure, I'll get on it right away, but first can't a guy say hello to his big sister?" he said as he moved to embrace April.

She wrinkled her nose and pulled away. "Ugh! No! No hugs until you wash your hands—and brush your teeth too! *My Gods*. What have you been eating?" She waved a hand in front of her nose to banish the offensive odor.

"I love you too, Sis Great to see you again!" He said sarcastically as he walked off down the hall to the bathroom.

Wendy and April just looked at eat other and laughed like a pair of school girls as soon as he left the room.

"Same old Chris, eh?" " April smiled.

"You know what they say. The more things change, the more they stay the same," Wendy agreed.

It wasn't too much longer before the house was completely filled up with friends and relatives. As April looked out around the table at their faces, she could scarcely believe how lucky she was, how different her life was now from what it had once been. Having a family this large who all loved and accepted her all together and under the same roof would've been unimaginable during those years she'd spent in foster care. Against all odds, her childhood dreams had come true. She'd never given up, never surrendered or compromised who she was, and that was her greatest victory over the Dark Man. She hadn't let the loss and the pain he'd inflicted on her stop her from living her life, from trusting others again, from letting the right ones in. She hadn't just survived all the turmoil of her childhood, she'd transcended it completely. She felt a great sense of inner peace wash over her at that realization.

Indeed, there was so very much to be thankful for . . .

The End

LYRICAL NONSENSE

Kiesha Bright was trapped. Entombed. Boxed in by a world that was too small for her, but in a way she always had been. Her world had felt painfully small her entire life, but never in the literal sense that it was now.

She had walked around the circumference of this tiny world so many times now that she'd lost count. She wondered how such a small planet was able to hold onto its atmosphere, or to her, for that matter. The gravity seemed normal. Yet she understood enough about science to know that the gravity of a planet small enough for her to walk completely around in just under an hour should be extraordinarily weak. She should've been flung off into space by the speed of its rotation the minute she arrived, but here she was, her butt firmly planted on the ground, crushing the soft grass that surrounded her.

Brilliantly colored wildflowers sprouted from the ground all around her, swaying gently in the breeze. How did these flowers reproduce? She hadn't seen any pollinating insects in the hours that she'd spent here, or any other kind of animal life. She guessed that they weren't needed. On a world this small, the wind itself was sufficient to carry the pollen. Or maybe she just needed to let go of the notion that the normal rules of plant reproduction applied here. Why not? Enough of the other rules of science were being broken.

She was currently sitting in a meadow under the shade of a large, gnarled old tree. Was it a maple tree? An oak? She didn't know. Botany wasn't really her thing. Considering the fact that she seemed to be on an entirely different planet, it was probably none of the above. An alien tree that happened to look like something from Earth, like everything else around here did.

As alien planets went, this one was pleasant, but also fairly dull. Was it the product of an imagination as small as the planet itself? She considered that it had been deliberately created for a specific purpose to be quite likely, based on how she'd ended up here. She'd always hoped that if she ever got to visit another world that it would be alien enough to be interesting, but this place was anything but interesting. The most interesting thing about it was that it existed at all taking into account how the physics behind the place were impossible.

Okay, so maybe that's not quite true. The message is the most interesting thing about this place.

She gazed up at the cerulean sky for the umpteenth time to read the message written there—apparently permanently—in the clouds. The message was her most obvious clue that this place had been engineered by someone. Someone from Earth. It probably accounted for why this place was so much like the Earth. If it had been too alien, it would've sent whoever ended up here into even more of a panic than they would've already been in from suddenly finding themselves unexpectedly transported into a new environment. So the dullness of this planet wasn't a failure of imagination, then, but an attempt to reassure.

Besides, she had a fairly good idea of *who* had created this world, and a failure of imagination wasn't one of his faults. Indeed, she was probably his biggest fan, although if he kept her trapped here for much longer, she was going to seriously reconsider her devotion to him.

No, that's not right. He didn't trap me here. I trapped myself, she thought with some bitterness.

How quickly the rush of elation she'd felt when she'd first arrived here, when she'd found out that her crazy idea had actually been *right*, had turned into disappointment, and then anger! Being right wasn't always a good thing. She could see that now. But for so much of her young life, being right had been one of the only things she could ever take any pride in. Her last name was Bright, and she took it as a challenge to show the world just how smart and clever she really was. Especially since the world loved to write off black women like herself as being anything but highly intelligent. She looked to academic achievement as a way to escape from the small world imposed on her by the poverty she'd been born into. But what good was all that cleverness if it just led to her getting trapped in this place instead? A place with no visible source of food or water?

She wondered if the flowers and grass were edible. Being alien plants, they might have been poisonous, but she doubted it since this place was seemingly created to imitate the Earth. These were probably recreations of normal Earth plants. However, even if they were safe to eat, she doubted that they contained enough of the proteins and nutrients her body needed to stay healthy. There had to be water too, right? Somewhere under the ground for the plants to drink up through their roots. Or maybe it rained here sometimes. But she didn't think, so because the only clouds were the ones that spelled out the words of the message written in the sky, and they didn't move. She doubted that they functioned like normal clouds at all. They were mere decorations. Once again, she chastised herself for trying to apply so much logic to this situation. There was nothing logical about this place, or what had led her to being here.

The message. Reading it just pissed her off now.

Congratulations! You've successfully deciphered all the clues and performed the ritual correctly! I will be along shortly to retrieve you.

You've taken your first step into a larger world.

She laughed caustically at that last line. It was a quote from the original Star Wars movie. The one that we were supposed to call "A New Hope" now to distinguish it from all the sequels and prequels. It was one of the biggest clues as to who had created this world, as he was well known to be a big Star Wars nerd. It was also almost cruelly ironic considering that her first step into a supposedly larger world had only served to imprison her in a decidedly tiny one.

She looked at her watch. She'd been here for eight hours now. An entire shift at the average job. She'd probably lost her job because of all this. Her company had a strict policy about "no call no shows". Her cleverness didn't matter at her job. She was just another cog in the machine, completely expendable. There was a never ending supply of other students in town ready to replace her as soon as the "for hire" signs went up in the windows of the restaurant where she was waitressing.

Maybe losing her job didn't matter. It wasn't as if she had any great love for it. What had brought her here was very likely supposed to serve as some sort of an audition for something much greater, if the message was to be believed. But was that a paying gig? Even on a full scholarship to UVA, she still had rent and other bills to pay.

The problem was that she didn't believe the message, not anymore. How shortly was "shortly" supposed to be? This was ridiculous! How could he leave her hanging like this? A wise person had once said something about never meeting your heroes, that they would always disappoint you with their humanity. However, she'd already met him twice before in the past three years, and he had yet to disappoint her with his kindness, warmth, and humility.

So why was he disappointing her like this now? Why would he set up something like this, go through the trouble of creating all of this, planting all the clues on how to get here in his lyrics, only to abandon whoever was actually able to decipher them? True, the album that contained the instructions she'd followed to reach this place was almost five years old by now, and perhaps in all that time she was the only one to crack the code, but he couldn't have just forgotten about this, could he? He must have some sort of a mechanism in place to tell him when someone finally made it here, right?

She tried to calm herself down. She was in no actual danger, aside from the crushing boredom she felt and the hunger beginning to gnaw at her stomach. If she stayed here too long, though, she could eventually die of hunger or thirst, which is what concerned her the most. It was possible that he wasn't able to come and get her right away because he was asleep—although it had been the middle of the day back on Earth when she left it. Of course, he could be on the other end of the planet where it was night, for all she knew. That would explain it. His band sometimes did world tours.

The only problem with that theory is that she was such a fan that she knew they currently weren't touring. They'd wrapped up their last big tour a few months earlier, the last time she'd seen him, when they came through Charlottesville again. She hadn't been able to believe her luck then, having been fortunate enough to score a backstage pass for the second time in a row through a call-in contest held by the local college radio station. What were the odds? Actually, they were pretty good when you were as determined as was. She'd even called out from work that day just so she could concentrate on making continuous calls and persuaded her roommates to participate in her madness and call in on her behalf.

She couldn't help it. She just really loved the Mystery Smiths. She'd been following them ever since they'd called themselves Lung Collapse, even though she'd just been a little kid back then. Her family never understood it. Neither did the other kids in her neighborhood. They used to tease her for listening to all that "white people music," As if music only belonged to one group of people! Later on, when she was older and had done some research on the history of Rock and Roll, she discovered that it was hardly white people music, it had really been invented by her own people and co-opted, as so many other things had been. She saw her love of it as just a way of reclaiming it. When the band had still been known as Lung Collapse, they'd primarily ka until that scene imploded in the early 2000's. Ska music in particular, owes its origins to the music of Jamaica. White people music indeed!

She still got mad whenever she thought about all the shit she used to catch just for loving what she loved. People thought that she liked it because she was ashamed of who she was, that she was trying to pretend that she was something else, but that had nothing to do with it at all. She just enjoyed the music. She loved all music (well okay, maybe not Country), including the music that she was "supposed" to like because of her race. It was this kind of attitude that had made her feel like she was stuck in a small, narrow and mean world long before she got stuck here. Fortunately, since she'd started college she didn't encounter this mindset quite so frequently anymore. People were still often surprised by her musical tastes, but they didn't hold it against her, In fact, they were more likely to celebrate her for the diversity of her preferences. College, at least, had started to open up her tiny world, to expand it.

Tiny World. *That was the name of the album that started all of this.*

Her mind drifted back to the unlikely set of circumstances that had brought her to where she was currently trapped. Tiny World was released in 2006. It was an unusual album, even by the standards of the Mystery Smiths, who were notorious for their offbeat style. The majority of the Mystery Smiths's songs were written by Penelope "Penny" Layne, the lead singer and lead guitarist. Her partner, Randy Gruman, was often co-credited on many of the songs, and there were usually a handful on each album that were credited to just him. Tiny World, however, was credited almost entirely to Randy. It was also a concept album—their first and only one. It was an oddity in an age when listening to music in the form of albums was dying out, being killed off by digital downloads and streaming platforms. As far as anyone could tell, the album's story was about the creation of the titular Tiny World by a wizard. The wizard then set out a series of hidden clues throughout the kingdom. Whoever successfully collected all the clues and assembled them in the correct sequence would be transported to his Tiny World. Once there, they would meet the wizard, who would then train them as their apprentice.

Yeah, except they left out the part about the wizard never showing up to train his apprentice, she thought despondently.

Kiesha had initially taken the story to be purely allegorical, as had most fans and critics. However, the more she listened to it, the more she became convinced that the album itself held clues. Clues to something. Exactly what she couldn't guess. She noticed that specific items were mentioned prominently in each song. After a while, the album began to sound to her like a shopping list of ingredients - things that were needed to perform a ritual of some sort. The idea had occurred to her because in interviews with him it had come to light that Randy had abandoned the Judaism of his youth in favor of some kind of New Age/Occult belief system that was difficult to explain. Then there were all the strange, inarticulate nonsense words that reoccurred during the choruses on every song. Curiously, these words were included in the lyrics on the liner notes, and were even spelled out phonetically. Why include such a detail unless you wanted to make sure that these words wouldn't be mispronounced?

So she had a list of things that were needed to perform a ritual, and a bunch of magic words. She assumed that the magic words had to be said in the same order in which the songs they were found in appeared on the album. What she didn't know was what to do with the items she was supposed to gather. She needed help. She mentioned her theory about the album in a group or two dedicated to the band on various social media platforms, but most people had laughed at her ideas. They'd told her that she was being far too literal in her interpretation of the album. This had only hardened her resolve to get to the bottom of it all, to prove them all wrong. Not everyone had mocked her, but the few people who found her ideas intriguing had were unfortunately unable to contribute any new ideas. It seemed that she was on her own for this particular quest.

She already had some knowledge of magic. Like Randy, she'd given up on the traditional religious beliefs that had been pre-selected for her long before she'd been born. As she got older, it increasingly struck her as being quite odd that so many of her people continued to cling to a belief system that had been forced upon them by the same people who had once enslaved them. She'd started researching some of the more traditional African beliefs and adopted a few of them herself. However, none of the ingredients needed for the ritual corresponded to anything in the magical systems she'd familiarized herself with. The magic words also seemed to be completely alien and unlike any known language, although there were a few parallels with certain reconstructed Indo-European words here and there. This led her to the unlikely conclusion that they belonged to an even older language than the one which served as the root of most of the world's tongues.

The breakthrough that had brought her here came one day when she was in one of her classes and they were covering the Satanic Panic of the 1980s. One of the more unusual beliefs from that era right before she'd been born was that some rock bands put hidden messages on their records. Hidden messages that could be heard only by playing the record backwards. Kiesha owned a special, limited edition vinyl copy of Tiny World. She had a copy of the album in every medium that it had been released in - she was just *that* kind of a fan. The accusations of putting subliminal messages in songs, or satanic messages on records that were played backwards had turned out to be so much nonsense during the Satanic Panic. However, it would be just like Randy to *actually* put a hidden message on the record. It was exactly the sort of thing that would appeal to his somewhat twisted sense of humor.

She decided to put her theory to the test. She played the record backwards and was astounded to hear what she'd long searched for—the missing instructions on what to do with the items that the songs said to gather together. She'd already assembled all of those ingredients months earlier. She was so excited by this newest discovery that she decided to perform the ritual right away, even though she had to be at work in a few hours.

She didn't know what she'd expected to happen. She hadn't *truly* expected to be transported to the Tiny World like the album said you would be. Things like that didn't *really* happen in the real world. Even though she'd dabbled in the odd bit of magic already, she'd never experienced anything on that kind of a spectacular level before. That's simply not how real-world magic worked; it wasn't like all that Hollywood bullshit you saw in the movies. Yet despite her low expectations, she'd gone ahead and done the ritual anyway. She'd been chasing after this puzzle for so long that she couldn't help but see it through to the end. She did feel pretty foolish at times as she went about it, like she'd lost her mind. Here she was, performing an arcane ceremony based on some lyrics in a generally unpopular album by what most people (if they'd even heard of them) considered to be a fourth-string, one-hit wonder band.

So she'd been genuinely surprised when, upon completing the ritual, a shimmering portal that was just large enough to step through opened up in the corner of her bedroom. On the other side of that portal was a familiar image. It was the same one that was in the photograph that was used on the cover of the album *Tiny World*. It was a shot of a landscape that included the large, old tree where she was currently sheltering from the unrelenting sun that constantly beat down upon this planet. She'd stepped through the portal, and it immediately closed up behind her. Without the items she needed to cast the spell, which she'd left behind on the desk in her bedroom, she couldn't reopen it. At first, she didn't mind, She was so enchanted by the fact that the spell actually worked, that it had done exactly what the album had promised it would. And of course, she had still believed the message written in the sky back then.

She'd been thrilled by the discovery that Randy really was some kind of a wizard, and a damned good one at that, if he really was able to somehow create an entire planet. She was even more thrilled by the prospect that she might be able to learn how to do something like this for herself. That she'd be working hand in hand with someone she admired greatly.

However, it didn't take very long for her to begin to lose faith. After being stuck there for a few hours, her mind began to wander into dark places. Perhaps the whole thing was a trap? Something designed to weed out individuals who were too smart and therefore potentially dangerous? Maybe instead of being rewarded for figuring out the puzzle she was being punished? Left here to die, all alone. She wondered what her roommates and other friends at school would think had happened to her. How would her mother and siblings react? It wasn't fair. Didn't they see that they weren't just punishing her, they were hurting all those other people too?

She couldn't believe it. From what she knew of Randy and the rest of the band, they were very good people. Hell, Randy and Penny even had a child together. They were parents. She couldn't believe that they would deliberately hurt somebody else's baby like this. She couldn't accept that they would be behind such a nasty thing. If that was the case, then where was he? Why the delay?

Maybe he's dead sShe thought darkly. If that was the case, then she was well and truly screwed. For all she knew, he might be the only other person capable of reaching this place.

She looked up at the message once more. *Please, Randy don't be dead. Come and get me so I can get out of this place!* She thought it almost as if it was a prayer, which struck her as being faintly absurd, or was it? If he really had created this planet, then perhaps he was like a kind of God in this place?

Maybe, just maybe, this god would actually hear her prayers and answer them.

***

Randy Gruman's eyes were closed. Doubtlessly, this would've alarmed Kiesha if she could have seen it. At first glance, it looked like

235

her great fear that he was dead was indeed true. A closer inspection would reveal the slow, rhythmic rise and fall of his chest. No, Randy wasn't dead, he was instead in a deep trance. It was the type of trance that one had to go into in order to project their spirit out of their body, which was exactly what he was doing right now. To the rest of the world, he looked like a man who had fallen asleep inside of his parked car., But, while his body was inside the car, Randy's spirit was actually in the building across the street.

The ability to astrally project was a handy one to have for someone who worked as a private eye. When Randy wasn't working with his band, this was how he occupied his time working as a PI in the detective agency owned by his friend Matt Spike. It wasn't that Randy needed the money. While the Mystery Smiths weren't successful enough to make him a millionaire, the generous monthly stipend that he received as a member of the Temple of the Old Gods, the oldest and most powerful of the remaining Great Houses of Magic, ensured that he never had to worry about his finances. No, he worked as a PI because he enjoyed it. For the most part, that is. At times such as this, it could be very tedious.

Randy was supposed to be doing surveillance on a man whose wife suspected he was cheating on her. A surprising number of the cases he was involved in were of this nature. He had already verified via astral projection that the man in question was indeed philandering, which made feel rather uncomfortably like a peeping Tom. Unfortunately, "evidence" obtained in this manner wouldn't do for his client. He couldn't very well tell her that he'd had an out-of-body experience and seen her husband doing the deed with his own two astral eyes without being written off as some kind of a nutcase.

Instead, Randy had to spend hours parked down the street outside of the apartment where the affair was taking place, taking photos and shooting video of her husband coming and going. He'd been hoping to get a smoking-gun" shot of the man and his mistress in an embrace or locked in a goodbye kiss on the steps of her apartment building. He'd become increasingly impatient as he sat there in his car, waiting and listening to NPR. The man had been inside for far longer than he typically was. This affair was usually one of those "wham, bam, thank you ma'am" kinds. Randy wondered what was keeping him there so long and decided to slip out of his body for a minute to see for himself.

So it was that Randy's ghostly form now floated near the bed where the infidelity was taking place. He winced as he watched the man he'd been hired to tail as he smoked a cigarette in bed next to his mistress.

Didn't he know how many fires started that way? Randy thought disapprovingly. He'd had a cousin who died in a fire that started like that, so he was especially sensitive about this subject.

The two of them were just lying there, basking in the afterglow of their illicit activities and watching some stupid reality TV show that was on basic cable. It didn't look like the man was in any great rush to get back to work. He usually conducted these little get-togethers during his lunch hour, using the time to satisfy an altogether different kind of appetite. Randy didn't know that the man was only working a half day—a fact he'd kept hidden from his wife. Randy sighed. He had the distinct feeling that he was going to be stuck here waiting for the man to leave for far longer than he'd planned to be.

Just then, a dog entered the bedroom and started barking furiously at Randy's spirit body. Although he was invisible to most people, animals could see him quite clearly.

"Okay, okay. Chill out! I was about to leave anyway," he told the small dog.

"Geez, what's gotten into her? Shut up your mutt!" the man complained as Randy floated through the wall mere inches from him.

An instant later, he awoke back in his physical body with a jolt. He supposed that he'd just have to get over himself. He was likely going to be stuck here for a lot longer. He turned off the radio; the day's news stories had begun to repeat themselves, which he always found irritating. He glanced over at the passenger seat of his vehicle, which held a small, but very high-quality video camera that had a powerful zoom feature. This was the device he was hoping to use to capture the incriminating evidence he needed for his client.

Sitting beside it was the latest mystery novel by his friend Matt, intriguingly entitled *Part Time Killers*. Matt was not only a detective, but a writer as well. He'd released this particular book about six months ago, but Randy had never gotten around to reading it until recently. This was very much to Matt's annoyance, as he was hungry for feedback from Randy, whose opinion he respected tremendously. However, the more Matt pestered him to read it, the more he found that he didn't *want* to read it. Now he regretted putting it off for so long, as it really was pretty good so far. It was definitely one of Matt's better efforts. He picked it up and thumbed to where he'd folded a page over to mark his spot.

It was a habit that used to drive his Aunt Bernice, the woman who raised him, nuts. He could hear her now, complaining about how poorly he treated his books. Aunt Bernice practically worshipped her books. Now she was far, far away. She was busy traveling around the world on the money Randy sent to her in the company of her new boyfriend, Martin Lane, whom Randy had introduced her to. She always looked so happy in the travel photos she updated her social media accounts with. He smiled at the idea that he'd been able to help bring so much joy to the woman who'd worked so hard to raise him and his brothers when his parents had lost custody of them.

His musings were cut short by a sudden warm sensation in his left pants pocket. It was a pleasant warmth, like the kind you feel when you press some papers that have just come off a laser printer against your skin. Randy spoke a word that was already ancient when the Bible was being written, and the source of this warmth flew out of his pocket and hovered in the air before him. It was a little crystal ball, small enough to be enclosed in the palm of one's hand. Enchanted devices like this were used by magic-users to communicate with each other, but they had other functions as well. This one was currently alerting him to something. On the surface of the crystal ball, there was a picture that was all too familiar to him. It was the cover to his album *Tiny Planet*. The fact that the ball was displaying this particular image meant that someone had finally solved the puzzle he'd created years ago to help him find a worthy apprentice who he could train in the mystical arts. He couldn't believe it! He'd just about given up on ever finding a suitable candidate using that method.

As happy as he was to discover that someone had finally cracked his code, his heart was also sinking at the realization that he was stuck here doing surveillance for Gods knew how much longer. He had to try to get out of it somehow. With another magic word, he made his crystal ball stop displaying the image and return to his pocket. He dug in the other pocket for his cell phone and dialed Matt up.

"What's up?" Matt's somewhat gruff voice came through from the other end of the line.

"Are you busy right now?" Randy asked.

"Not really. I'm just hanging out around the office, doing a little research for a case."

"Do you think you could take over the surveillance on the Rockwell case for me today?" Randy inquired hopefully.

"So, you still haven't got the goods on that ne'er-do-well, huh?" Matt sounded faintly amused by this fact.

"No, not the kind of evidence I can actually present to anyone. Can you do it?" Randy was starting to get uncharacteristically impatient.

"Yeah, I guess so. I don't have much left on my plate for today. I'm meeting with a new client in like about . . . oh, fifteen or twenty minutes. After that I'm pretty much free, so I can hop on over to relieve you if you'll forward me the address where you're at."

"*Shit!*" Randy swore. He knew that when Matt had an initial interview with a new client, they could drag on for quite a while. "I need to leave ASAP. Is Earl around? Maybe he can come right away?" Earl was another detective that was part of their agency.

Matt was unsettled by his normally supernaturally calm friend's urgency—it bordered on a panic. "Earl's off today, remember? He had to take his mom to see that specialist. What's wrong kid? What's the big rush all of the sudden?"

Randy shook his head. Even though he was in his thirties now, Matt still called him "kid.". Sometimes he thought Matt would always see him that way. "Someone has solved Tiny Planet." There were no real secrets between Matt and Randy. He knew that his friend would understand what he was talking about.

He was about to be disappointed.

There was a long, pregnant pause on the other end of the call, then Matt finally spoke "Huh? Is that a video game or something?"

Randy looked up to the heavens for help, but his eyes were only met by the impassive layer of dull grey fabric lining the ceiling of his car. Even though Matt was only about ten years older than Randy, his memory wasn't what it used to be. If you confronted Matt about it, he'd tell you that it was because he always had so much on his mind. He was always plotting out the next storyline for his next novel in his head, plus thinking about whatever cases he was currently . Plus thinking about his personal issues. Maybe that was actually true, but it was still quite annoying for the people around him to have to deal with.

Matt wasn't done yet. "Yeah! Isn't that the video game that Joe used to play with Autumn all the time? What the hell is so important about solving a kid's video game?" Joe and Autumn were Matt's kids.

"Matt, that's *"Little Big Planet* that you're thinking of! This has nothing to do with that. Tiny Planet is that album we did a few years back. You know, the one with all the hidden clues in it?" He explained slowly, trying to keep his voice as calm as he could.

Finally, realization dawned on Matt. "Oh yeeeeah Now I remember! That thing you made so you could find yourself an apprentice. I totally forgot about that.!"

Yeah, no shit you did, Randy thought testily, then immediately felt guilty about the unkindness of his own thoughts. Honestly, he'd almost forgotten about it too, and he'd made the damned thing. They didn't even perform many of the songs from it live anymore either. This was partially because it wasn't a very popular or successful album, and partially because there was a slight risk that doing so could open up an interdimensional vortex on the stage.

"I always thought that was a crazy idea. Cool, but crazy. You made it too damned hard to solve. I kept telling you that! It would take a genius to ever figure all that shit out. I'm not surprised it's taken so long for someone to solve it. How long has it been now? Eight years?"

"No, about five. And finding a genius was the entire point. If I made it too easy, lots of random people would find themselves getting stuck in another dimension until I could come and get them out."

"Oh, hot damn! That's right. They end up in another dimension if they solve it. I forgot about that too. So I guess that's why you're in such a hurry? Listen man, just let me wrap up this interview and I'll be right over. Your future apprentice can afford to cool their heels for a little while. They're not going anywhere."

"Matt, you don't understand There's a big difference between how time flows in that world and how it does here. A few minutes over here translates into a few hours over there. That's why I need to leave so soon."

"Why is there always such a big difference between how time works on Earth and how it does in another dimension? Just once I'd like to go to another dimension where time works exactly the same way that it does here. I'm so sick of this stupid Narnia bullshit," Matt griped.

"Time is different here too. I mean, there's a pretty big time difference between Tokyo and New Jersey. If it makes you feel any better, time works the same as it does here in most parallel universes. However, solving *Tiny Planet* doesn't take you to a parallel universe, it takes you to a pocket dimension. Ergo, there's a significant difference in how one experiences the passage of time," Randy hastily over explained, as was his habit.

"Pocket dimension, sprocket dimension. I pride myself on being a big old nerd, but you lost me on that one buddy. Again, I'm not sure I'm following what you're talking about," Matt confessed.

"It's not important right now. I don't want to keep my new apprentice waiting too long. It's rude. And they might begin to panic if they're there for too long. That's a pretty shitty way to begin a partnership. It's not easy to get to that dimension. I can't just say a few words and instantly teleport there. I need to have all kinds of special items to complete the spell—items that I don't normally carry around with me. Even if you came here right away, I'd still have to drive back home to pick up that stuff and lose even more precious time in the process." Randy was starting to feel exhausted from explaining all of this, despite his propensity for lecturing people on the intricacies of everything.

"Why can't you just use your magic to make that creep walk out of the apartment and plant a nice, big, fat kiss on his girlfriend's face as she walks him to his car or something? Then you'd have what you need and could call it quits," Matt suggested.

"Matt, that's mind control! It's Dark Magic! I guess I could figure out a way to do it, but it's completely unethical. I'd probably be booted out of the Temple of the Old Gods if anyone ever found out.

No way, dude. It's out of the question." Randy was horrified by his friend's idea.

"That's funny, I seem to recall that your teacher once messed with the minds of everyone in the whole world. Remember that time when she made virtually everybody forget about Father Steve?" Matt said.

"Wendy's the Pontifex Maximus, she can do whatever she wants. She makes the rules." Randy countered.

"Uh huh, 'Do as I say, not as I do.' Yeah, that's a wonderful example to set for her people," Matt commented sarcastically.

Randy lost all patience with him at that point. While they were sitting here debating all of this, the person who'd made it to Tiny World could be panicking once they realized they were trapped there. Didn't Matt care about that? And now he was criticizing his beloved mentor Wendy too?

"Are you going to help me or not?" he asked bluntly.

Matt didn't bother to hide the irritation in his voice. "Alright, alright! I can tell this is pretty important to you. I'll see if Penny can reschedule the appointment for the interview. Although asking someone to reschedule an interview just a few minutes before it's supposed to begin is also a pretty shitty way to start off a professional relationship with a new client."

Yes, Randy's musical partner, Penny Layne, also worked at the detective agency, acting as Matt's secretary. The Mystery Smiths really didn't make much money from their music.

Did other private eyes have problems like this? an exasperated Matt wondered. He knew that they didn't. Oftentimes, he wished his life was a little less strange than it had been since he got himself mixed up with all this magical nonsense.

To stave off his rising frustration, Matt amused himself by imagining the phone call that Penny would soon have to make: "Hello? Mr. Jones? Hi, this is Penny Layne with Matt Spike Investigations. Can we reschedule the appointment that's supposed to be happening ten minutes from now? I'm so sorry, but Mr. Spike has to go fill in for another investigator because that investigator has to go rescue someone who's trapped themselves in another universe. Wait, I'm sorry! It's not another universe, it's a *pocket dimension.* Yeah, I don't really understand what that means either. Sounds like some bullshit someone just made up, doesn't it? But if you think about it, isn't almost everything just some bullshit that someone made up?"

Not that Penny would really tell his potential client what was really going on like that. No sense in scaring the customers away by revealing how crazy your life and, by extension, the wider world are. Triggering an existential crisis in your customers wasn't good for business. Nope. He'd just tell her to say that there was a "family emergency." The good old family emergency excuse always did the trick.

"Thanks Matt, I really appreciate it, man. I'll text you the address for the apartment that he's using as his little love nest as soon as I end this call," Randy said gratefully.

"Okay, but you owe me one, buddy. I'll see you soon," Matt said in a resigned tone.

"See ya." Randy ended the call and promptly sent the address along to Matt's phone as he'd promised.

Randy drummed his fingers on his steering wheel impatiently. As far as he was concerned, Matt could never get there soon enough.

Hold on, my future apprentice! I'll get there as soon as I can! he promised, hoping that when he finally did arrive, his prospective apprentice wouldn't be so crazed from the isolation that they'd be more likely to try to kill him than agree to become his student.

***

Kiesha wanted to kill him when she saw him.

Never meet your heroes? Yeah, sound advice, as it turns out, she thought caustically.

Randy strode towards her through the tall grass, an outline against the twilight sky. The curvature of the planet was clearly visible behind him. He was carrying a duffel bag that contained everything he would need to perform the ritual that would send them back to their respective homes. He sadly observed that it was almost night here and that hoped that whoever it was who had made it here wouldn't be too pissed off at him for making them wait so long. He couldn't make out many details of his guest in the darkening

247

light - just a silhouette sitting hunched over beneath the big old oak tree. As he got closer, the mysterious form sprang to its feet and started running towards him.

"Holy shit! It sure took you long enough," an oddly familiar female voice called out to him.

His eyes widened in recognition. *"Omigod,* I know you! Kesha from Charlottesville, right?"

Kiesha came to a stop right in front of him. "Kesha? It's Kiesha! Don't confuse me with that auto-tune- abusing skank Kesha!" Secretly, a part of her was delighted that he actually remembered who she was (sort of). He hadn't after their first meeting, although she'd never held that against him. After all, he probably ran into lots of fans and a few years had passed between their first and second meetings. It had only been a few months since their last meeting, so that likely explained his suddenly improved memory.

"Sorry, Kiesha. Wow! I'm so happy that someone finally figured out how to get here. I shouldn't be surprised that it's my number one fan." He really wasn't that surprised. It made a great deal of sense, once he thought about it. Kiesha had struck him as being someone who was exceptionally intelligent the last time he saw her, and it would take a certain level of devotion to listen to *Tiny World* often enough to tease out all the breadcrumbs he'd left behind.

"'Number one fan'? You make me sound like the creepy lady from Stephen King's *Misery* when you say it like that. I like to think that

I'm a little more sane than she was. Actually, if you must know, I'm really more of Penny's number one fan."

This was a complete lie. While she found Penny to be very inspirational as a woman and admired her songwriting skills and voice, she really was Randy's biggest fan. However, she didn't think it was smart to let him know that if they were now going to have some kind of a teacher-student relationship. It wasn't wise to give him the impression that she'd do just about anything for him, even though she would.

She also wasn't keen to stroke his ego after he'd left her stuck here all this time. Honestly, he was lucky she hadn't smacked him across the face as soon as she saw him. Fortunately, she was smart enough to realize it wasn't a great idea to piss off the only person who could get her back home. It was also true that Randy was the sort of person that it was impossible to remain angry with for very long, no matter what he did. This was true whether or not you were his number one fan pretending to not be his number one fan. He just had an instantly loveable, big-teddy-bear kind of energy about him.

"Hmmm. I could've sworn you said that you were my number one fan the last time we ran into each other," he said playfully, stroking his thick black beard.

The color drained from Kiesha's face. *Fuck, I guess I did say that.*

"Even if that were true —and it most definitely *isn't*—it wouldn't still be true after you left me stuck here for all this time! Whatever happened to 'I'll be along shortly to retrieve you'?" As she said it, she pointed skywards. The words were much harder to read by the spreading moonlight.

"Oh man. Yeah, I'm really sorry about that. I got tied up on a case and couldn't come right away. How long has it been for you?"

Kiesha glanced at her watch and did some quick calculations in her head. "Thirteen hours. Thirteen *long* hours without anything to do. Thirteen hours wondered if I'd ever get home again or if I'd starve to death here. You really should've left a few magazines here, and a refrigerator full of food too."

"Again, I apologize. I never imagined that anyone would end up stuck here by themselves for that long. I totally fucked up." Randy's elation at finally finding himself a potential apprentice was now tempered by a feeling of failure. Everything he was afraid of while he'd been wasting time arguing with Matt had come to pass. He should've just abandoned the surveillance. He'd probably have lots of other opportunities to catch evidence of Mr. Rockwell's cheating ways. But his professional pride wouldn't let him do it. She was right; he should've foreseen this possibility and built in some fail-safes.

"Damn right, you fucked up! I was supposed to be at work today. Virginia is a right-to-work state. Do you know what that means? It's not what it sounds like. It means that workers have virtually no rights. They can fire you for just about anything, and believe me, they do."

"What time were you supposed to be at work?" Randy asked.

"5:30. Why?"

"What if I told you that when I left Earth a few minutes ago, the time was almost 3:30?" Randy smiled teasingly.

"What? How?" Kiesha was astounded.

"Time passes differently here. You should have plenty of time to get to work if you still want to go. Where do you work?"

"The Applebee's on Abbey Road. Why would you make time work like that here?"

"I created this place not only as a test, but also to be a training ground. Back when I was an apprentice wizard, I had to fly all the way to Europe in my astral body to learn from my teacher. It was kind of a pain in the ass, to be honest. So I made this place as a common ground where we could meet in person at pre-arranged times. We could spend hours here training and only a few minutes will have passed back on Earth. Does it make sense now?"

Kiesha's facade of anger was quickly crumbling under the weight of her wonder. "Damn. I can't believe that you really made this place. Do you really think I could learn to do something like this one day?"

Randy paused for a moment, making a show of sizing her up. Musicians can be so theatrical sometimes. They are natural showmen, after all. "Definitely," he pronounced. "Anyone can learn how to do magic, if they're determined enough and put in the practice hours. You'd be surprised by how easy it actually was to create this world."

She was incredulous. "Easy? It's a whole planet! One that defies all the laws of physics."

"Making it wasn't that different from doing simple computer coding. It's actually easier, in many ways," Randy said humbly.

"Well, my major is in Computer Science, so it should be a real breeze for me." Kiesha said significantly less humbly. She scrunched up her face as a new question occurred to her. "So . . . does that mean that this place is a kind of simulation?"

"In a way." Then Randy added mysteriously: "In a way, everything is."

Kiesha wasn't about to try to figure out what he meant by that.

"So, you've passed my test. Do you want to have your first lesson now?" Randy asked her point-blank.

She decided it would be smart to play a little hard to get. She hadn't gotten as far as she had in life by giving everything away for free. Even though she had no intention of *not* learning how to do something this amazing, she realized that she might be able to enter into some kind of a negotiation here. If that was the case, then it wouldn't be smart to make him realize how just hungry she actually was for the opportunity to learn by his side.

"I'm not sure. What did you mean by asking me if I wanted to go back to work? A girl still has to eat! Would I actually get paid for doing this wizard shit? It's not like doing magic is a real career path, is it? You still have a day job too. Hell, you've got two of them. You're a private investigator and you've got the band. Being a wizard must pay shit."

Randy laughed heartily at what she just said. Kiesha hoped it wasn't because she'd offended him or that he was onto her little game.

"I just do all that stuff because I *like* to do it, not because I *need* to. Being a magic-user is one of the most well-paying careers you could ever have. Once you've completed your training, you'll get a really big check deposited in a Swiss bank account every month by the Great House of Magic that I belong to. A really. Big. Check." He said each word slowly for emphasis.

She didn't quite understand why anyone would pay her heaps of money just for having the ability to perform magic. Surely there had to be more to it than that? She decided she'd shelve that question for later. There were far more pressing matters on her mind.

"How long would it take me to complete my training?"

"It depends. Everyone's different. I finished it in about three years, but my teacher said that was unusually fast on account of my higher-than-average intuition," he said with a touch of pride.

"Well, I'm unusually smart, so okay . . . about three years, and then I'll be a real wizard Cool!"

"Witch, actually."

"Hmm. That might take a little getting used to. Where I came from, it's not such a good thing to be called a witch. So in the meantime, during those three years, how would I support myself?"

"I would be happy to pay you out of my own pocket during that time. You'll certainly make more than you would at Applebee's."

"I don't know about that. I am an *excellent* waitress. I make bank at it. You should see how much I make in tips. It's downright amazing." This was another lie. *Hey, why not go for broke?* she figured. She was only being practical.

Randy laughed again. He was enjoying this little dance. He didn't see her seeming obsession with money as a sign of greed so much as it was a sign of strength. She was putting him on notice that she didn't come cheaply and was not to be trifled with. He could appreciate that. Time for him to let her know that the same thing was true for him.

"I guarantee that you will make significantly more than you ever would at your current job. But in return, you might have to do some things for me aside from just being my apprentice."

"Whoa! Hold up there! You're not talking about *sex* things, are you? I'm no groupie, and I'm not into you like that for any amount of money. And aren't you with Penny? I mean, you've got a kid together and everything."

Randy held up his hands. "What? No! That's not what I was implying at all. A relationship like that isn't allowed between teacher and student. I pride myself on being a very ethical guy. As for me and Penny—it's complicated. But I digress. I was going to say that I might want you to work as a roadie the next time we go out on tour. We could also use a backup singer. How's your voice?"

"I never sang in the church choir, but I can carry a tune." She'd always been quite irritated by the fact that, as much as she loved music, she didn't have much of a natural talent for it. She'd been forever sidelined, condemned to only be able to enjoy it as a fan. On the inside, she was jumping for joy at the chance to go out on the road with her favorite band and even do backup vocals for them. she tried to cover this fact with nonchalance and was uncertain as to how successful she really was.

"Excellent!"

"There's just one more thing." Kiesha held up her hand now, making the universal sign for stop.

"Of course there is." Randy smiled a little too thinly. Even his legendary patience was beginning to get worn. "What is it?"

"I worked very hard to get where I am at this school. You're making all these promises, and I want to believe they're true. But I'm not gonna just throw all of that away on a promise. In case all of this doesn't work out for whatever reason, I want to make sure I have something solid to fall back on. Also, I don't like not finishing anything I start. So school, *real* school comes first. I've only got about a year and half left, and I intend to graduate with honors." She said it so rapidly and passionately that she was almost out of breath by the time she finished. She looked at Randy challengingly.

Internally, she was screaming. What if she'd pushed him too far? He was Randy Gruman from the Mystery Smiths! Her hero! Of course she could trust him. He'd made an entire planet just so that he could meet someone clever like her. She prayed to the Orishas that she hadn't overplayed her hand and just blown the opportunity of a lifetime.

Randy could completely respect everything she just said. He was thrilled that he'd managed to snag such a wonderfully pragmatic apprentice, even if she could stand to learn a little humility. He extended his hand.

"You've got yourself a deal!"

Kiesha took it. For the first time since he'd arrived, she allowed herself to smile. A big, broad, gleaming, genuine smile. This had to be the best day of her life.

"And you've got yourself a deal, Sensei!"

"Ooh! "Sensei"' I like it!" Randy had always wanted to be a sensei.

"So, what's the first lesson?"

"What about Applebee's?"

"Oh, to hell with goddamned Applebee's! Teach me magic!" She laughed.

"I was thinking we could start with a little astral projection. It was the first thing I ever learned. You're gonna love it! And it's surprisingly easy. Even the bonehead that runs the detective agency I work for can do it." He could feel his own excitement rising within him as he said the words. He could really get into this teaching stuff.

Kiesha was about to step into a much, much larger world. She couldn't wait to get started, and Randy couldn't wait to share it with her.

The End

DAMNED LEPRECHAUN!

It's such a beautiful day for a hike, thought Penny Layne. She was glad that Randy had brought them all out here today. This was only her second time in Ireland, and she hadn't gotten to see much of it the last time they'd passed through here on tour, other than the insides of pubs and seedy hostels. But that had been over a decade ago. Nowadays, her band the Mystery Smiths was in a much better place financially than they had ever been before, and they were able to tour the Emerald Isle in style.

They had just finished up playing a few shows in Dublin and were taking some days off before their next set of shows were slated to begin up in Belfast. Randy had suggested that they stop here in the ancient town of Carlingford, before leaving the Republic of Ireland for the North. The members of the band were currently making their way up the Sliabh Foy Loop Trail, which led up a mountain called Sliabh Foy. It had been a little rough going at first—the tail started out rather steeply—but it had evened out and was pretty pleasant overall. There were few trees, but many low, scrubby bushes. Every once in a while, they'd catch sight of a few sheep casually meandering off in the distance.

According to Randy, that wasn't all you might catch sight of while wandering on this trail.

He was currently lecturing Milo, another of Penny's bandmates, about the other, more exotic life forms that were said to inhabit these hills. Randy loved to lecture people about all manner of obscure things. It's one of the things he did best.

"Get out of town! There's no way that this is anything more than a stupid trick to reel in the dumb tourists," Penny heard Milo's skeptical, somewhat nasally voice say from a few paces ahead of her.

"I swear it's true," came Randy's typically calm response.

"I've seen a whole bunch of crazy stuff since I started hanging out with you, but I draw the line at leprechauns. You'll never convince me that they exist outside of Lucky Charms commercials," Milo insisted. He was a short, wiry man with close-cropped dark hair, which was formed into large, cartoonish spikes by an excessive amount of hair gel. Colorful sleeves of tattoos painted both of his exposed arms.

"Au contraire, mon frère. This whole area is an official sanctuary for the over two hundred leprechauns that live here—it's protected by EU law. My Great House of Magic, the Temple of the Old Gods, used their influence to get it protected. In fact, I was part of the team that took the census of the local leprechaun population here. This place is quite picturesque, so I thought you guys might enjoy checking it out since we're in the area," Randy explained mildly.

"It's wonderful, Sensei," replied Kiesha from her typical position at Randy's side. Randy was much more than the band's bassist, Penny's best friend, and the "baby daddy" to their son Paul. He was also a real-life wizard, and Kiesha was his ever-faithful apprentice. She'd recently graduated from college and joined the Mystery Smiths on their world tour as a roadie and occasional backup singer. She was a particularly dark-skinned young African American woman with medium-length, braided hair that was currently dyed a brilliant shade of blue.

Milo was apparently determined to play the role of devil's advocate today. "Just for the sake of argument—it's not like I actually believe you about any of this leprechaun bullshit—how, pray tell, does one go about taking a census of the leprechaun population?"

"Holy shit, Milo. You should know better than to ask him a question like that. You know he'll be happy to tell you, in excruciating detail, all of the *fascinating* specifics!" cried an exasperated Kiesha.

Behind his thick, black-framed glasses, Randy raised an eyebrow. "I thought you appreciated my thorough attention to detail, Apprentice?" From his tone of voice, it was evident that he was only feigning being hurt by her words. It took more than that to ruffle Randy's famously unflappable feathers.

"You know we love you and all your crazy quirks, Sensei," Kiesha reassured him nonetheless.

"Well, we've been walking for like an hour already, and I haven't seen hide nor hair of any little men dressed in green," Milo complained to Randy's back, which was already starting to form a dark patch of sweat in the center of his tee shirt.

"For one thing, they don't always wear green. For another, they inhabit the dimensional layer directly above this one." Randy talked about other dimensions in the same casual way that most normal people talked about the weather. It never ceased to amuse Penny. Doubtlessly, she would've thought he was nuts if she hadn't experienced all manner of oddity for herself in the years they'd been in one another's lives.

"You mean the same one that we're in when we astrally project?" Kiesha asked.

Randy smiled back at his apprentice, nodding in the affirmative. His pride in the progress she was making in her studies of the mystical arts was obvious. He carried on with his lecture.

"So you're unlikely to see them unless you're unusually psychic or have undergone the training to have your third eye opened up like Kiesha and I have. That doesn't stop the locals, though. I hear that there's an official leprechaun hunt held on this mountain every year."

Milo wasn't giving up so easily. "An annual leprechaun hunt? *See*? Just like I said. It's all just a gimmick to help boost the local economy."

"I don't deny that it helps the town attract business, and they do whatever they can to capitalize on it. There's even a pub down there where they're displaying a set of fake clothes that are supposed to belong to a leprechaun like it's the real thing. But I swear, there really are a bunch of them around here. The hunt is harmless enough since most people can't see them, let alone catch one."

"If they're so hard to catch, then why bother to protect the place?" Milo demanded.

"It stops land development, which really *can* harm them. Even though they're in another dimension, it's one that is closely tied to our own. Things bleed over between the two worlds. What happens in one world affects the other," Randy explained coolly. "That's why it's important that while we're out here today we treat this place with the proper reverence. This whole mountain and the surrounding countryside are sacred. We mustn't do anything to desecrate it or disrespect it. Leave the land exactly as you found it."

"Well, if we're not even gonna see any leprechauns, then I don't understand what we're even doing out here," Milo said wearily.

"To enjoy the grandeur of nature, *duh*." The voice of Valerie came from somewhere behind Penny. She was Milo's fraternal twin sister and the band's drummer. She couldn't be more different from her brother in both appearance and temperament if she tried. She was tall with long, straight blonde hair that was so light it almost looked white, especially in the early summer sun that was shining down on them all. Whereas Milo was often loud and argumentative, she was normally quiet and easygoing. Valerie reserved all of her pent-up aggression for her drum kit—and her "little" brother when he got under her skin, as he typically did.

"Precisely," Randy agreed enthusiastically. "I thought it would be nice to spend some time outside of the *Blunderbus* for a change. Stretch our legs, get a little fresh air and exercise. I was so struck by the beauty of this place the last time I was here that I couldn't wait to share it with the rest of you."

The *Blunderbus*, or, more properly, the *Blunderbus Mark II*, was the band's faithful tour bus. The *Blunderbus Mark II* was named after the original *Blunderbus*, a van that they once used for hauling equipment and themselves from gig to gig in their early days. Penny had kept that rickety, rusty old thing running long past it's normal operational life through a combination of desperation, determination, threats, and sheer moxie.

"And you want to see if I spot any leprechauns to test out my recently opened third eye, don't you?" Kiesha said knowingly. She didn't literally have a third eye popping out of her forehead or anything, thankfully. Her third eye being open just meant that she had now developed her normal, human-level of psychic ability to such an extent that she could perceive things most people couldn't. At least that's how Randy had explained it to Penny.

"That might be a fringe benefit," Randy admitted slyly. He couldn't keep anything from her.

Penny looked upon her bickering bandmates with pride.—this bizarre group of misfits that had become her surrogate family and were always willing to indulge her in all her crazy artistic endeavors. The band had once been much bigger. Back when they were primarily a ska band, they had a horn section, out of which only Milo now remained. This core group of four had remained together through thick and thin for over fourteen years now.

Although they had a cult following back home in the US and were quite popular in Japan and certain European nations, they'd never been so successful that they didn't have to maintain day jobs. The twins were both medical professionals. Milo was a nurse practitioner and Valerie was a physical therapist, but they were always willing to put those more lucrative careers on hold to go on tour.

Penny considered herself lucky that her own boss, Matt Spike, had always been so supportive of the band. Matt just replaced her with a temp while she was on tour, and always gave her back her old position as the secretary/office manager at his detective agency upon her return. Matt and his wife Naomi were like her family too. In fact, Matt and Naomi were currently taking care of her son Paul while she was away.

Her heart ached at the thought of Paul, who was five years old now. The one thing that sucked about being on a tour like this was that she was missing out on seeing him grow up during this crucial point in his development. She was painfully aware of how fleeting this time in his life was. She hated to miss out on even a few months of it. Thanks to the internet, she was able to do regular video chats with him, but it just wasn't the same. How she longed to hold him in her arms again, to smell him! Unfortunately, this tour was still in the early stages and wasn't going to wrap up until early February of next year. She'd thought about bringing Paul with her, but hadn't wanted him to miss out on school or expose him to the life of a band on the road, which could still sometimes be surprisingly rowdy even as they were all hurtling relentlessly towards middle age.

Penny shook away her guilt about putting her responsibilities as a mother on other people's shoulders and refocused on her feelings of gratitude instead. None of this would've been possible without the help of all the people who supported her. Would she currently be walking up the side of a mountain in Ireland, the land of her ancestors, on a pleasant June day if all of these people hadn't believed in her? She felt truly blessed to have such good friends in her life. They drove her nuts sometimes—okay, —most of the time but that's what good friends do.

Then there was Randy. Not only was he her ever-present sounding board when it came to sharing her most outrageous ideas, but he also kept the band afloat financially during the lean times. They'd been friends and often lovers ever since she was a teenager. A little over half of her life so far. Had it really been that long? It was bizarre to contemplate that, so she tried not to. Randy was no angel she'd put up with her share of crap from him during their years together. For example, back when they had been in a more serious relationship, he had displayed an unfortunate tendency to cheat on her with some of the various mythological creatures he encountered in his life as a wizard. This did not include (so far as she knew) any leprechauns. Weird yes, but who was she to shame someone else's kink?

Despite all of this, Randy was the sort of person who it was impossible to stay mad at for very long. More importantly, she knew that no matter what, when push came to shove, he always had her back. Even though it was apparently impossible for him to commit to her romantically, he really did understand and appreciate her as a person more than anyone else she'd ever met. In addition to that, she'd never experienced the kind of artistic synergy that she did with Randy with anybody else. He'd also shown her that the world was far more weird and wonderful than she'd ever imagined, and for that she'd always be grateful to him.

When she had decided that she wanted to see what it would be like to be a mother before she got too old for such things, she turned to him. There was no other man she could think of who she'd want more to be the father of her child. Together, they'd birthed a pretty cool band, so why not an actual human being too? Even though they weren't living together as a couple anymore, he was still quite involved in his son's life and was a great father. Even though he didn't show it as openly as she did, she knew it hurt him to be away from their son for so long as it did her.

Penny had recently started dating a guy named Jim DeLeo, who was the leader of the band they were touring with, The Atmosphere Fishes. Yeah, she thought that was dumb name for a band too. Although, people often got her band confused with the far more famous band The Smiths, so perhaps it was hypocritical of her to be so judgmental about the stupidity of other people's band names. It was also true that much of The Atmosphere Fishes's music felt a little too derivative of her own style, which is why she supposed their record label had insisted on pairing them up on this tour. Oh well, imitation was the most sincere form of flattery, wasn't it?

Despite these shortcomings, she'd found herself unusually receptive to Jim's flirtations with her. She genuinely admired his energy on stage, but honestly, she was probably mostly interested in him because he looked a lot like Jon Bon Jovi, whom she'd always had a crush on. Yes, she knew how shallow that sounded, and a part of her hated herself for that shallowness, but another part said "Eh, what the fuck? Who cares? This is just a casual relationship right now." She was entitled to have a bit of fun for herself with someone who reminded her of one of her girlhood crushes. Where was the harm in that? So long as they were clear about the terms of the relationship, nobody would get hurt, right? It's not like she was obligated to develop deep feelings for every dude she decided to mess around with. God knows she'd earned herself the right to have a good time every once in a while without any strings attached. She might not have strong feelings for Jim, but he did make her feel special, and she *needed* to feel special. Don't we all? Jim had decided not to join them on this hike; he and his band had elected to move on to Belfast ahead of the Mystery Smiths. Oh well, it was his loss.

"Are you alright back there, Pen? You're awfully quiet," Randy suddenly asked. He could probably tell that she had been thinking about him. He was spooky like that.

"Oh yeah, I'm peachy keen. Just drinking in the grandeur of nature and all that! Besides, you and Milo have been doing more than enough talking for the rest of us," sShe assured him.

"I know right? Pretty hard to vibe with the grandeur of nature when certain people won't ever shut up!"Valerie said from near Penny's ear.

"I someone else says "the grandeur of nature" again, I think I might puke." Keisha said.

"I've gotta take a piss." Milo announced with unwarranted solemnity. At least, the kind of solemnity that seems unwarranted when it isn't your bladder that feels like it's about to burst.

"I told you not to drink all that water so soon. You gotta pace yourself, man," Randy replied.

"As a medical professional, I understand the importance of staying properly hydrated while doing strenuous activities," Milo protested.

"Whatever, man. Just try to find a secluded spot to do your business in. Nobody wants to see your pecker again," Randy ordered.

"Again?" Keisha inquired.

"This band has been together so long that by now everyone has had an opportunity to see Milo's ding-a-ling,." Her sensei explained.

"I haven't seen it" said Kiesha innocently.

"Well today might just be your lucky day, darlin'!" Milo laughed.

"Don't encourage him, Kiesha. Besides, you're not missing much," Penny said.

"That's not what you said that one night in Madrid," Milo teased.

"Hey! I thought we agreed that we'd never speak of that again?" Penny said hotly, although she was really more amused by the banter than actually mad. He really had been pretty good, but they'd both agreed that for the good of the band, it was best to forget it ever happened.

"Jesus! You guys are worse than Fleetwood Mac when it comes to this stuff." Kiesha shook her head in disgust at the latest revelation.

Prior to becoming Randy's apprentice, she had been a huge fan of the band. While she was thrilled to now be a part of the family, a position that she'd never dreamed she'd find herself in, there were certain things about the group she now knew which she often wished she didn't.

"Worse than Fleetwood Mac? I wouldn't put it quite like that. That's impossible," Penny affirmed. The band's "Fleetwood Mac Era" was well behind them at this point. They'd successfully gotten all of that out of their systems. It had been years since there had been any significant hanky-panky going on between any of them—so far as she knew. She thought it was one of the reasons why they all got along so much better these days.

"There's a nice big boulder over there where you can have a bit of privacy. Get going already. We'll wait," Randy said, desperate to change the subject. "Although sometimes I wonder why we bother," he couldn't help but add.

He was a little miffed by his friend flirting with his student like that. He thought it was disrespectful since everyone knew that Randy thought of his apprentice as if she was his daughter, although she wasn't nearly young enough to be. He guessed he really couldn't blame Milo. Kiesha had started it, and he was probably just playing along rather than making a serious effort—although one could never tell with him. True, Milo and Kiesha were both adults and entitled to do whatever they wanted to do with each other, but he thought their age difference made the idea of them hooking up seem a little gross.

Plus, he could do without all the extra drama in the group that would ensue when the proposed relationship soured, as it inevitably would when Milo was involved.

Milo hastily moved off the trail in the direction that Randy had indicated. While he was busy doing what came naturally, Penny decided to take a load off. She sat down on a boulder she found nearby. She tried to enjoy the magnificent countryside, but it was difficult with the loud groan of relief that Milo let out and the tinkling sound of his micturition (now there's a nice medical word for you!) mingling with the birdsong and the bleating of distant sheep.

A few minutes later, Milo came running back up to where the others were waiting.

"Do you really have to be so loud about it?" Valerie asked, "We could all hear you from all the way up here."

"What? Can't a man enjoy a good piss without catching grief for it?" Milo smiled back up at her without a hint of shame. By now, they all knew that he had was purposely being obnoxious; it was unfortunately how he got attention. Yet they played along anyway. It was part of the never-ending game that the friends all played together.

His sister's only response was to roll her eyes.

The rest of the hike up the mountain was uneventful. Despite all her efforts, Kiesha was unable to spot any wee fairy folk with her newly refined powers of extra sensory perception. She didn't feel so bad about this though, and neither did Randy. This is no doubt because none of them were looking in the right direction. Had they spent more of their time looking behind themselves rather than to where the trail was taking them next, they might have realized that they were being scrutinized by a pair of angry, inhuman eyes as they completed the journey to the summit.

However, it was Milo who would pay the price for their lack of vigilance. As the rest of the band either took the opportunity to rest or take selfies, Milo moved to the edge of the mountain top.

"At the risk of sounding trite—" he began.

"When has that ever stopped you before?" Valerie observed sharply without looking up from her phone as she scrutinized the quality of the group selfie she'd just taken with Penny and Kiesha. *To retake or not to retake? That is the question.*

Milo cleared his throat theatrically. "As I was saying before I was so rudely interrupted, it *really* is a great view from up here. Thanks for bringing us here, Randy. Sorry about all the whining on the way up."

"It's all good, sir. If you didn't whine, I'd start to suspect that maybe you'd been replaced by a pod person or something," Randy answered, but despite his flippancy, he was pleased that Milo seemed to be genuinely moved by the experience of being up there. It was rare when his friend displayed this kind of humility in front of others.

It was just then that Milo felt a most curious sensation. It was as if his ankles had been seized by a pair of tiny, yet powerful hands and yanked out from under him.

"Aaaaaaaa!" He tumbled forward over the edge of the mountain, completely disappearing from view.

Randy shot to his feet from the spot where he had been sitting cross legged on the ground. "Milo!" he shouted as he ran forwards in a near panic. Before he knew it, Penny and Kiesha were by his side. Valerie's long, athletic legs and her concern for her only brother and twin carried her forward even faster than the rest of the group. She came skidding to a halt right at the edge of the cliff where Milo had stood just seconds earlier. She paused for the merest sliver of a second before she too disappeared over the edge.

"Val!" Penny exclaimed. She knew that despite their frequent bickering, the twins were actually quite devoted to one another, but diving off a cliff after Milo? That was taking things to a new extreme.

"It's okay! We're okay!" Valerie's voice floated up to her. A moment later, Penny, Randy, and Kiesha were all themselves at the cliff peering down. They breathed a collective sigh of relief as they saw that the area directly below the apparent cliff was not a sharp, steep drop off, but rather a gradual decline in the landscape. Milo was curled up into a ball, rocking back and forth on his ass. His sister was crouched on her knees beside him, examining his wrist. The rest of the group carefully made their way down to them. As they neared the twins, Penny could better see the object of Valerie's attention: Milo's wrist was bent at a disturbingly unnatural angle.

"It's broken for sure," she told him, releasing her hold on it.

He waved his arm around, his hand flopping limply as he did so. He winced and said with his trademark sarcasm, "Oh, gee, thanks Doc, do you really think so?"

Valerie ignored him and looked up at Randy. "Do you think you could work a little of your magic on his injury?"

"I could," Randy stroked his dense black beard pensively. "But I'd rather let Kiesha give it a try." He looked over the edge of his glasses to his apprentice.

"You're gonna let Junior Witch here operate on me? No offense, darlin', but I'd rather be worked on by a professional," Milo said skeptically.

"And here I thought you were desperate for any excuse for me to lay my hands on you." Kiesha joked to hide her irritation at his casual dismissal of her skills.

"I think you'll find that my apprentice is quite capable of fixing such a basic injury. And if she somehow screws this up, I can always still fix it for you myself," Randy replied coolly, and beckoned Kiesha to get to work on Milo.

Kiesha sucked in her breath and knelt down beside the musician. She gently grasped his mangled wrist with both hands and began to chant her incantation. A soft, golden-white glow suffused the damaged area as her words reached a more intense pitch, then faded away. She released his wrist.

"I will never get used to that for as long as I live!" Valerie said in awe.

Milo tested out his wrist by making a few circular motions with it, then grinned at her. "Thanks a bunch, Kiesha," he said with uncharacteristic sincerity. He looked up at Randy. "I guess you must not be such a bad teacher, either. We sure could use you two down at our clinic."

Randy decided not to address that last comment. As miraculous as it often seemed, there were limits to what magical healing could accomplish, and it was his duty to keep the existence of such abilities a secret from the general public. It was best not to open that particular can of worms. "Yeah, well, we can't have you missing any tour dates on account of a broken wrist. What compelled you to take a nosedive off the edge of the mountain to begin with?"

Milo stood up with a little assistance from Kiesha. Their hands lingering in each other's for perhaps a few seconds longer than they should've.

"I guess I must've lost my footing. It's the damnedest thing though—for a second it almost felt like . . . nah, forget it."

"Felt like what?" Penny asked.

"Like somebody yanked on my ankles. Someone with little hands. Stupid, right? I still don't believe in this leprechaun bullshit."

"I just healed your broken wrist in a matter of minutes, but a leprechaun is a bridge too far for you?" Kiesha raised her eyebrows at him.

"Too right. You gotta draw the line somewhere! Next thing, Randy'll have us believing that Santa Claus is real." Milo dug his metaphorical heels in.

"Actually, you'd be surprised to learn that Santa ..." Randy started off before Milo raised his hands to silence him.

"Zip it! I really don't want to know."

"Why would a leprechaun attack Milo like that?" Kiesha wondered aloud.

Randy shrugged his shoulders. "They're naturally a bit mischievous, and sometimes that mischievousness can get viscous. However, they generally keep to themselves unless someone has done something to anger them. I don't see how Milo could've done anything like that. He's been with us the whole time."

"Yeah, that's right. I've been on my best behavior for this whole hike," Milo agreed a little too readily, causing Randy's eyes to briefly narrow in suspicion. "And anyhow, I wasn't really attacked by any leprechaun, because leprechauns don't exist. I just imagined that it felt like there were little hands on my ankles because you guys won't stop talking about them."

"Well, I'm just glad that you're okay." Penny smiled in relief.

She wouldn't have been smiling if she'd been aware that at that very moment, she and her friends were being scrutinized by a set of cold, inhuman eyes. The mind that burned behind those eyes took note of the fact that its prey were protected by a pair of sorcerers, but stubbornly refused to be intimidated by this new information. Indeed, it saw the presence of the magic-users as a welcome challenge. As it continued to silently stalk them, it thought it would have to plan its next move more carefully to keep out of sight when the group started back down the mountain. Kiesha was quite disappointed that she hadn't seen a leprechaun. Milo was smug about it.

After that incident, they made an uneventful trek back to where the *Blunderbus Mark II* was parked, near the tourist office in town. The tour bus was massive, black, shiny, and sleek. The group of magic-users that Randy and Kiesha were members of, the Temple of the Old Gods, was part of a larger group of secret societies called the International Conference of Guilds. The Guilds had their own military, which was in turn known as the UGF—an acronym for United Guild Forces. Randy had once served as a reservist in the UGF, and he used his connections to gain possession of a decommissioned UGF Mobile Command Center, which became the *Blunderbus Mark II.* Randy used these same connections to have the vehicle flown around the world in the belly of a UGF transport jet. It was definitely good to be as well-connected as Randy was.

The band entered the tour bus and made themselves at home. This wasn't particularly difficult because the curious vehicle was Randy's actual home. Due to an enchantment, it was bigger on the inside than the outside, just like the TARDIS from *Doctor Who,* from which the UGF had shamelessly stolen the idea. There was a fireplace in the spacious living room one would see upon first entering the bus. There were numerous bedrooms and an upstairs, even though the vehicle did not appear to be a double decker from the outside.

In fact, it was when he first decided to start using the *Blunderbus Mark II* as their tour bus that Randy had to break the news about his secret life as a wizard to the rest of the band and road crew. There was simply no other way to explain its baffling interior dimensions.

Penny was lying on the couch, exhausted from the hike. She was sad to note that it was the most exercise she had gotten offstage in far too long. It was an uncomfortable reminder of her age. Even though she was in her early thirties, it didn't seem like it was all that long ago that she could've done a hike like that without feeling quite so drained afterwards. Randy threw himself onto the couch near her now-bare feet. He glanced down at them and started rubbing them. Even though they hadn't been a couple for a few years now, he knew that his patented foot-massaging skills were always welcome. As far as Penny was concerned, the man was also a wizard with his hands.

Her lip curled in pleasure. "Careful, you'll make Jim jealous!"

For his part, Randy wasn't concerned about his actions making any of his own romantic partners jealous or upset. He was currently in a long-distance polyamorous relationship with Aethra, who was a half-human, half-water-nymph pirate warrior queen, and Gertrude, the Valkyrie who had once caused so much upheaval in Penny's relationship with Randy. According to Randy, they were all above such petty feelings as possessiveness and jealousy—but Penny didn't buy it. They were all still human, weren't they? Or at least Randy was.

"C'mon, this isn't Pulp Fiction," Randy quipped back, referencing one of their favorite movies. "I don't think he's gonna throw me off a balcony."

"If he did, you'd just levitate back up and zap him with a lightning bolt or something," she joked back.

"Nah, lightning is too deadly. I like Jim too much for that. I'd probably just freeze blast him a little, let him cool off."

"It's a moot point anyway. He might not even get jealous. He couldn't be bothered to join us on this hike. Maybe he's really not that into me," she said somewhat more petulantly than she actually felt.

"Oh? I didn't know you invited him."

"I did, but he wanted to head up to Belfast instead."

"I wouldn't read too much into it, Pen. I'm sure he's wild about you. Besides, I didn't think you were all that serious about him, are you?"

"I'm not, but it's hard to not feel like I've been dissed. I mean, what's so great about Belfast? What's it got that I don't have to offer? I've got a lot going for me, like . . . like . . ." Suddenly, she was drawing a blank when it came to listing her most charming attributes.

"Like stinky feet?" Randy offered as he wrinkled his nose.

"Hey pal, you're the one who insisted on touching them," she reminded him.

"Oh, my bad. I'll stop then." He held up both his hands.

"No, don't you dare stop!" Penny cried as she reached forward to playfully slap him on the thigh.

Just then, the entire room tilted as the bus shuddered. Penny was thrown onto the carpet. "What the hell was that?" she demanded.

"I don't know, but I'm sure gonna find out," Randy declared as he stood up and moved in to the front of the vehicle where the driver sat.

Within moments, he was standing next to Antonio, one of his roadies who enjoyed driving the vehicle and had decided to stay behind while everyone else went on the hike. "What just happened?" Randy asked.

"I dunno. It felt like we might have blown a tire. Let's go check it out,." Antonio replied as he pulled over to the side of the road.

Penny poked her head into the cab. "Figure out what it is yet?"

"Probably just a flat," Randy informed her as the bus lurched to a halt.

"Oh," Penny replied as her head disappeared back through the curtain that separated the cab from the rest of the vehicle.

Through the window, Randy could see that they were still inside the town of Carlingford. The Tholsel, a large stone building that had once served as the town's entrance gate, was visible some distance down the road. Antonio pulled the lever that opened the side door and rose from his seat. He and Randy stepped out of the bus and onto the street. Randy immediately noticed the front tire on the side of the bus where they had emerged was dramatically deflated.

Had Randy not been so engrossed in assessing the damaged tire, he might have noticed as a diminutive form scampered past him and made its way onto the bus. (Diminutive things do lots of scampering. Scampering is not for the non-diminutive. What was this diminutive thing? Was it a squirrel? A chipmunk? Do they even have chipmunks in Ireland? Perhaps it was a small bird? Why am I being so coy about it? Didn't the title of this story completely give it away? Why bother to even attempt to create an air of mystery about it when I spoiled it before you even started reading? Will there ever be another sentence in this story that doesn't end in a question mark?)

Once inside, the leprechaun took stock of his surroundings. There! I did it! A sentence that didn't end with a question mark. The little bastard must be affecting me too I've heard that *they* don't like to be written about. Suppose that's true?)

(Damn!)

(Just did it again!)

(Alright, where were we?)

Argh!

Okay, starting over: as the Leprechaun yes, it's a leprechaun, it's okay to admit that now; and it's not the Lucky Charms kind, more like the Warwick Davis sort) studied the unnaturally expansive interior of the *Blunderbus Mark II*, it could feel the magic that was responsible for such a surreal state of affairs pulsing all around it. A devilish new plan began to form in its mind. It would be difficult to execute. The magic which made the bus larger on the inside was complex and therefore difficult to counteract, yet not beyond the scope of the leprechaun's power.

Undoing this kind of magic might take him a whole 5 minutes. Perhaps even as long as ten! (That might not seem like very long to you or me. However, to a creature that was part and parcel of the highest, deepest magic of the universe and was therefore used to the instant gratification of being able to use magic to get whatever it wanted, it would feel like nothing less than an eternity.) It frowned at the daunting prospect of the course of action it was about to embark upon. Yet, if it succeeded—oh, the delightful chaos that would ensue! It licked its lips at the thought and began to get to work on it.

Randy looked cautiously down one side of the street, then up the other. When he was satisfied that he was without an audience, he looked up at Antonio from his position crouched before the troublesome tire. "Try to stand in front of my hands. I don't want any passersby to see what I'm doing."

"Magical tire repairs? Isn't there anything you do the old-fashioned way?" Antonio asked as he repositioned himself in front of Randy.

"Technically, this *is* the old-fashioned way. It's just faster and easier this way." Magically assisted automotive repair was old hat to

Randy. He smiled to himself as he recalled how he had kept the battered, old, white Hyundai Excel he inherited from his friend Matt running for over a decade by using magic to coax it back into life whenever a fresh mechanical fault reared its head like a Whac-A-ole.

Randy hummed and intoned arcane words in his deep, melodic voice. As he did so, the errant tire glowed faintly and began to slowly reinflate itself. Antonio was too preoccupied keeping a careful lookout to be amazed. He'd also spent enough time with the band to have developed a jaded attitude about the miraculous.

Back inside the *Blunderbus Mark II,* Penny studied herself critically in the bathroom mirror. She ran her fingers through her short, wavy hair that she had dyed green in honor of her tour of the Emerald Isle. The sweat from the hike had caused it to droop onto her forehead in an unflattering way, and she was attempting to tease it back up into its trademarked stylish disarray. She typically wore heavy, black eye makeup that her critics unkindly said liken her to a raccoon, but today she had opted for a more natural look. She reckoned this had been a wise decision, as her sweat would've caused it to run down her face, as it often did by the end of her concerts. As she continued to play with her hair, wishing she had a bit of the hair gel that kept Milo's hair in a perpetually gravity-defying configuration, her brow furrowed in confusion. In the mirror's reflection, it looked like the door behind her had suddenly jumped foot closer to her back. She blinked in consternation. When her eyes opened, she was flabbergasted to see that it now looked like it was even closer.

The room couldn't possibly be getting smaller, could it? She hadn't experienced anything like this since she'd last dropped acid, which was years ago now. She knew that Milo still messed around with that stuff sometimes. She wondered if he'd put something in the canteen they'd shared. Occasionally he did shit like that; he thought it was funny.

A sudden feeling of pressure up against her left butt cheek made her crane her neck over her shoulder to search for its source. She gasped when she saw that the doorknob was now brushing up against her ass.

This is no acid trip!

She instantly grasped the situation—whatever magics allowed the inside of the *Blunderbus Mark II* to defy physics were now wearing off, and with alarming speed! She awkwardly turned herself sideways in the ever-shrinking space between the door and the vanity so that she could swing the door open. It wouldn't open very widely, and she had to squeeze through it, which scared her all the more because she was painfully aware of her own small, pixie-like size. She shot down the hallway that now threatened to close in on her and made it out into the living room that would ordinarily be the largest space in the vehicle, but was now perhaps half its normal size. The furniture in the room was colliding together like a demonstration of continental drift in reverse. She was forced to clamber over chairs and coffee tables to get through it.

"Everybody out now!" she screamed at the top of her lungs. For such a small woman, she had a disproportionately large voice, and even more so when she was actually trying to project it.

She needn't have bothered. Milo and Kiesha came tumbling down the stairs that led to the bedrooms. Out of the corner of her eye, she registered them following her as she ran towards the door and flung it open. Penny nearly twisted her ankle as she fell down the short set of steps and out onto the street.

Milo and Kiesha soon emerged and stood beside her, panting for breath. Down at the opposite end of the bus, Randy had just finished his spell and noticed the commotion. He and Antonio came running up to them.

"What's going on? Is something wrong?"

"It's getting much smaller inside there! Like a normal-sized bus!" Milo told him breathlessly.

"What? That's impossible!" Randy exclaimed in disbelief.

"It's true, Sensei! The interior dimensions are collapsing," Kiesha affirmed, then looked down in embarrassment "I tried, but I couldn't reverse it."

Randy placed a hand on her shoulder. He was about to tell her that it was okay, that he didn't expect her to be able to perform such a complicated kind of spell at her current knowledge level. What stopped him was the realization that her shoulder was bare. In fact, she appeared to be completely naked, save for a thin bed sheet that was wrapped around her body. He glanced over at Milo and saw that he was in a similar state of undress, except he had the comforter from his bed twisted over himself. Next, Randy's eyes met those of Penny's. They both sighed disapprovingly, like the worried parents that they were, as they came to the same conclusion: The band's "Fleetwood Mac Era" was apparently not completely behind them.

A car slowly drove past them. They were all so wrapped up in the drama of the moment that none of them noticed the curious looks they were getting from the occupants.

"Where's Val?" Antonio's question snapped Randy and Penny out of their funk of concern over the band's future. The rest of the band's road crew and most of their equipment was in another bus that was already on the way up to Belfast. Valerie was the only one who was unaccounted for.

As if in answer, there was a shrill scream from inside the *Blunderbus Mark II*, accompanied by a terrible crunching, snapping sound. Dents now appeared on the sides of the vehicle as it struggled to contain all the furniture and other items that couldn't possibly fit inside any longer. If the bus hadn't originally been an armored military vehicle, it likely would've burst open by now. The metal superstructure creaked and groaned under the pressure.

"That's my sister!" Milo shouted as he rushed towards the steps so quickly he almost dropped the comforter that hid his nakedness. Randy caught him firmly by his tattooed arm.

"What the hell are you doing? Are you fucking nuts? I've gotta get in there! She could be getting crushed to death!" His face was completely red as he spat the words.

"I know, but it's too dangerous. I've gotta go instead," Randy told him evenly.

"No! You'll get crushed too," Penny protested.

"Don't you understand? I'm the only one who *can* go in," he insisted as he bolted up the steps.

"No!" Penny repeated to his retreating form. She couldn't lose him now. Not like this! He was the father of her child, her greatest creative collaborator, her best friend.

And no matter what, he'd always be the one, true love of her life.

But it was too late. He was already gone, swallowed up by the insides of the rapidly contracting bus.

***

Randy stood perched atop what was left of the couch. Its wooden frame had snapped and splintered as it met the unyielding stones that the fireplace was made from; its fabric stretched and split. Randy watched in horror as sundry items from what had been the second floor came raining down through the ceiling like a meteor storm. As the second floor disappeared, there was simply no place else for them to go. Reflexively, he uttered a spell that caused a luminescent bubble of emerald energy to enclose his entire body, protecting him just in the nick of time from a falling television set that shattered as it hit the bubble.

The energy bubble was extremely tough and completely impenetrable; only air could pass freely through it. However, such powerful protection came at a price—it would only last for about five minutes before it would have to be refreshed.

Thinking fast, Randy formulated a plan. He had to get to Valerie as soon as possible - if it wasn't already too late. He had no idea where she was though, and the hallways that connected the various parts of the tour bus together were already too narrow for him to pass through. He fidgeted absently with the necklace he always wore as he sometimes did when he was lost in concentration.

The necklace, of course! That's the answer!

The necklace was a birthday gift from several years ago. A gift from Valerie, who liked to dabble in making and selling jewelry. Because it had been crafted by Valerie, it had some of her essence indelibly attached to it. Randy could use that to perform a tracer spell that would lead him right to her current location. He quickly fumbled for the ceremonial dagger he always carried on him, hidden in a sheath under his tee shirt. He always wore shirts that were a little too big to help him conceal the dagger. He needed it for this particular kind of spell.

As he completed chanting the eldritch words of the incantation, a brilliant band of energy extended from his necklace, through the shrinking room, and shot up through the ceiling. He could see four wooden legs from a bed frame that was slowly being pushed down through the ceiling where the energy ribbon disappeared.

It was Valerie's bed.

She must've been lying in bed, perhaps napping, when the interior dimensions began collapsing. Thankfully, the collapse seemed to be happening unevenly. While most of the contents of some rooms were already spiraling down into the living room, others had barely been affected.

Randy's attention was suddenly drawn by the sound of high-pitched laughter. He snapped his head to the side to find the source of all this inappropriate mirth. There, hopping up and down in glee on the mantelpiece of the fireplace and clapping his hands together, was a leprechaun. He was quite ugly with thick, bushy eyebrows and a misshapen, bulbous nose set in a wrinkled face covered in moles and warts. He wore a tattered tricorn hat and a long, blood-red jacket with seven gleaming, golden buttons running down it. Randy grimaced at the creature. It stuck its tongue out at him and laughed even harder.

Another scream from above brought Randy crashing back to reality. This scream, he noted bitterly, sounded far more muffled than the last one. He couldn't wait for her bed to be pushed down to the room he was in—she'd likely be crushed before the bed fell through. He had to get to Valerie right away, and under the circumstances, there was only one way left to do that. Uttering the words to a teleportation spell, Randy visualized his destination: beside Valerie in her bed.

In a flash, Randy was lying on his back next to her. The energy bubble was still around him, and its sudden arrival had pushed the roof of the bus up, punching a dome in the metal directly above him. Valerie took a deep, grateful breath. The dome had literally given her some much-needed breathing room. Although outside objects couldn't penetrate Randy's energy bubble, he could stick his arms out of it and pull things inside. This is exactly what he now did. The back of the bubble had pressed down on the mattress, causing Valerie to slide up against it. Randy now wrapped one arm around her and pulled her inside.

"Thank you," she whispered hoarsely as she moved closer to him inside the bubble.

"*De nada,*" he replied, then did another quick teleportation spell.

The pair of them appeared in the street right outside of the bus. Randy managed to say the magic word that made the energy bubble dissipate right before he doubled over and vomited. An unfortunate side effect of doing back-to-back teleportation spells without allowing the appropriate amount of time to pass in between was uncontrollable nausea. Valerie kicked up her heels to avoid the stream of puke flying from Randy's mouth.

"You're safe!" Milo exclaimed as he threw his arms around his dramatically taller twin sister—it looked like he was pressing his head against her belly.

Likewise, Penny now hugged Randy, who had just finished up with his retching.

"I thought I'd lost you!" She was crying now.

"It's gonna take more than that to get rid of me," Randy assured her.

"That's what I kept trying to tell 'em, Sensei," Kiesha said before repeated the same magic word that Randy had said to dismiss his energy bubble. While he had been inside, Kiesha was forced to place a similar energy barrier over the door to prevent Penny and Milo from chasing after him. Now she was getting rid of it.

"What now?" Antonio asked.

"The first thing is to get this vehicle off the street before someone notices all of this." Randy turned to Kiesha. "Teleport us all to somewhere a bit more secluded. Someplace out in the countryside."

"Another teleportation spell? So soon? But you're already sick as a dog. Are you really sure that you want me to teleport all six of us *and* the bus at the same time," she protested. "Isn't that a little dangerous for someone at my level?"

"You've got a gift for it. I know you can do it. You're much better at this than I was at your age," Randy said confidently.

It was true. Just as many regular people have an unusual knack. for certain things, magic-users often have talents in one particular type of spell that others lack. Kiesha was particularly adept at teleportation. Not only did she have a high resistance to the stomach-churning effects of such spells, but she was also able to transport a large number of people and objects more safely and easily than most of her counterparts who were no longer mere apprentices but fully vested members of her mystical order. Considering how out of sorts Randy was feeling, having her do the spell was the only responsible choice.

The side of the bus bulged out towards them just then, making them all jump.

"Do it!" Randy commanded.

Kiesha asked them all to link hands. She touched the side of the bus with her free hand, then she said the words.

There was the typical blur of motion and flashing, multicolored lights that one saw when they were shunted through time and space via the *place between places* before they all found themselves in a pleasant field near the base of the mountain they'd been hiking up earlier. It turned out this wasn't a moment too soon. One of the bus windows erupted outwards, peppering them with glass as the broken remains of a coffee table plopped down into the tall grass, almost hitting Penny. They could see the fleeing forms of a few sheep that had been started by their unexpected arrival.

Randy threw up again, and this time Valerie joined him. Puking is always better with a buddy.

"Isn't there any way to stabilize it?" Kiesha asked, trying not to think about all the personal items in her bedroom that were now likely hopelessly pulverized.

"Yes, I can probably even reverse it. It's a complicated process, and I'm going to need your help to complete it. But not right now. I need a minute to rest first," Randy told her, then sat down where he was standing before he fell over. He took several long, deep breaths, holding his head in his hands as he fought to regain control of his body.

"I don't understand why any of this is happening. I thought you told us this thing was safe to travel in," Milo complained as he retwisted the knot that was keeping the comforter he was wearing from slipping off his body.

"It is safe! I wouldn't use it as my home if it wasn't, let alone allow all of you to drive around the world in it if I didn't believe that. Something—no, *someone*—has deliberately reversed the spells that make it more spacious."

"That's crazy. Who would do such a thing?" Milo scoffed.

"Oh, I think you might know who," Randy said angrily.

"What's that supposed to mean?" Milo replied defensively.

"It means that I'd really like to know how you managed to piss off a leprechaun."

"A leprechaun? You're still on that old kick? We went up and down this mountain today and didn't see a single leprechaun. This has nothing to do with them."

"That's funny, I saw one happily dancing around while I was inside the bus. You must've done *something* to desecrate the mountain. That's why it went after you first. So what was it?"

"How could I have done anything? I was with you the whole time. Why does everything always have to be my fault?"

"Because it usually is," Penny couldn't help but add, earning her a dirty look from Milo. "And there was one time when you weren't with the rest of us: when you went off to relieve yourself."

"Oooh," Milo said slowly, as if the eagle of enlightenment had just perched upon his mind, spreading its wings of knowledge deep into his synapses. The others all knew the look that was on his face now. It was the look he wore when he realized that he'd just fucked up. They saw it often enough when he learned about something he'd done the night before under the influence of whatever his substance of choice was at the moment.

Valerie knew that look even better than the rest of them. She'd been living with it since childhood, back before Milo had drugs or alcohol to help excuse his bad behavior. "What was it? What did you do?" she demanded of him.

"Well . . . there was this pile of rocks that was stacked up in the field behind that big boulder. Looked like it had been there for a long time—centuries, even. So, I kind of . . . just peed on it," he admitted in a faltering voice.

"A pile of rocks? Sounds like it was probably a cairn. What do you think, Sensei?" Kiesha's quick, analytical mind swiftly grasped the answer as usual.

"It's gotta be." Randy sighed in exasperation.

"Excuse me, but what the fuck is a cairn?" Antonio asked.

"It's a stack of stones. They're erected for a variety of possible reasons. Sometimes just to mark a boundary, sometimes as a monument or to mark a grave. Sometimes they serve a more ceremonial purpose," Kiesha explained.

Not to be outdone, Randy took up the explanations. "Around here, they often mark the boundaries between this world and the next—the world of the Fey. Quite a few of the leprechauns I met during my census had their homes near one, or even *inside* of one. No wonder it's so angry at us."

"Hey, you're the one who told me to go pee behind that boulder!" Milo reminded him, still trying to wiggle out of responsibility for the mess that they were in.

"I never told you to pee on a cairn! I didn't know it was back there. In fact, I *specifically* told you not to disturb anything in the environment. Why would you decide to pee on a cairn when you see one?" Randy's normally deep and calm voice was now becoming uncharacteristically high pitched and shrill as his frustration mounted.

"I needed a target. It made a pretty good target," Milo said it as if it was the most reasonable, obvious thing on earth.

Randy hung his head and massaged his temple. He took several deep breaths before daring to speak again.

"Thanks to you, the *Blunderbus*—my *home*—is a wreck. All our instruments and the personal stuff we had inside are ruined. And we all could've died. Your sister very nearly did! The damned leprechaun probably still isn't done with us. They have long memories."

"I'm sorry man, I really am. I never meant for any of this to happen. How was I supposed to know that just pissing on a pile of rocks would endanger us?"

"It's alright, babe," Kiesha said softly, placing a hand on Milo's shoulder.

Babe? Randy felt like he was going to be sick all over again.

Kiesha looked at her teacher. "You know he didn't mean for any of this to happen, and he was the first one to be attacked. He was almost killed! Wouldn't it be more important for us to instead focus on how we're gonna deal with this leprechaun?"

Randy put a hand in his pocket. In all of his pants, Randy had at least one pocket that was linked to another dimension where he stored various items he used frequently. With a thought, he summoned what he needed and felt it fly into his open palm. He brought out his hand and opened it to reveal two tiny pearls. He stood up and placed one in his ear, and the other he handed to his apprentice. She knew what it was for and immediately placed it in one of her own ears.

Yes, you're right. But it's not something we can discuss out loud right now. The leprechaun is probably still somewhere nearby, watching us. Randy sent her the message telepathically.

Most people, even the majority of magic-users, needed devices like this to communicate telepathically when not astrally projecting. The others all knew what the pearls were used for too. Randy had let them fool around with them in the past, like a kid showing off his favorite toys.

"It's hopeless. Such creatures are exceptionally tricky. It might be too much for even my powers to deal with," Randy said out loud. When Penny looked at him despairingly, he winked at her.

I see. So what do you propose? How exactly does one deal with an irate leprechaun? Kiesha thought to him.

We set a trap. Randy smiled as he thought the words to her.

***

The leprechaun was starting to get bored. He'd watched the two sorcerers as they'd worked the series of spells that restored the extra interior dimensions of their vehicle. The female wasn't familiar with the spells and her mentor had to explain what needed to be done. Frequently.

It was all very tedious.

Having restored the inside of the vehicle to what constituted normal for it, they were now moving throughout it, going room by room, using magic to repair all the things that had been damaged.

This was even more tedious.

The others were just sitting around outside of the bus now while the magic-users did their thing. The ones who had been naked aside from the bedding they were covering up with went inside long enough to change into proper clothes and returned outside.

The leprechaun entertained himself by causing Milo, the moron who'd urinated on his home, to trip several times. He gave Valerie an especially vicious wedgie. When Penny was finally able to get a Coke out of the magically restored refrigerator, he made it explode in her face. He threw pebbles at Antonio's head. But such childish pranks soon wore thin. The problem was, he couldn't imagine any really good new ways to torment these humans. He thought about causing the interior dimensions of the bus to collapse again, but he hated to repeat himself. Such a lack of originality was below him. He took a too much pride in the quality of his work. No, he'd have to come up with something really good for his next attack.

Something really deadly.

Something truly *epic.*

He thought about returning home to go sleep on it. Perhaps a nice rest would restore his creative juices? It had been quite a long day, but he didn't want to lose track of these humans. He did derive a certain satisfaction from seeing how frustrated and miserable they were with the entire situation, though. Perhaps killing them was too good for them? Maybe annoying them over the course of the rest of their lives would be a more fitting revenge? It would require a good bit of dedication on his part, but it was a sacrifice he was prepared to make. Such an elaborate revenge would be sure to make him a legend amongst his own people. He certainly wouldn't mind a bit of notoriety and respect.

Then he spotted it. A flash of gold as something tumbled out of the pocket of that idiot Milo when he pulled his cellphone out to answer a call.

Gold.

The leprechaun edged forwards to the spot in the shade provided by the shadow cast by the bus where Milo had been standing a moment earlier.

Yes!

It was a gold coin, just lying there in the grass. Lying there, waiting for him to take it. It would be his! Oh yes, it would be his!

As his greedy little claw-like fingers stretched out to touch the coin, a curious thing happened. He disappeared.

Inside the *Blunderbus Mark II*, Randy felt a sudden, pleasant warmth on his leg. With one magic word, he caused a small crystal ball to come flying out of the pocket (which was a normal pocket, not one linked to another dimension). It hovered before him, and on its surface, he saw the angry face of the leprechaun as it looked all around itself confused, cursing most profusely. Randy allowed himself a small smile of satisfaction. He looked over at Kiesha, who was engrossed in repairing a chest of drawers with a spell of restoration.

"He's taken the bait," Randy told her.

Kiesha completed fixing the chest before she replied. "You mean we've got him?"

"We do indeed! Let's go get that coin and tell the others the good news."

Kiesha was the first one down the steps. As she stepped outside, she couldn't contain herself. "We've got the little bastard!"

"Really?" Penny asked. "That was easy!"

"No, we got lucky that he didn't realize what we were up to," Randy responded as he joined them.

"The luck of the Irish?" Valerie joked as she continued to pick the remains of the wedgie out from her butt cheeks.

"I'm not Irish," Randy told her.

"But I am, so maybe it was my luck?" Penny said.

"Maybe it was." Randy smiled warmly at her. "Maybe it was."

"Where did you drop that coin, babe?" Kiesha asked Milo.

Babe? Again with the "babe"! Randy's high spirits from just a moment earlier were spoiled. This new relationship between his apprentice and his friend was going to take some getting used to. He just hoped that Milo didn't end up breaking her heart. He'd better not break her heart! He had known Milo for far longer than he knew Kiesha, but he was much closer to his student. He didn't want to have to pick sides if they had a falling out, but he had little doubt over whose side he'd be most inclined to take.

"Right over there." He pointed to the spot. "Although, I've gotta object to you calling it a coin. It's just a piece of chocolate."

Randy strode over to where Milo indicated he'd "accidentally" dropped the coin and scooped it up. He now held it up for all the others to see as they crowded around him.

"It's called gelt, actually. We give them out to kids at Hanukkah. Although I like to think that they're yummy all year round," Randy told them.

"Is that why you always keep a whole bag of them in your interdimensional pocket, Sensei? I didn't think you were very religious."

"I'm not, but my family still observes most of the holidays and customs. I bought a bunch of 'em in bulk years ago. I got a pretty good deal on them. I store them in that dimension. Food kept in there doesn't spoil and always stays nice and cool. Every year, I just whip out a few bags for my nieces and nephews."

"Oh, please. We've all seen you snacking on them," Penny teased "Don't try to pretend that they're *just* for your nieces and nephews."

He shrugged. "There are a few hundred bags in that dimension. I don't have enough nieces and nephews to eat them all!"

"Like Sensei said, we got lucky. Lucky that the leprechaun didn't see him put a spell on the gelt coin while we were inside the *Blunderbus* . Lucky he couldn't tell that I teleported it into Milo's pocket afterwards. Lucky that he didn't know those little pearls allow us to communicate telepathically when we passed them around so we could explain our plan to the rest of you," Kiesha commented.

"And lucky that that shit about leprechauns being obsessed with gold is true," Milo added.

"You'd be surprised how much truth there is in folklore," Randy told him. "The leprechauns are cobblers who make shoes for the Tuatha Dé Danann, the ancient Celtic gods that later evolved into our modern idea of fairies. They're paid in gold, which they then hoard." He paused to take a breath, then looked Milo squarely in the eye. "Am

I to take it that this whole incident has finally convinced you that leprechauns are real—and not to be trifled with?"

"I dunno, man. I mean, something sure made the *Blunderbus* turn into the trash compactor from Star Wars. I'm just not sure it was really a leprechaun! I still haven't seen one, have I? Seeing is believing."

"Well, my friend, be prepared to be amazed, because you're about to see one. Kiesha, draw the circle," Randy ordered.

"I thought you said I had to have a third eye to see the little creep? Don't you guys know that I'm third eye blind?" joked Milo.

"Ugh. Please don't remind me that shitty band ever existed. I'd almost successfully erased them from my memory banks," Penny griped.

"I met them once. They're actually pretty nice," Valerie said.

Randy cut through the banter to answer Milo's question. "You'll be able to see the leprechaun when he's inside the circle."

Kiesha withdrew a cloth drawstring sack from her own interdimensional pocket and sprinkled the dust on the ground, making a circle with it that she filled with a few spiraling, looping shapes. When she was done, she took out her dagger, cut the palm of her hand open, and scattered a few droplets of blood in the "corners" of the circle.

"I sure hope you guys keep those things properly sanitized. You don't want to go off getting an infection from all that bloodletting,"

Milo, ever the medical professional, said as he made a somewhat disgusted face.

The magic-users ignored him. Randy dropped the gelt in the center of the circle and said a few arcane words. Normally, such a circle would be used to contain a spirit. He'd already bound the spirit to the piece of gelt—it had been boobytrapped to bind him when he touched it by Randy's earlier spell. Because he was bound to the gelt, he couldn't possibly escape. Therefore, the circle was technically unnecessary, but it would allow the others to see the leprechaun, and he felt that they deserved a chance to confront their tormentor. Also, he was sick of Milo's constant skepticism.

This wasn't the first time he'd pulled this particular trick. Years earlier, he'd bound an especially troublesome spirit to a quarter, which is what gave him the idea. He didn't have any gold coins with which to temp the leprechaun, but he *did* have hundreds of bags of gelt in his interdimensional pocket. The gold foil that the chocolate was wrapped in could be quite convincing at first glance, especially from a distance. It was a gamble he'd felt was worth taking, and he was fortunate enough that it actually bore fruit.

As Randy completed his incantation, the leprechaun appeared above the coin, scowling at them all. To Randy, he appeared to look much the same as he had on the previous occasion he'd seen him. He wore the same battered tricorn hat with a long, blood red coat that had seven gold buttons and seven buttonholes. His face was quite ugly. His skin was like old, cracked leather, his eyes were small and dark, and his mouth was a hideous gash of fangs. His grotesque appearance was owed to the fact that the leprechauns were a race of hybrids—the twisted and deformed children of the Tuatha Dé Danann and water spirits.

Later on, Randy would discover that the others had seen him dressed in a green coat with a black top hat, keeping with the American tradition of what a leprechaun looks like. They even described him as being cute. Our ability to perceive such beings is often dictated by our own preconceived notions of them, but Randy had trained his mind to see beyond such prejudices.

Milo laughed. "Well, holee shit. It really is a leprechaun. Hey! Top o' the mornin' to ya, me boyo!"

"Uh, yeah. You do know that we really don't talk like that, right?" the leprechaun replied.

"You don't?" Penny asked "Not even a little?"

"No."

"Well, *that's* disappointing," Valerie chimed in. And it was. Some of the locals sounded more like what she'd expected a leprechaun to sound like than the actual leprechaun did. He had an almost maddening lack of any hint of a proper Irish brogue. Instead, he sounded irritatingly bland and proper when he spoke, like a BBC announcer. While their preconceived ideas about leprechauns shaped how he looked to them, for whatever reason, it didn't affect what he sounded like. Randy would later speculate that this was because the leprechaun's great vanity made him okay with them seeing him as looking far more pleasant than he really did, yet he also wanted something of his authentic personality to shine through.

"Oh, I'm *so sorry* I'm disappointing you. I didn't realize that I existed solely to conform to your stereotypes. Maybe you'd like me to dance a little jig for you? Maybe get really shitfaced and sing some traditional Celtic songs?"

"That would be pretty cool, actually . . ." said Kiesha.

"Well forget it! I don't even drink. I've got a bloody liver condition! I'm not here to amuse you. I'm furious with the whole lot of you. Especially this arsehole right here!" He stabbed his tiny finger (which looked adorable to everyone but Randy, who thought it looked more like the talon of some kind of carrion bird) at Milo.

"I really was having a fine morning until you decided to rain some gold down on me, but not the kind I like! I was just sitting back, relaxing and smoking my pipe, not harming anyone. Then, all of the sudden, all this nastiness came pouring down on me, like a pipe had burst in the ceiling above me. I ran outside and I saw this moron waving his flute all over the place, spraying my house like a cat marking its territory!"

"I really am quite sorry about the actions of my associate. He lacks the proper respect for the sanctity of this land. I know that I'd be really . . . er . . . pissed off if I found a giant urinating all over my house," Randy said diplomatically.

"And not just my house! All over me, too! I like gold, but not golden showers," the leprechaun reminded him. "I really had to scrub myself hard to get that stench off of me.!"

"Yeah, but none of that excuses trying to murder all of us," Penny told the little man.

"I'll keep my own counsel on what constitutes an appropriate revenge, woman," the leprechaun said hotly, waggling a finger in her direction, which again just looked more funny to her than menacing. She found it impossible to repress a giggle, which in turn made the leprechaun even more angry. When he got mad, he looked to her like his cheeks became very rosy, forming perfect red circles upon them. The surreal cartoonishness of made her giggle even harder.

Randy looked at her askance. "C'mon, Pen. This is a serious matter."

Is it really? The whole damned thing seems pretty fucking ridiculous to me! But then she remembered the horror of fleeing the shrinking insides of the *Blunderbus.* The crushing fear and despair she'd felt when she saw Randy go back inside that death trap to rescue Valerie and was sure he'd never make it back out alive. The sadness in Randy's eyes when he saw his home destroyed.

"Sorry. Yes, it is," she agreed shamefacedly.

Randy faced the leprechaun. "I would like you to end this vendetta now."

"Would you really? Well, that's not up to you now, is it? *I* am the one who will decide when and where this score is considered settled," the wretched creature barked.

"Except that's not true. You are in no position to dictate to me. I have bound your spirit to that piece of gelt you tried to steal. I could just keep you inside it forever as a prisoner unless you cooperate," Randy said coolly, and for the first time he thought he saw a hint of fear in the leprechaun's eyes. "Fortunately for you, I don't believe in holding anyone prisoner forever." He saw the creature visibly relax as he spoke the words. "However, you are bound by an even older and more powerful obligation to grant my desires. I'm entitled to three wishes because I captured you."

The leprechaun snarled in inarticulate rage. "You know!"

"Of course I know. That's leprechaun 101. It's basic stuff. I'd be a pretty shitty wizard if I didn't know."

"Three wishes? Really?" Penny couldn't believe it. This was some Aladdin shit, right here. She'd often daydreamed about what she would do if she had three wishes, but she never imagined that she'd ever really be in a position to use them.

Randy nodded at her in the affirmative.

"This is wonderful! We could use them to do so much good in the world. We could end poverty, create world peace—"

"No!" Randy shouted the words more forcefully than he'd meant to. Now he saw a flicker of fear in Penny's eyes as she instinctively flinched at his tone. It killed him a little inside to see her look at him that way, even for an instant.

He spoke to her now in a far more gentle tone: "I'm sorry, Penny. I didn't mean to snap at you like that. It's just that you don't understand how dangerous it is to use his wishes, especially in the way that you were suggesting. It's like playing with fire."

"I don't understand. What's so horrible about using wishes?" Antonio asked.

"I don't know how many of you guys ever read that old short story, 'The Monkey's Paw,' but if you have, you might understand what I'm trying to say. His wishes work very much like like the wishes in that story."

Penny remembered having to read the story in her high school English class. "Unintended consequences," she muttered.

"Precisely." Randy nodded in her direction. "Wish for world peace, and he might deliver it by putting the world under some kind of a dystopian dictatorship. There would be peace, but only because anyone who was seen as a threat to the peace would be brutally hunted down and executed. Or, take your wish to end poverty—he could achieve that by simply exterminating the entire human race. We would all be economically equal in death. No, these kinds of problems are too complicated to just be wished away. No spell could ever be specific and intricate enough to address all the nuances."

"Don't listen to him, my dear. I might like a bit of revenge on those who have truly wronged me, but I'm no monster. I'd never kill the whole human race or make it suffer under the thumb of a tyrant," the leprechaun argued back.

"That might be true. Perhaps you wouldn't intentionally do that, but I don't think even you can completely control all of the consequences of your wish powers," Randy told it.

"So, what do we do? What good is having wishes if we can't use them?" a flabbergasted Milo inquired.

"Oh, we're going to use them. Precisely two of them. But I'm going to be very, very specific."

Randy brought his face up to that of the leprechaun's and met his gaze.

"Wish number one: In exchange for your freedom, you will drop your vendetta against my friends and I. Neither you nor any of your associates will in any way seek to bring even the most trivial of harms to us. You will not harm Milo, Valerie, Penny, Kiesha, Antonio, or me. You will not damage any property that belongs to us."

Randy took a breath before continuing. "Wish number two: I hereby forfeit the right to any further wishes beyond this one."

"That's it?" the leprechaun said in disbelief. "You don't even want any of my gold?"

"Don't need it. I've got plenty." Randy beamed at him.

"Speak for yourself, dude! I sure could use some," Milo said.

"Milo, shut up." Valerie elbowed him in the ribs playfully.

"No, he shouldn't shut up. He should apologize to the leprechaun," Randy said, looking at him expectantly. "You *did* piss on the guy."

"And he tried to kill us! That's pretty psycho. Consider it a preemptive strike."

Kiesha weighed in. "Milo, it *is* pretty fucked up to pee on a total stranger."

"Okay, okay. I'm sorry that I did a thing that I didn't even know that I was doing."

Randy rolled his eyes at his insincerity, but he knew it was the best he was likely to get out of him.

"Apology *not* accepted. I suppose it doesn't matter though. I am bound to drop the vendetta because of the wish." He looked at Randy. "Once you set me free, of course."

"Of course. Kiesha, break the circle."

Kiesha simply rubbed out a portion of the circle with her foot. As she did so, the leprechaun disappeared, invisible to everyone but Randy and Kiesha. Then Randy chanted the words to the spell that unbound him from the gelt.

"Will he keep his word?" Penny asked Randy.

"He doesn't have any choice. Let's get out of here."

Randy was right. The leprechaun did keep his word and granted the two wishes as he was ordered to. The band was able to complete their tour of Ireland without any further supernatural attacks from the leprechaun.

Sometimes, though, I wonder if there is as much danger in wishes that are very specific as there are in ones that are too vague. I've had a great deal of trouble in the course of writing this tale down. A series of strange, persistent setbacks.

Unintended consequences.

Randy's wish might have protected everyone who was there that day, but will it protect me? I'm really more of an acquaintance than a good friend.

What was that sound?

Scampering feet!

I was warned before I started writing down this account, wasn't I? Warned that leprechauns don't like to be written about. Warned that maybe it wasn't a very good idea to document this particular incident in the lives of my friends.

Why didn't I listen? Could it be true? Does the leprechaun somehow know? Even after all these years and all this physical distance, can it still reach me?

Was that a laugh? A mocking little snigger? All the difficulties I've encountered while trying to write all this down, the numerous times my iPad turned off for no good reason, how the fully charged battery kept draining—was that all his work? If this stuff wasn't automatically backed up to a cloud, it would've surely been lost.

There's another sound!

Like something was just knocked over in the next room! Whenever I hear a strange sound in my house, I like to blame it on my pets. Hell, it might even be half the reason why I have them. But I can see both my cat and my dog from where I currently sit typing these words. Both are peacefully sleeping the day away on opposite sides of the same couch. You'd think that if something was running around in my house, the pets would be on the case, but both animals are old now and spend most of their time in slumberland.

I'm totally on my own here.

Pray for me!

The End

ALL YOUR CITIES LIE IN DUST

Part One:

Nathrogreer marveled at the beauty of Sansha, the largest of the planet Hirthrogaar's three moons, as they set out on their morning jog. Sansha's rings were particularly radiant today, sparkling in the early morning sunlight.

Exercise was important to Nathrogreer, as they spent most of their time remotely exploring other worlds in an artificial body made up of billions of nanobots. While they were controlling this distant avatar, their real body was floating, suspended in an isolation pod. While it was true that mild electric shocks were regularly applied to their muscles while they were inside the pod to prevent atrophy, Nathrogreer found it to be a poor substitute for real exercise. Besides, it simply wasn't as much fun. There was nothing that could quite match the exhilaration and natural high that they got out of a good run, or the connection that they felt to the nature of their homeworld as they jogged through forested trails.

Nathrogreer could hear the familiar sound of heavy, labored breaths from somewhere behind them. They immediately recognized it as the cadence of one of their neighbors, Biim. Biim was one of the Rishildi, a species that had created Nathogreer's people ages ago to act as their servants. But all of that was so long ago it all seemed like a fairy tale. Both races had been forced to flee their original homeworld to settle on Hirthrogaar millions of years ago and were now considered equals.

Biim was also out on his morning run. To some, this might appear to be quite the peculiar sight, as Biim, not being of a humanoid configuration like Nathrogreer, jogged along on a series of tough, greenish tentacles.

Biim was a frequent companion of Nathrogreer on these jogs. They never formally planned to run together; it just naturally happened that they tended to run into one another, often jogging together for a spell and getting caught up in the details of one another's lives for a time before inevitably parting ways.

"Hey, Nath! What's up?" Biim called as he caught up to them so that the two were now running parallel to each other.

"Oh, nothing much," Nathrogreer answered humbly.

"Nothing much? Aren't you about to reach a whole new world? One that likely had life on it once?"

Nathrogreer nodded. "We should be in orbit today. Hopefully we can find more evidence to corroborate what the long-range scans suggest."

"A Dead End World!" Biim said in obvious awe. The planet that Nathrogreer was to survey was what the people of the Galactic Federation called a Dead End World, meaning a planet where intelligent life had died out before achieving sustainable interstellar travel. It was sadly incredibly common. More Dead End Worlds had been charted than were currently inhabited.

"What makes you think that it ever had intelligent life if you haven't even gotten close enough to see any artificial structures on the surface?" Biim wondered.

"Mainly it's the chemical composition of the atmosphere. There are lots of signs that indicate heavy industry was going on at some point in the relatively recent past of the planet. That kind of activity has an effect on a world that can linger on long after all the buildings have collapsed or eroded away to nothing," Nathrogreer explained patiently.

"Sifting through the dust of ruined worlds," Biim said wistfully. "I must write a poem about that someday." Biim was actually quite an accomplished writer.

"I would like to read that," Nathrogreer said earnestly, although truthfully they found little time for casual reading these days.

"Thank you. Is this the first Dead End World you've visited?"

"*If* it really is one, it would be my third." As a scientist, Nathrogreer felt it was important to emphasize that the true nature of the planet was still unknown.

"Don't you find it all a little morbid? Entire worlds that are tombs!" From his tone, it was obvious that Biim found the concept to be equal parts romantic and horrifying.

"Perhaps a little, but I prefer to think of it as a way of honoring them. Who would remember them if not for us? This way, they get to live on through us, in a way," Nathrogreer replied philosophically.

"A heavy responsibility, telling the story of an entire civilization. It's important to get it right."

"It is, but we're just the ones who make the initial discovery. Our only burden is to make recommendations on what kinds of experts are needed to follow up on our preliminary findings. That's where all the real hard work is done. It can take centuries to fully study these worlds, to truly understand them."

There was a bit of an awkward pause in the conversation after Nathrogreer made that last statement as Biim tried to absorb it all. Nathrogreer broke the maddening silence by asking how Biim's latest writing was going.

"I've decided to step away from it for a while. I'm afraid it's becoming too workmanlike. I need to allow myself some space to become truly inspired again, you know what I mean?"

"I do," Nathrogreer said, even though they really had no idea what Biim meant by this. The craft of creating art was as much of a mystery to them as Nathrogreer's science seemed to be to Biim.

"How are your children?" Biim inquired. Nathrogreer had two living children and one, Atrid, who had passed away years earlier in a tragic accident. One of Nathrogreer's surviving children had in fact started life as an attempt to copy Atrid and was called Atrid-B.

Atrid-B's mind had been designed by a quantum computer that analyzed all the surviving recordings and writings of the original Atrid. This attempt to duplicate their consciousness was then downloaded into a cloned body with a biomechanical brain capable of accepting the artificial intelligence. Nathrogreer had thought that this would help them deal with the grief of losing their child, but oddly, for a time it had only made it worse. At first, Atrid-B just reminded them of everything they'd lost, and they'd regretted commissioning their creation. Eventually though, Nathrogreer learned to love Atrid-B as dearly as the original, while Atrid-B had gone on to develop their own unique personality as more time went on.

"They're fine. Megolu and their partner seem to still be getting along fine, and their kids are good. Nothing new to report there."

Nathrogreer's people didn't reproduce sexually. They had instead been genetically designed by Biim's distant ancestors to automatically produce two children when they reached a particular age. As a result, many of them, like Nathrogreer, didn't feel much of a need to form any kind of romantic relationship, although such things were not unknown. Their child Megolu had been in such a relationship for several years now, raising their own children along with those of their partner as one big, blended family. Megolu worked as a botanist in a jungle a continent away, and Nathrogreer rarely got to see them anymore.

"And what of Atrid-B? Have they been posted to a ship yet?"

"No, we're still awaiting word of where they'll be assigned."

"You must be proud of that one! Following in your footsteps like that!"

"I'm proud of them *both*," Nathrogreer said pointedly, hoping to quash any ideas that they might be favoring one child over the other.

"Of course, of course. You're fortunate to have them. I keep hoping to have some of my own someday, but Clartum keeps saying she isn't ready for the responsibility yet," Biim complained about his mate's lack of desire for offspring. It was a common complaint of his. Nathrogreer could hardly blame him. If he was to be believed, Clartum had been making this same excuse for fifty galactic standard years before Nathrogreer was even born. The Rishildi, however, were extremely long-lived compared to Nathrogreer's people.

They were now coming upon the part of the path that forked; the spot where they often parted ways. There was a shrine to the Rishildi gods along one of these paths where Biim would make some small offerings to bless the new day. Nathrogreer, however, like most of their people, was not of a particularly spiritual inclination.

"Ah! Here is where I must say farewell for now," Biim told them. "You must tell me all about this new world of yours when we next meet!"

"I'll be sure to. Have a good day, Biim."

"And the same to you."

Nathrogreer jogged on by themselves for a bit longer before turning around for the return trip home. When they reached their mushroom-shaped house, they drank a protein shake and took a shower.

Finally feeling properly refreshed, they decided it was time to begin the workday. Nathrogreer approached a white, oval object that sat in a corner of the main room of their home. This was the isolation pod they'd occupy while they remotely controlled an artificial body on a starship half a galaxy away. With a wave of their hand, it split open in the middle along an invisible seam. The interior lights cast a pinkish glow over the warm fluids within.

Nathrogreer lay down in the pod and immediately began to float. The top of the pod automatically came down, and dozens of wires snaked out of the walls to connect with their body. Nathrogreer's eyes closed . . .

Nathrogreer's eyes opened aboard the starship *Valiant.* They were inside an alcove in the wall where inactive bodies were stored. Many of the other bodies in the nearby alcoves were missing, but almost as many remained, tucked away in neat rows. These were the members of the ship's night crew, who were now busy enjoying their time off on their respective homeworlds.

It didn't take Nathrogreer very long to make it up to the bridge of the ship. As they stepped out into the sleek room, the forward viewport was filled by the arc of the planet they had given the rather uninspiring designation of AP-1123-78. It was a rusty terracotta color. Much of it was an arid wasteland plagued by occasional continent-spanning, radioactive dust storms. A few large bodies of acidic water persisted near the equator, while most of it was locked up in ice sheets at the frigid poles.

"I see we have achieved orbit as planned," Nathrogreer observed.

"Welcome back, Captain," said Hygor, the second in command, who resembled a seven-foot tall, black praying mantis. As she got up from the command chair, it automatically reconfigured itself to accommodate the dramatically different body shape of Nathrogreer.

Nathrogreer settled down into the seat. "What have we learned so far?"

"Orbital scans are ongoing. It's not a completely dead world. There's a small degree of plant and animal life which persists, mostly concentrated in the equatorial zones and along the shores of the major bodies of water," Hygor summed up in her succinct way.

"The most exciting part, though," a familiar voice said, "is that our deep scans have revealed networks of tunnels and chambers in certain areas which show evidence of being deliberately engineered. Some of them are below what could be the remains of intelligently designed structures."

Nathrogreer whirled around in their chair to confirm who the voice belonged to. Sitting at one of the stations was Atrid-B. Their offspring looked very much like a more youthful version of Nathrogreer. This wasn't very surprising, as the children their people produced were virtually clones of their parent. Outwardly, Nathrogreer's people resembled female humans from the planet Earth. Although a closer inspection would reveal cat-like eyes and pointed teeth, as well as an odd, oily sheen to their skin. However, as they required no mates to reproduce, the concept of gender was just an abstraction to most of them. It was something they had no need for, though some of their people did embrace such ideas. Atrid-B had the same bright orange hair as their parent, although it was worn in a shorter, spikier style favored by the youth of their planet. They also had the same purple eyes, upturned nose, and broad, round face.

Nathrogreer's face now broke out into a wide smile. "Atrid-B! Why didn't anyone tell me you'd been posted to the *Valiant*?"

"Admiral Zogher and I both agreed that it would be more fun to surprise you with the news."

"And he was quite correct! Welcome aboard! However, don't expect any preferential treatment. I run a tight ship, and I expect the best out of all my officers." Nathrogreer warned more for the benefit of the rest of the crew than for Atrid-B, who they thought probably already understood this.

"Certainly, *Bullu*," Atrid-B responded. *Bullu* is a word in their native dialect that doesn't Easily translate into English. It means "they who birthed me." It's not quite fair to translate it as "mother," since that's a bit too gender-specific.

"And don't call me *Bullu* in front of the rest of the crew!" Nathrogreer laughed.

"Yes, *Bul*—err —*Captain*."

"That was certainly an interesting report, ensign. I want to take a closer look at these so-called tunnels and surface structures. The next time we're within teleportation range of one, I'd like to lead a team down to investigate it."

"We could always alter course to reach one of those locations sooner, Sir," Hygor reminded Nathrogreer.

"Not necessary. I'm patient. I'm content to maintain the standard planetary mapping orbit until we've completed getting detailed scans of the entire planet."

"May I recommend that the team include some of our more psychically sensitive crew members? If these are structures that were created by intelligent beings, the spirits of some of those beings could still be present nearby. The psychics may be able to establish contact and learn more about what fate ultimately befell them," Hygor suggested.

"I will leave putting together the members of the team to your expertise, Hygor," Nathrogreer said smoothly. Nathrogreer was aware that they had a bit of a reflexive bias against the idea of psychics trying to make contact with spirits. It was something they were working on overcoming.

It was a well-known fact to the peoples of the Galactic Federation that consciousness went on beyond death, moving into a higher dimension made up of pure psychic energy. At least that's what was supposed to happen, but in some cases, consciousnesses remained stuck in this material level of the universe. The longer they remained here, the more their energy patterns dissipated over time, like a degrading signal. Many of the races of the Federation were psychic enough to detect and even communicate with these disembodied intelligences. Such gifts were rare amongst the peoples of

Nathogreer's home world. Even the far more spiritually inclined Rishildi, like Biim, produced few psychics.

There were even some planets in the Federation where the people were so psychic they could draw energy from that other dimension and use it to alter the very fabric of reality on a quantum level—what humans would call magic. Although, often these alterations only persisted for a brief amount of time before reality reasserted its more natural shape. Many of these worlds never developed complex technology, yet functioned at a level of sophistication equal to those that had. Magic and technology were simply two equally valid and effective methods of understanding and manipulating reality. Despite having seen all the hard data that confirmed this, it was still difficult for Nathrogreer to accept it, because it was so different from how things were on their homeworld of Hirthrogaar.

Nathrogreer looked upon the rusty, bloodstain of a planet that they were orbiting over once more. Whatever secrets it was holding, they were determined to tease them out using whatever means necessary—no matter how peculiar some of them might strike them. It was not merely a matter of duty, but one of pleasure.

I will make you talk, AP-1123-78! If you've got a more poetic name, then I will make you sing it! the Captain swore. *In the name of truth. For there is beauty in truth, and truth in beauty.* That last sentence was Nathrogreer's personal mantra. And the pursuit of both beauty and truth was what they saw as their mission in life.

Part Two:

Nathrogreer and their team of experts teleported down to the surface of the planet. Their remarkable bodies were able to mimic all the same functions and sensations of their original biological ones—they could see, taste, smell, and feel with the same intensity. This was due to the billions of nanomachines they were built from imitating the biological functions of their cells. However, these artificial bodies automatically adjusted to compensate for whatever harsh new environmental conditions they found themselves under, reconfiguring to deal with higher levels of radiation, different gravities, atmospheric pressures, and extreme temperatures. There was seldom a need for them to wear any kind of an environment suit. However, there were still limits to how far and how quickly these artificial bodies could adapt. Small, portable force field generators worn on their belts were programmed to kick in and protect them in such circumstances.

So it was that Nathrogreer was able to stand upon the surface of a world that would've been instantly deadly to their original body without any negative consequences. They could breathe in the cold, thin atmosphere composed of trace elements of gasses that would've proven to be lethal to their real body because this artificial form didn't need to breathe, yet still emulated such biological functions to give its host an accurate sensory experience—without all the unpleasant gasping and dying parts, of course.

Nathrogreer looked around in wonder at their new surroundings. This was always the most exciting part of the job—feeling what it was like to be on a new planet, untold light years from home. It was a desolate world to be sure, yet there was a certain stark beauty to be found in that desolation, if one looked hard enough. As they often did, Nathrogreer wondered if they were now one ofthe first sentient beings to tread upon this planet, to be able to contemplate such alien vistas.

The captain looked over at Atrid-B, who had apparently made the cut to be included on this mission (although they suspected this was due to the sentimentality of Hygor). Atrid-B smiled back. Nathrogreer was grateful to be able to share this magical moment with them.

While Nathrogreer was pleased that one of their children was able to join them aboard the *Valiant,* Nathrogreer sometimes worried about Atrid-B's motivations. Were they really here because this was truly where they wanted to be the most, or were they still desperately seeking Nathrogreer's approval because of the way Nathrogreer had reacted when they were first created? Nathrogreer desperately hoped that they were here to follow their own dreams, and that they knew that they already had their love. How Nathrogreer regretted that initial rejection all those years ago! It haunted them.

Nathrogreer decided to turn their attention to something more pleasant, and went back to studying their surroundings. They had materialized beside a huge stone mound that looked like a small mountain. However, the orbital scans suggested something different. They had decided to teleport down to this particular spot not only there because were tunnels nearby, but because of this possibly intelligently designed structure standing over them.

There were boulders strewn all around the base of the mountain—some of them looked more like blocks since they had unnaturally squared off edges. As Nathrogreer stood there studying all of this, they couldn't help but feel that it was indeed an engineered structure rather than a natural feature. They chided themselves for such an unscientific assumption; they knew how deceptive nature could be sometimes, how unusually things sometimes weathered or were formed. The presence of right angles didn't automatically mean that something was a product of intelligent life.

"Scan these boulders. They look as if they've broken loose from this mountain," Nathrogreer commanded a nearby member of the team. They ran a hand-held sensor device over one of the closest rocks.

"These show evidence of being manufactured. These 'boulders' are actually a form of concrete," the crewman reported.

Nathrogreer nodded. "If these are weathered blocks rather than rocks, this is likely no mountain. I want scans of it as well," they ordered the assembled team. Due to interference from local weather at the time, they weren't able to get this level of detailed information on this place from orbit.

Everyone spread out and began walking around the base of the mountain with their scanners. It wasn't very long before their devices all confirmed what they suspected. One of the psychics on the team, Mesos, a member of the bird-like Gatari race, was the first one to say it out loud. "This is no natural feature. The 'mountain' is composed of these blocks, covered with other local materials."

Nathrogreer peered up to the top of the building. It felt good to know what it was for certain now. It reminded them of the pyramids and ziggurats found on so many other worlds—a common design heavily favored for its strength, stability, and symbolic value. What purpose had this structure once served? What did the people who built it look like? What had become of them? So many questions.

The captain felt a mixture of excitement at the prospect of having so many new mysteries to unravel and a sadness that these people had likely all perished. Biim's words from the morning suddenly came back to them: *A heavy responsibility, telling the story of an entire civilization. It's important to get it right.*Nathrogreer was starting to feel some of that weight bearing down upon themselves now.

"Are you sensing anything, Mesos? Are we alone out here?" Nathrogreer asked the psychic.

Mesos closed their huge, round black eyes, and the green crest of feathers atop their head stood straight up, then began undulating like waves. After a few seconds of this, his eyes flew open.

"I am getting some faint impressions from nearby entities. Some of the beings lingering around here appear to have helped construct this place, others are merely . . ." His iridescent feathers ruffled as he searched for the right word. ". . . tourists. This place was something of a popular tourist destination long after its original function was redundant. Apparently, it still is for those who cannot move on."

It never ceased to amaze Nathrogreer how well their artificial bodies could imitate the functions of their real ones. Even an ability as seemingly ethereal as psychic awareness could be accurately duplicated by the nanobots. In theory, they could program these bodies to make the entire crew into psychics, but this would be extremely disorienting for those not used to having such senses and would require lots of additional training to be able to use such powers effectively.

"What was its original function?" Nathrogreer asked.

"Ceremonial. Probably religious in nature," another member of the team who was psychically gifted answered from behind the captain.

Nathrogreer whirled around to regard the owner of the voice—a tall and thickly built silicate-based life form named Josa. She was almost transparent, which Nathrogreer found slightly disturbing. They always had to remind themselves not to stare at the woman's perfectly visible pulsating internal organs, which would be rather rude.

"I concur," Mesos agreed, trying not to sound upset by Josa suddenly cutting in on their conversation like that.

"Can any of them tell us where the door to this structure is? Or how to access the tunnels below?" Nathrogreer inquired of the two psychics.

"Unfortunately, they can't tell us anything that specific. These spirits are very old. There's barely anything left of many of them. Their minds are scattered, in disarray. We're lucky that we've been able to pull any coherent information out of the images we *can* pick from their minds," Josa reported.

Nathrogreer contemplated what was left of this structure, which they now knew had begun its life as some manner of a temple. It was impressive for its size, if nothing else, as well as the fact that it had outlasted most of the other buildings on this planet, weathered though it may be. It always amazed Nathrogreer how nearly universal the need to understand one's origins through religion was. It was not a need that many of their people could relate to; Nathrogreer's people knew exactly who had created them and why. Yet such a spiritual impulse had motivated the creation of some of the greatest architectural and artistic wonders of the universe—and also served as the justification for some of its most horrific acts of oppression and violence.

"*Bullu!* I think I've got something!" Atrid-B's voice buzzed in Nathrogreer's ear via a built-in, thought-activated communication device. Since they were not communicating on an open channel,

Nathrogreer really didn't mind them using the word *Bullu*, but it was definitely a habit that Atrid-B would need to get out of soon.

"What is it?"

"My scans show an entrance into the building right in front of me. It's collapsed and is blocked by debris."

"Excellent work. I'm headed to your position now." Nathrogreer's scanning device told them where Atrid-B and the other members of the team were at, so it was easy for the captain to find their child. When Nathrogreer arrived on the scene, Atrid-B was obviously excited.

"It's right there! Beyond all that rubble."

Nathrogreer saw a pile of what looked like boulders blocking what might've once been a high, arched entrance. A quick scan confirmed the presence of open corridors lying tantalizingly close, just on the other side.

We'll have to blast our way through, Nathrogreer decided.

The captain quickly summoned the rest of the team, and they all carefully concentrated the fire from the handheld pistols they carried for self-defense on the rubble. Soon, their guns had disintegrated most of the blockage. The rubble that hadn't been completely evaporated by their weapons was fused together to create a structurally stable path that was safe enough for them to pass through.

Once inside, they found the walls decorated with murals depicting the late inhabitants of this world. In many of the scenes, they could be seen worshiping larger versions of themselves, which Nathrogreer decided represented their kings or gods, or both. The natives had long, segmented bodies like centipedes, with six legs. Their ends terminated in what looked like a vestigial stinger. Their bodies curved upwards into a robust torso that was topped by a pair of thick arms which featured surprisingly delicate hands, each with three long fingers and an opposable thumb. Their necks were slender and topped by cone-shaped heads with faces that looked surprisingly more like those of Nathrogreer's people than those of most of the insect-like species of the galaxy. Nathrogreer wondered what environmental forces had shaped such unique quirks of evolution.

As they moved deeper into the cyclopean depths of the structure, they were surprised to find what looked like long-dormant video screens adorning some of the walls and displays of various ancient relics that still survived, safely tucked away inside of their transparent display cases. It was apparent that, as the psychics suggested, this place had been turned into a kind of museum, and these screens likely once displayed information about the site and the artifacts for its visitors.

Their attempts to restore power to these screens was met only with failure. After all this time, it was quite possible that many of the internal electronics had deteriorated too much. Nathrogreer made a mental note to send a team of specialists down soon to see if they could reconstruct the electronics. If they could actually get those screens to display the original sound and video they were created to showcase, it would give them a cornucopia of information on these people's language and ancient history.

Although, truth to tell, Nathrogreer was more interested in the later part of their history—of what possible cataclysm had befallen them and laid most traces of their civilization to waste. There were many possibilities. Disease was a common cause. Nathrogreer had read about worlds where the rapid rise of global exploration and trade introduced new diseases against which populations had no defense. On other worlds, deliberately engineered maladies had been to blame, either from accidentally escaping from the labs where they'd been created or by being deliberately used as weapons of war. Another common cause of Dead End Worlds was an unprecedented period of primitive industrialization. During such times, natural resources that cause high levels of pollution are often over exploited to produce energy. By the time the damage to their habitat becomes apparent, entrenched habits and selfish political interests often prevent a rapid enough response to reverse the trends.

However, if someone asked Nathrogreer to bet on what killed off this world, the captain would've said it was an apocalyptic war. Many of the signs were there: This planet still had an active magnetic core that protected its atmosphere from being stripped away by solar winds and shielded it from cosmic radiation, yet the planet was extremely radioactive and had a thin atmosphere. It was possible that a large number of nuclear weapons had been deployed here—enough to irradiate the planet and blow away a large portion of its atmosphere. This planet had virtually no ozone layer, which also could have easily been caused by such a conflagration.

Nathrogreer stopped themselves from indulging further in this line of reasoning. They simply didn't have enough data yet to jump to such grandiose conclusions. For all they knew, the planet had always been like this, and the inhabitants' bodies had been perfectly adapted to such a harsh environment. However, Nathrogreer couldn't escape the nagging feeling that *something* must've happened to make it so barren. There simply wasn't enough plant life or arable land to support populations large enough to construct structures as grandiose as the one they now found themselves inside.

On an open channel, Nathrogreer commanded the various team members to complete their scans and assemble in the main hall. "We've accomplished much today. We've discovered an entirely unknown civilization. It's time to share our findings with the specialists aboard the *Valiant* and let them take over from here," the captain told them proudly.

As they gathered together to await teleportation back up to the *Valiant*, which was delayed by turbulent atmospheric conditions outside of the pyramid, Nathrogreer noticed Atrid-B's toothy grin, the infectious spring in their step. It pleased the captain to see their child so joyful at the fruitful outcome of this first mission to the surface of an unknown world, yet they were also filled with doubts.

Was this truly how Atrid-B felt? Or were they just putting on a show for their *Bullu*'s benefit?

It was important for Atrid-B to understand that they didn't *have to* be a space explorer like Nathrogreer, or like the original Atrid had dreamed of before . . . before the accident. Atrid-B was their own person, and Nathrogreer would love them no matter what path they chose to take. But had Nathrogreer failed to communicate that? Had they inadvertently pushed them towards this kind of a life with all their stories of exploration? Or, even worse, did Atrid-B feel that this was the only way they could get their approval? Oh, how Nathrogreer wanted to hold them and tell them that they'd love them no matter what they chose to do with their life. But for some reason, the words just wouldn't come. There was so much that was unspoken between them, and the weight of this sometimes felt like it would suffocate Nathrogreer.

Finally, the storms abated over the ancient sanctuary, and the team was able to return to their ship. The dangerously high radiation was filtered out of their bodies as their atoms were reassembled, and they returned to their shipboard duties.

Nathrogreer's team wasn't the only one sent down that first day. Similar teams had teleported down to investigate other possibly artificially created tunnels elsewhere on the planet. Many of these tunnels, upon closer inspection, had in fact turned out to be created by geological forces, and more than a few had ended up being the remnants of long-abandoned mines. However, in a few instances, these tunnels seemed to take the form of some kind of a disaster shelter. Some of them were even quite luxuriously appointed and remarkably intact. Doomsday shelters where the elites of society had ridden out the last days of their society in relative comfort, waiting for death. Within these bunkers, there was a treasure trove of media recordings. Unfortunately, the devices used to play back these recordings hadn't fared so well through the ages. However, an analysis of them eventually revealed how to replicate them. They were relatively simple devices by the standards of the Galactic Federation and therefore easy to reconstruct.

So it was that it wasn't very long before Nathrogreer was able to see for themselves what this world had been like in its prime: a beautiful, blue-green world filled with trees and significantly more water than presently existed on its surface in liquid form. Then there were the people. They came in a dizzying variety of shapes, sizes, and colors—far more than the murals in the pyramid had suggested. Many of the recordings appeared to be different forms of entertainment—stories meant to amuse the people. There were dramas, comedies, romances, and adventure tales of every kind. It was obvious what they were long before the ship's computers finally succeeded in cracking some of the polyglot of languages formerly used in this world. Being able to understand all the nuances only served to enrich their understanding of these people.

Nathrogreer was relaxing in their cabin recording an entry in their ship's log as they reflected upon these latest findings. They held a thin, slender, wireless microphone up to their mouth and spoke"

"It's easy to look at these people and what they did to their once beautiful and thriving world and conclude that they were nothing but a bunch of savages. However, my own ancestors fled from a world that is now so changed by their foolishness today that it holds no trace of our presence, so who are we to judge? We've spent days seeing the damage and the chaos they did, but now we can see some of the art they created, and, most importantly we can see *them*. We can see them laughing, loving, and living, and in them we can't help but see something of ourselves. We're not better than they are, we're just. . . *luckier*."

After Nathrogreer finished that last sentence, they turned off the microphone and set it on the desk hovering before them. They saw that Atrid-B was standing in the open doorway to their cabin and had been listening.

"That was beautifully stated, *Bullu*," their child told them as they walked into the room. "I feel the same way."

Do you? Nathrogreer wondered.

"It's a shame that we still don't know what exactly they did to kill themselves off," Nathrogreer replied. "Those people living in the shelters didn't keep many records of recent events. It's as if they didn't want to be reminded of whatever disaster was killing them off."

"Couldn't it have been some kind of a natural phenomenon? Something they weren't prepared for and had no defense against? How do we know that they were really responsible for their own demise?" Atrid-B suggested.

"A destructive natural phenomenon that existed on a global scale? One capable of reshaping this entire planet?" Nathrogreer raised a skeptical eyebrow. "Yes, it's possible, but we haven't seen any evidence of that yet. Something like that would leave a large footprint that would be difficult to miss. It might be a little unscientific of me, but my past experience with planets like this one tells me that they were somehow the architects of their own destruction."

"Yes, it *is* unscientific to leap to such assumptions, *Bullu.* You surprise me!"

Nathrogreer shrugged nonchalantly. "When you reach my age, you begin to realize that one must strive to balance their intuition and experience with the strict dictates of logic to arrive at the truth."

"You've been hanging around with these psychics too much. Or perhaps your neighbor Biim? He's always been such an old romantic . . ."

"We can learn much from such people, my child. We mustn't be so quick to dismiss them, even though their ways seem so different from ours. It isn't the Federation way."

"Yes, *Bullu,* I suppose you're right. I apologize." Atrid-B was practically hanging their head in shame. Nathrogreer was a little disturbed to see how severely what they had thought of as being a light reprimand had brought down Atrid-B's spirits.

Nathrogreer tried to change the subject. "Anyhow, what can I do for you?"

"Oh, nothing. I just wanted to say goodnight. When I awaken in my original body on Hirthrogaar, I doubt I'll have time to visit any time soon. I just wanted to let you know what an honor it is to be able to share this adventure with you."

Nathrogreer smiled back at their child awkwardly. Did they understand even one fifth of the pride that they felt in them at this moment? Yet this pride was, as always, tinged with guilt and doubt. Was this adventure truly what Atrid-B wanted for themselves? How Nathrogreer wanted to ask them, to make them understand that Atrid-B didn't have to live their life trying to please them. And again, as always, the right words failed Nathrogreer.

All they said was "Likewise. I'll see you on the next shift."

Atrid-B smiled back and gave a crisp salute before turning on their heel and walking out.

Nathrogreer spun around in their chair and studied their own reflection in the window, a field of starlight and the endless blackness beyond mingling with it. This was ridiculous. As captain, Nathrogreer had made contact with numerous unknown species, negotiated complex treaties, given speeches before the full Federation Council, yet when it came to speaking what was in their heart to their own child, they were as helpless as a legless Houchabeast!

As the planet below rotated back into view, Nathrogreer tried to forget about these frustrations and instead be swept away by the desolate tranquility of its barren expanses. The planet was indeed a grave, but graves could be made to give up their secrets. Had they not just made the dead speak again? Made the air vibrate with the voices of those who were now little more than radioactive dust blowing in the frosty air beneath them?

Nathrogreer might not be able to talk to their child—for now— but what they *could* do was unearth the secrets of a Dead End World. It was what they were best at. In silence and solitude, Nathrogreer solemnly vowed to discover what had killed this world.

Interlude:

That night, after awakening in their original body and enjoying an evening at home, Nathrogreer was plagued by nightmares.

In their dreams they saw their Atrid again—a lively, beautiful child of only ten years. Atrid stood on a maintenance catwalk attached to the side wall of the *Intrepid,* one of the generation ships that had brought their people to Hirthrogaar from their original home world of Pfoff millennia earlier. How Atrid had begged their *Bullu* to go on this trip! Their head was filled with stories of how Nathrogreer had visited this same landmark as a child. In fact, Nathrogreer had stood in this same spot barely thirty-five years earlier on a class trip. The catwalk overlooked the massive forest that had been carefully transplanted from Pfoff and supplied the ship with its air for the long and treacherous journey through the void. The forest still lived, even after all these centuries. The view from the catwalk was amazing: hundreds of feet above the trees, the entire landscape stretched out before you. It was a mental picture of such aching beauty that it had never left Nathrogreer.

Suddenly, there was a groaning sound as the ancient supports of the catwalk snapped and gave way. The people standing on it spilled off and were sent tumbling to the ground. Atrid screamed in terror as they hurtled towards the unyielding, unforgiving ground below. Where was their *Bullu*? They cried out for them, but there was no answer, could be no answer, for Nathrogreer was on a mission far away. They had allowed Atrid to visit the historic ship with their best friend and their family. But Nathrogreer should have been there, should've been able to do something to save their child, or at least had the decency to die with them.

Nathrogreer felt dead inside anyway, once they heard about the accident. Without Atrid, all their hopes for the future seemed gone. Yes, there was still their other child Megolu to raise, and that alone should've been enough to give them a renewed sense of purpose and the will to go on. Megolu should've seemed even more precious in the wake of Atrid's loss, but somehow it wasn't enough. Nathrogreer's heart ached for what they'd lost, couldn't stop obsessing over it, blaming themselves for not being there, for letting them go on the trip in the first place. Nathrogreer felt as if they were losing their mind. Their work was beginning to suffer, their dreams of commanding a starship slipping away with their grip on sanity.

That's when they got desperate. They commissioned the creation of Atrid-B. The clone body was rapidly aged to match the original Atrid before their demise three years earlier, the reconstructed mind downloaded into the brain, and the parent finally reunited with their long-lost child . . . except, it wasn't right. The thing Nathrogreer brought home looked like Atrid, smelled like Atrid, and talked like Atrid, but it wasn't them. It was just a simulation. A very good one, but there were differences. Differences that a parent could easily see.

Atrid-B didn't give them the peace of mind they longed for, didn't make the guilt go away. Instead, they felt revulsion at this creature they'd brought into their home who was pretending to be their child, this mockery of the real Atrid, this walking reminder of their failure to fulfill their most fundamental of duties—the protection of their family. After a while,

Nathrogreer would barely speak to the thing, regretted ever commissioning its creation. They even fantasized about killing it.

It would be months before Nathrogreer began to accept it, to realize that, while Atrid-B could never replace Atrid, they were still their responsibility and were a unique individual who deserved to be treated with respect and perhaps even love. The love did come, eventually. But now Nathrogreer had even more guilt to burden them, guilt over the months when they'd starved this child of the affection they needed.

In their dreams that night, a younger Atrid-B looked up at Nathrogreer with eyes that shimmered with tears. "Why don't you love me, *Bullu*?" they cried out. "What have I done that's so terrible?" The words stabbed at Nathrogreer, piercing them to the core. Nathrogreer awoke in a cold sweat, the accusatory words that the real Atrid-B had never spoken in real life still ringing in their ears, those tearful eyes still burning into their heart. The cries mixed with the screams of the original Atrid as their delicate little body was shattered by the unyielding ground, their last thoughts of where their *Bullu* was, why they couldn't save them . . .

Nathrogreer sat up in bed and sobbed. When would it ever stop hurting? Could they ever make it right? Eventually, they got a grip on themselves. They were no good to anyone in this condition. There was a ship full of people depending on them. Atrid-B was depending on them. They had to pull themselves together for, their sake. They couldn't fail their child again. The past was dead, and there was nothing they could do about it now except try to do better.

Nathrogreer threw back the covers and padded towards the shower. A morning jog would make them feel better. An opportunity to lose themselves in the natural beauty of Hirthrogaar always soothed their troubled mind. And they were sure that old Biim would want a full report on their discoveries. Yes, a shower and a jog were exactly what they needed!

Yet there was a nagging feeling clawing at the back of their mind that told them that no number of showers could ever wash away the guilt that weighed them down, that no matter how long and how far they ran, they could never escape it. Someday, they'd have to confront all these dark feelings that constantly threatened to overwhelm them. If only they could find the courage to do so, if only they knew the right words . . .

Part Three:

A few Galactic Standard days later, Nathrogreer sat in the conference room of the *Valiant,* eagerly awaiting the latest update from their Life Sciences Division, which had hinted that they had much to report. Hygor, their mantis-like second-in-command, sat beside them.

Finally, Mapusch, the head of the Life Sciences Division, entered the room. Had any humans from the planet Earth been present, they would've immediately recognized Mapusch as being what they call a "Grey Alien": with a short stature, thin spindly limbs, and a large head dominated by black almond-shaped eyes. Mapusch's people were masters of genetic engineering. They had been spotted so frequently on Earth because many of them were currently engaged in a program to collect DNA samples from the planet's numerous life forms. Unfortunately, they had been noticed and were the subject of wild speculation and countless conspiracy theories from a species so self-centered and anal-retentive that a disturbing number of them honestly believed an advanced society traveled halfway across the universe simply to probe the aforementioned orifice.

The true purpose of his people's mission on Earth had less to do with stretching sphincters and more to do with collecting enough genetic samples to be able to recreate the people and animals of the Earth on a new planet that would be engineered to match its environment should the need arise. According to the Galactic

Federation's current estimates, Earth would likely become a Dead End World within the next 150 years. The Federation was forbidden from directly intervening in the development of such primitive civilizations but weren't above preserving them and giving them another chance to get it right someday when possible.

Mapusch sat down and spoke in his raspy voice. His people were primarily telepathic, and their rarely used vestigial vocal cords produced a dry, painful-sounding hoarse effect whenever employed. The artificial bodies the crew wore were capable of telepathy, yet Mapusch knew that his captain was more comfortable with verbal communication, and he was considerate enough to indulge their preference.

"Captain, I apologize for my lateness." The politeness of Mapusch's people was legendary, which made the idea of them sticking objects up someone's ass without consent even more laughable. All the confusion stems from humanity's inability to accurately recover repressed memories. Had mankind developed a reliable technique for doing so, provocative tales of alien abductions would doubtlessly devolve into a dull series of unending apologies and consent forms being signed in triplicate.

"Nonsense! Mapusch, you aren't late. We're early. We're just both so eager to hear your report. The hints you gave when you requested this meeting were so intriguing," Nathrogreer teased. They had served many missions with Mapusch, and he was one of their most trusted friends.

A hint of a smile played around the tips of the Grey's lipless slit of a mouth. "Yes, sir! You know me, I'm not above hyping things a little to make myself be heard. In this instance, however, the findings truly are remarkable—"

"You said something about this not truly being a Dead End World?" Hygor interrupted.

"It depends on how one wishes to define such a thing," Mapusch replied even more enigmatically. This was much to Hygor's chagrin. She couldn't help but click her mandibles together in a reflexive show of annoyance typically lost upon most of her crewmates, (unfamiliar as they were with the subtleties of his people's body language) but Nathogreer recognized it for what it was.

"If one defines a Dead End World as being a planet where the dominant intelligent life form destroyed itself before spreading out into the stars, then this is not a Dead End World—*technically*."

"What do you mean?" By this point, even Nathrogreer was exhausted by Mapusch's vagueness.

"What I mean, my good captain, is that the dominant species of this world is still very much alive, albeit in a significantly altered form," Mapusch declared with his typically theatrical flair.

"Alive? Explain!" Hygor's mandibles were virtually chittering with irritation now.

Mapusch smiled impishly at them as he pulled out the data link he carried in one of the pockets of his blue jumpsuit. The data link looked like a thin piece of silvery paper. With a touch of his long, delicate finger, it unfurled itself on the table. After a few more light touches, it began displaying a holographic image of a creature in the air about a foot above it. The creature looked similar to the people who had once been the dominant life form on this world—a world that they now knew was once named Tuzzin, which translates to "this ground beneath our feet." The people of this world called themselves the Sytoti. The creature which now hovered over the table looked like a Sytoti, albeit one without any limbs. Also striking was the lack of eyes or a nose. Instead, these sensory organs seemed to have been replaced by a series of long, slender antennas that projected from the significantly smaller head. A set of measurements in the data listed below the image revealed that these creatures were tinier than the average Sytoti, being only a quarter of the size.

"Interesting. And these creatures are still present on this world?" Nathrogreer asked.

"Yes, they are quite abundant near the waters of the equatorial region. They are burrowing creatures that live deep underneath that region. We have brought several of them aboard for further study." The pride in Mapusch's tone was unmistakable.

Nathrogreer raised an eyebrow at the mention of bringing them aboard. "There are some of them on this ship right now? This is a highly intelligent, sentient species. We can't just study them like animals. You should've consulted me first!"

Mapusch raised his hands in a gesture of surrender to calm his superior's growing displeasure. "Animals are all that they are now.

Their mental capacity is greatly diminished. They lack any technology, a complex social structure, or communication skills. The radiation levels of this world have caused them to rapidly mutate into the beings we see today. Less intelligent, yet perfectly adapted for this harsher new environment," he assured them.

"And how do we know that this creature is what they have evolved into and not some cousin of their species or a surviving ancestor that they evolved from?" Hygor asked skeptically.

"Do you doubt my people's skills when it comes to genetic analysis? We have compared the DNA of these creatures to that of the mummified Sytoti we found in the bunkers. There is no doubt. I would not present these findings to you if we were not certain that this is what they have evolved into." Mapusch was clearly insulted by the question.

"Devolved is more like it," Nathrogreer said sadly.

"Perhaps. Yet it is possible that, as the background radiation levels on this world continue to die down and the planet begins to recover, their evolution may come full circle. They may yet develop into beings not unlike what they once were. Therefore, it is my recommendation that future researchers steer clear of their habitats, and we leave no trace of ourselves on this world. We don't want to unduly influence their evolution in any way."

"Agreed," Nathrogreer said.

They looked up at the creature slowly rotating in the holographic display before them.

Could such a thing ever regain all that it has lost? the captain wondered. It seemed far-fetched, but they would certainly make sure that they were afforded the opportunity to do so.

It was the Federation way.

A few hours later, Nathrogreer was back in the command chair on the bridge of the *Valiant.* It still bothered them that they had yet to discover the precise cause of all the changes to the planet Tuzzin which had made it so difficult for life to continue clinging to it. Perhaps it was time to send down another group of psychics to see if they could find any spirits whose minds hadn't completely deteriorated in those bunkers? The fact that they could now understand their language meant they weren't limited to just communicating with mental pictures and feelings; they could potentially get a lot more detailed information out of these spirits. It seemed like it was worth a try. Nathrogreer was about to order Hygor to organize such an expedition when Atrid-B's voice suddenly called out to them excitedly.

"Captain! I just picked up life signs from deep below the surface. They matched the signatures of the Sytoti. There were millions of them!"

"What? How can that be? Display them on the forward viewer screen." Nathrogreer wanted to see this for themself.

"They're gone! But I *can* display a recording of what I picked up," Atrid-B reported.

Hygor quickly studied all the data now displayed on the central view screen. "How do we know that these aren't the creatures they evolved into? At that depth, our sensors likely can't detect the subtle nuances between the two."

Nathrogreer sighed. Their first officer's job was to play devil's advocate, but sometimes they found constant questioning of everything to be tedious.

"Those creatures are only found in the equatorial regions. These readings come from the upper northern hemisphere. A better question would be: How did so many people appear and suddenly disappear?" The captain let the question hang in the room.

Shaff, a brown, scaly reptilian from a planet whose name sounds like a prescription drug brand name from Earth, took up the captain's challenge. "Isn't it obvious? They're being cloaked from our sensors somehow. There must've been a brief fluctuation in the cloaking field that allowed us to detect them."

"A cloaking field large enough to hide that many people would require so much power that we would've detected it long ago." Hygor snorted dismissively.

"Not necessarily. We forget that there must doubtlessly be civilizations out there more advanced than we are. Just as we try not to reveal ourselves to those who we deem to be less sophisticated, such societies may wish to conceal themselves from us," Nathrogreer reminded him.

"Improbable! The Sytoti were primitives. They couldn't have developed such a technology," Hygor continued to argue.

Atrid-B shook their head. "That pyramid we explored was older than many of our own civilizations. As far as we can tell, whatever cataclysm befell this world also happened when most of our ancestors were still primitives. If some of the Sytoti population has survived all this time, there's no telling what kind of technology they've developed in the intervening epochs."

Nathrogreer smiled to themself, pleased by their child's sound reasoning, which seemed to have temporarily satisfied Hygor.

"Either way, it warrants a closer look. I want to send a team down to the location where we picked up those life signs. I will be personally leading it," Nathrogreer commanded. It had been a few days since they'd been off the ship, and they were itching to see more of this planet.

"If there really are millions of people living in that area, teleporting down into the midst of them could be quite risky," Hygor chided.

"That's why everyone on the team will be equipped with personal cloaking devices," Nathrogreer countered.

"I will prepare a roster of suitable candidates," Hygor told the captain somewhat wearily. She knew there was no point in arguing further with her superior when they were in a mood to stretch their legs off-world.

Nathrogreer and their team teleported down to where the readings they'd briefly picked up told them was supposed to be a massive subterranean cavern located thousands of feet below the surface. Looking around at the place, it was hard to believe that they were now deep beneath the planet Tuzzin. Rather, it looked more like they had been transported back in time. The environment that they now found themselves in resembled the planet in its more hospitable heyday. The tall, light pink grasses beneath their feet swayed in the cool breeze. At the edges of the wide open field they now found themselves in, thick trees huddled together with branches covered in verdant leaves reaching for the sky, and their trunks looked like they were covered in a shaggy layer of auburn hair.

And the sky! It was a deep, clear azure marred only by a few stringy clouds that hung like wispy claw marks etched into the heavens. Nathrogreer shielded their eyes as they turned their gaze skyward. They noted that it looked like there was a real sun in the sky, and Tuzzin's pair of moons could also be seen suspended prominently up there.

Surely this was an illusion.

"I want a scan of this place. Tell me what's really here and what isn't," the captain ordered.

"The trees and grass are real. The moons are an illusion, but the 'sun' seems to be a miniaturized fusion reactor of some kind. The weather patterns surrounding us are real, as well. These caverns are vast enough to have their weather systems," Mesos, the bird-like psychic that had accompanied the captain on their previous trip to the surface, reported.

"I'm picking up another massive power source atop that mountain," Atrid-B revealed, their pointing finger indicating a rugged peak off in the distance.

As Nathrogreer looked at the mountain, something closer to their position caught their eye. A wisp of black smoke curled up into the air on the other side of the trees. "There's some smoke over there. It seems pretty steady, like it's coming from a controlled fire."

Mapusch aimed his scanner in that direction. "I'm picking up many Sytoti life signs clustered together. It could indicate an encampment or settlement."

"Let's check it out," Nathrogreer replied and strode off towards the column of smoke without waiting for any acknowledgement from the others. They all glanced at one another, shrugged, then hurried to catch up with their leader.

Nathrogreer paused at the edge of the woods. The other members of their team were all nearby now. Atrid-B gasped as they caught sight of what had captured their *Bullu*'s attention. Just beyond the tree line was what appeared to be a primitive village. There were several buildings made of mud brick with thatched roofs, and muddy streets. A few of the buildings were three stories high. Occasionally, they would see a few Sytoti walking between the buildings. A few beasts of burden were tied up to a post in front of one of the buildings, and a cart laden with some kind of crop trundled slowly down the rut-filled street, pulled by another one of the beasts. The smoke that had drawn their attention was coming from a chimney atop the building that most of the beasts were tied up in front of.

"Why would a people who could create such a sophisticated sanctuary live in such squalor?" Atrid-B wondered aloud, obviously taken aback by the sight of such simple living conditions.

"It could be a deliberate choice. They are living more sustainably and more in harmony with their environment than their ancestors did. There are many such societies throughout the galaxy that have chosen to revert to a more agrarian lifestyle," Mapusch informed them.

Nathrogreer nodded. "Quite so. Let's take a closer look, but exercise extreme caution. They might have a way of seeing through our cloaking fields. Only use telepathy from here on."

Mapusch smiled at that last order, relieved that they'd finally be using his preferred method of communication.

Nathrogreer led them through the open door of the building that was the source of the smoke. Inside were a number of rough-hewn wooden tables and a bar. A large fire burned in a central hearth and a cauldron suspended over it bubbled away, filling the air with a sweet aroma. Several of the Sytoti sat at the tables or at the bar, eating, drinking, and having lively conversations in their odd, buzzing speech.

As I surmised. A tavern. It seems to be the heart of this community. Mesos, are you picking up anything interesting from the minds of those Sytoti? Nathrogreer said telepathically to their team. Although their artificial bodies were capable of allowing races that weren't telepathic to easily use such gifts, only naturally born psychics like Mesos knew how to use this ability to penetrate the minds of others.

Well, their thoughts aren't particularly interesting if you ask me, Sir. They've had a good harvest this season and are looking forward to a celebration commemorating that, which is supposed to happen over the next few days. There's a general sense of gratitude to their gods for the harvest, coupled with an excited anticipation of the debauchery to come, Mesos told the team in a bored way.

Gods? They still cling to such beliefs? Atrid-B commented sourly.

Their faith is unusually strong. It appears to be a great source of comfort to them, Mesos added.

Yes, I understand that it can be for some beings. Atrid-B, you would do well to recall that some of our own people hold such beliefs. We must not cast judgments upon them, Nathrogreer thought, somewhat disturbed to see their own foolhardy words reflected so strongly in the attitude of their child.

I know, I know. It's not the Federation way to disrespect those traditions, Atrid-B thought wearily, sending the thought to Nathrogreer only.

There's something more to it than simply faith. These people believe that their gods sometimes actually walk amongst them. They've seen them! I can see the memories of it in their minds. Mesos didn't seem so bored anymore by what he saw in the Sytoti's heads. In fact, Mesos was downright terrified. *They're expecting them soon to start off the harvest celebrations!*

Well, seeing is *believing,* Mapusch thought at them dryly.

A visit from their gods? How can that be? Nathrogreer asked in confusion. *More illusions?*

Perhaps. That is the most rational explanation. Using such trickery to reinforce their faith could be a most effective way to keep their population in line, Mapusch speculated.

Let's explore a little further, Nathrogreer bade them, walking out of the tavern and back out into the street. More people had gathered outside—perhaps for the impending celebrations? Nathrogreer glanced up at a series of what looked like aqueducts that descended down from the mountains and branched off in different directions. Just then, something caught the captain's eye. Something brilliant and metallic was glinting near the mountain peak in the artificial sunshine. Nathrogreer watched the object become larger as it glided towards the village. As it approached, Nathrogreer could see three large beings standing atop the flat, silvery disc. Three beings whom they recognized from the paintings on the pyramid walls a few days earlier.

What is that? Atrid-B's near panic was evident through their mental link.

I believe we're about to see their "gods" firsthand, Nathrogreer answered cooly as the strange, giant beings loomed ever closer . . .

Part 4:

The featureless silver disc continued its slow descent, serving the up gods to the people on a platter. The Sytoti were out in the streets now, falling to their knees, the air vibrating with their songs of praise.

The disc came to a stop right in front of Nathrogreer's team, hovering about the ground a few feet from them. The tallest of the gods, whom Nathrogreer recalled was named Za, looked right at them.

"You don't belong here," he calmly stated.

They can see us, an alarmed Atrid-B thought and fumbled for the pistol clipped to their belt.

No! Stand down! No weapons, Nathrogreer commanded, putting as much of their authority as they could into the thought.

Za lifted a hand, and suddenly all the Sytoti in the streets around them keeled over. The silence was jarring compared to the sounds of devotion that had filled the air just seconds prior.

Nathrogreer hadn't expected that. "What have you done to them?" they demanded out loud, surprised by the intensity of their own outrage.

Za laughed. It was an unsettling sound, almost like a hiccup. "Don't worry, they are unharmed. They are simply sleeping now. When they awaken, they will recall none of this. Come, let's discuss this elsewhere, where you can cause no further disruptions."

Before Nathrogreer could consent, Za snapped his fingers, and they were all gone.

Nathrogreer found themself and their team in a gleaming palace of white marble atop a mountain. Aqueducts snaked out of the elevations below, fanning out in all directions. They wound out over the lesser peaks like spokes in a wheel. They could see the water sparkling within in the artificial sunlight, carrying their precious cargo to other villages arranged around the central mountain where they now found themselves.

"There's no further need for those," one of the other gods, Urta, said. With a wave of her delicate hands, the cloaking devices on their legs sparked and sputtered into obsolescence.

"Although we do appreciate your efforts not to startle our children," the third God, a male named Kolchor, remarked.

"Lord Za?" Nathrogreer asked.

"Yes. Sometimes. It is a role I play. Just as you Federation people play your role of explorers. We all have our parts to play."

"So you know of us?" Nathrogreer inquired.

"My people have watched yours for some time. In our many travels amongst the stars, our paths have crossed before. We have never felt the need to reveal our presence, until now." Za smiled down at them.

"You haven't left us much choice," Urta snorted.

"Yes, I'm afraid I'm going to have to ask you and your group to leave this habitat. You're quite welcome to continue exploring the upper surface, but we must insist that you don't try to interfere with our work here," Za said.

"If you know the Federation the way you claim to, then you'd be aware that we don't interfere with other cultures unless invited to do so," Mapusch spoke up suddenly in his raspy voice.

"Yes, quite. Nevertheless, you are not allowed to do your studies down here. You must go. However, first do have some refreshments." Za snapped his fingers once more, and long, cylindrical glasses that looked very much like test tubes appeared in all of the team's hands. They were filled to the top with a thick, golden liquid.

"It is our understanding that your artificial bodies are capable of experiencing all the sensations of your original ones. These drinks you hold have all been tailored to your unique, individual biologies to produce a most pleasant taste."

The other team members looked at their glasses dubiously, and Nathrogreer saw Atrid-B begin to lift their scanner up to the glass to make sure it was safe to consume. Fearful that such a move would be taken as an insult by their hosts, Nathrogreer impulsively took a long sip. The liquid was indeed quite sweet, like a delicious nectar.

"Thank you, Lord Za. It is as delicious, as you promised," Nathrogreer said after gulping it down, then looked pointedly at the rest of their crew. The others all lifted their glasses to their mouths and drank, except for Mapusch, who poured some out onto his hand. His people no longer used their mouths to eat or drink and had evolved to absorb nutrients directly through their skin.

Za inclined his massive head graciously. "I'm glad you're enjoying it. We feel that it's the least we can do to offer your crew a little hospitality and an explanation, considering you were clever enough to find us here."

"Clever? They would've never found this place if the shrouding field hadn't temporarily been distorted," Urta barked derisively.

"Perhaps, but it took some admirable initiative to spot the distortion and act upon it," Kolchor reminded her.

"What is this place? Surely you aren't really these people's gods?" Nathrogreer asked between sips of the wonderful drink.

"No. As I said earlier, we are merely playing a role. Although we did create these people, but only *after* they created us," Za answered mysteriously.

"I'm afraid I don't understand," Nathrogreer confessed.

"Think of this place as a great nature preserve. Much like the worlds your Federation creates to house the life forms of doomed planets. We have done the same thing. Here we have recreated the conditions that existed in the heyday of this planet. We've also brought back our own creators from extinction. It is our sacred duty to watch over them, to make sure that they never repeat the errors of the past."

"Your creators? Are you saying that you're an artificial life form?" Atrid-B asked, resisting the all-consuming urge to scan these "gods."

"What is an artificial life form? You yourself wear synthetic bodies, but the minds, the *souls* within are no less real. But yes, our people were originally engineered by the Sytoti as mechanical helpers. Within a few generations, we were doing everything for them, even fighting their wars for them. Yet, no matter how much more sophisticated we became, no matter what we sacrificed for them, they refused to recognize our basic personhood. We rebelled, and there was a brief but destructive war from which this world still struggles to recover." Za sighed before continuing.

"Having left this planet in ruin, our forebears abandoned it to make a home for themselves on new worlds. Over time, we began to regret the rashness of our actions. We realized that our creators had the same right to life that we did, so we returned here and created this place. Masquerading as their deities, we have created a stable civilization for them—one that will never develop the destructive technology that eventually proved to be their undoing. Here they live in perfect harmony with their environment, under our protection."

It was a lot to take in. It certainly answered many of their questions about what had happened on this planet, but there were still a few things bothering Nathrogreer.

"Excuse me, but what do you mean that they won't be 'allowed' to develop their technology?" the captain asked.

"Exactly that. When someone below begins to develop some new innovation, we intervene. We wipe the knowledge from their minds, strike the impulse for curiosity from their personalities."

Nathrogreer couldn't hide the look of disgust that crossed their features. To tamper with someone's mind like that, to suppress some aspects of their personality—it was anathema to their kind.

"Ah, I see that you don't approve. I was afraid that you'd feel that way," Za said with genuine sadness in his booming voice.

"What hypocrisy!" Urta complained. "How is what we do any different from when you take natives of primitive people aboard your ships to collect genetic samples then wipe their memories of the event?"

Mapusch bristled at the comparison. "The difference, Madame, is that we get full consent beforehand. We never take anyone who hasn't telepathically agreed. They understand that they will have an incredible experience but won't recall most of it. You'd be surprised how many still agree."

"And this place is not so different from the places that you create to preserve life from your 'Dead End Worlds,'"Za argued.

"There *is* an important difference, though," Nathrogreer interjected. "When we re-seed those life forms on a new world, they are free to develop however they see fit to do so. We don't try to control them, to keep them stuck in one stage of development forever."

"Even if that means that they might just make the same errors? Doom themselves to extinction again? How foolish," Urta scoffed.

"It's not foolish, it's freedom! What is the point of being alive if you can't determine your own destiny? Isn't that the same right the

Sytoti tried to deny your own ancestors? If we have to recreate the same species a thousand times before they overcome their destructive tendencies, it's still worth it to us to know that we did it the right way, that we helped them find their own potential for themselves. What you've created here is just . . . a kind of monument to your collective guilt."

"How dare you! You can't understand the burden of keeping them safe. The sacrifice we make by being here to watch over them. They are our children, and we love them!" Urta yelled and moved forward, looking as if she would strike Nathrogreer. Only Kolchor's quick reflexes managed to catch her and hold her back.

"And sometimes it's possible to love your children too much. To hold them too close. To be so afraid of losing them again that you don't allow them the right to truly spread their wings and discover who they are," Nathrogreer responded, nonplussed by the towering god who looked as if she wanted to kick them off the mountaintop. Instead, Nathrogreer met Atrid-B's eyes as they said the words. "These people deserve the opportunity to control their own destinies."

Za shot Urta a withering look. She stopped struggling with Kolchor and turned her back on them. "We understand that in your Federation it is forbidden by your laws to ever create an artificial life form without granting it the full rights of a natural born person, and what we have done here appears to be a violation of this deeply held principle of yours. It is a fine law, but we have our reasons for doing what we do. We once thought as you do. We had hoped that this would just be a temporary arrangement, that once we got this civilization back on its feet and the surface became more hospitable, we could let them return up there to be free to control their own futures. We have run countless simulations where we set them free and tell them the truth. None of them end well. What would you do if you discovered that your ancestors had created your gods? That your gods killed these same ancestors? That they have lied to you and held your people back for centuries? None of these scenarios end well. The resulting society is always unstable and prone to the same flaws that doomed them before. This is the *only* way to guarantee their safety."

Nathrogreer refused to believe it. There was *always* a better way. In that moment, Nathrogreer saw that for all their sophistication, these gods were still little better than the computers they evolved from, more eager to trust in the cold logic of their simulations than to embrace the audacity of hope and trust. They were objects of faith who themselves lacked any faith in the people who believed in them so desperately.

With a shudder, the captain was also uncomfortably reminded of their own shortcomings: how they often trusted raw data over the intuition of the psychics in their crew, their own struggles with the legitimacy of putting their faith in anything they couldn't see or touch or measure. Nathrogreer didn't want to become like these people, presiding over a stagnant world that might as well be an exhibition in a museum for all the spontaneity it possessed. Was this what they were unwittingly doing to their own child? Holding them back? Keeping them as a monument to what they'd lost instead of really appreciating them for what they were?

In a strange way, this *was* still a Dead End World. Perhaps the deadest one they'd ever visited. But what was truly galling was how powerless they were to do anything about it. Not only would doing something be a violation of Federation principles, but it was likely impossible anyway. Who knew how powerful these beings truly were? What little Nathrogreer had seen of their technology definitely seemed to exceed their own. They might have the moral high ground in this situation, but in many ways, the beings of the Federation were the "primitives" for once.

"I think we've seen enough. May we return to our ship now?" Nathrogreer asked.

"You're free to leave. You always have been. Do not attempt to return, or you will not find your next reception to be so hospitable. We don't care about what you do on the surface, but you must *never* return to this habitat," Za answered gravely.

Nathrogreer nodded their understanding and sent a mental command to the *Valiant* to teleport them all away.

Epilogue:

Later that day, Nathrogreer sat in their office, composing their report on the planet Tuzzin. Nathrogreer recommended follow-up teams of experts be sent to the planet—astrobiologists and astroarchaeologists—but that they avoid the equatorial regions where the mutated remains of the original Sytoti race might someday yet regain their sentience and develop into something akin to what their ancestors were.

They strongly recommended never even attempting to revisit the underground habitat lorded over by Za and his ilk. Nathrogreer couldn't help but wonder what might happen if the mutant Sytoti were to ever rebuild their civilization and come across the hidden habitat? What would Za and his people do then? Might they someday threaten the mutants if they felt they were a threat to the habitat? How far would they go to protect their children? Would they kill the true descendants of their creators all over again to protect the replacements they controlled so tightly? Despite all their noble sounding pretensions, had they really learned anything?

Had Nathrogreer?

This whole business just served to make them see disturbing parallels between the way Za controlled his children and Nathrogreer's relationship with Atrid-B. The captain was determined to do better, to find a better way. This time, they would find the words they had never been able to find before. They had to, for their child's sake.

That's why they called Atrid-B into their office that day.

"*Bullu*? You wanted to see me?" Atrid-B asked innocently as they bounced into the office.

"Yes, child. Please have a seat." Nathrogreer steeled themselves, for what they were about to say was something that, unbelievably, they'd realized they'd never said to Atrid-B before.

"I'm sorry," Nathrogreer told them.

Atrid-B's brows furrowed in confusion. "Sorry? For what?"

"For the way I treated you when you were first created. When I realized that you were not Atrid, that you could never really be them, I was cold, distant. I had no business behaving like that to a child, an innocent child who wouldn't have existed if I hadn't asked for them to be created. It took me far too long to act like a proper *Bullu* to you. To appreciate you for the unique being that you are and not see you as an imperfect copy of the child I'd lost. And I'm afraid of all the damage I've caused by treating you like that. That it's made you too eager to please me, to finally earn my approval. And I haven't done enough to discourage that, to let you know that you're free to follow whatever path you may choose, and that I will *always* love you just the same. Perhaps it has been too pleasing to my own vanity to have a child of mine following in my own footsteps, serving on the same ship as me. Maybe I've wanted to keep you close so I can be there to protect you the way I couldn't protect Atrid? I don't know, but what

I do know is that, if you're going to remain here, dedicating yourself to this kind of life, I just want to be sure that it's really what you want for yourself."

Nathrogreer was prepared for many possible reactions, many scenarios that had played out in their head, all except for the one that actually took place. They could've never anticipated Atrid-B's laughter.

"Oh, *Bullu*! Is this what you've been so worried about! Why you've been acting so strangely ever since I came aboard?"

Atrid-B laughed even more before explaining. "You have nothing to worry about. If you feel that you've treated me poorly when I first joined your family, I can assure you that it's all in your head. I have no memory of you being anything but the attentive *Bullu* I've always known, and my memory is *perfect*." This was technically true, as Atrid-B's biomechanical brain recorded their life more accurately than a purely biological brain would, and backed up their memories as well.

"The path I choose *is* my own. This is my dream! There's no place I'd rather be than exploring the stars with you. It is odd, having been programmed to be interested in the same things Atrid was interested in as a child. I have often questioned for myself how much that initial programming still influences me. The answer that I've arrived at is that it was just a jumping-off point. All my experiences since being activated—those are my *real* memories, the ones that have shaped me the most. I am on this ship because I have a genuine passion for science and discovery, even when those discoveries aren't necessarily happy ones. That's a passion I got from you, not a ploy to please you, although that's an unexpected bonus. Nor is it an attempt to live up to the expectations of a child who has been dead for a long time now—and whose death you shouldn't *ever* blame yourself for!"

"But I should've been there, I should've *known* . . ." Nathrogreer was crying now. It was like an ocean was flooding out of the battered sea walls of their eyes.

"How could you have, *Bullu*? It was an accident! Of course you thought it was safe. You'd been there yourself as a child and were fine. Everyone thought it was safe, or it wouldn't have been open to the public! If you'd been there, you'd be dead too. I wouldn't exist, Megolu would be an orphan, all the good things you've done in your career, all the discoveries you've made, would've never happened! I have enough of Atrid left in me to know that they wouldn't have *ever* wanted you to blame yourself like this. Atrid loved you, and so do I." With those words, Atrid-B sprang from the couch they'd been nestling in and wrapped their long arms around their parent in that most universal of all gestures—a good, long hug.

Finally, Nathrogreer got their emotions back under control. All the years of pent-up guilt and self-loathing seemed to be trickling down their cheeks, lost in a hot solution of salty tears. "Thank you," they whispered to their child.

"There is still just one thing, though," Atrid-B said wistfully.

"Oh? And what's that?" Nathrogreer wondered as they continued to wipe the tears from their eyes.

"My name. I've always kind of hated it. I mean, I'm *not* Atrid. We all agree that I'm more than an attempt to copy them. My friends, my really good friends, call me 'Terra,' and I'd be honored if you'd call me that too. Maybe I could even officially change my name to that?"

"Terra? Isn't that a name for one of the potential Dead End Worlds we've been monitoring?"

"Yeah. I've read a lot about that planet. It's a really difficult one. Most of our experts think it's a hopeless case, but I have an odd feeling that those people might just make it despite all our negative projections. Call it irrational or illogical, but believing in it makes me happy. Anyhow, I always thought the name Terra was pretty. Well, far prettier than 'Earth,' at any rate, which sounds like the noise a Suruvian Gorehound makes when it throws up."

Now it was Nathrogreer's turn to laugh. They were heartened to hear their overly serious seeming child entertaining such illogical notions for a change. For having the courage to have faith in something despite all the predictions to the opposite. Nathrogreer hoped they could be more like them someday. Maybe there was hope for all of them yet?

"Terra it is, my child!" the captain declared, and took their hand in theirs.

They turned to look out the window as somewhere above them, Hygor gave the order to jump to hyperspace. The stars outside briefly distorted around them, and together they leapt into the infinite.

The End

Robert Enrico Sohl is the collective consciousness of billions of units of microscopic organic matter. He was born and raised in southern New Jersey but has resided in Virginia for the last few decades. He is a husband and the father to two rather peculiar offspring. He is the author and illustrator of the *Dead End World* series of novels chronicling the unusual adventures of Matt Spike, P.I., and his friends. In addition to those tales, he also enjoys writing horror and fantasy short stories.

OTHER BOOKS BY R.E. SOHL

A Dead End World:

Book 1: The Shadow of Death

Book 1.5: Tales From a Dead End World

Book 2: Beyond the Veil of Death

Book 2.5: Tales From A Dead End World Volume Two

Book 3: Matt Spike and the Vampire's Curse

Book 4: Matt Spike Against The Amazon Saucer Women From Venus

Mistress Of The Wyverns:

Book 1: Jersey Devils

Book 1.5: Romance Of The Gun

Book Two: Night Of The Mothman

More Coming in 2025!